CAST IN FIRE

A Phoenix of Hope Novel

by Zora Marie

STARCATCHER
— PRESS —

CAST IN FIRE

For contact information, please visit:
www.starcatcherpress.com

Ingram Paperback Edition, April 2021
ISBN: 9781087876009

First Paperback Edition, April 2020
ISBN: 9798623530486

Case Cover Edition, April 2020
ISBN: 9781078786058

CAST IN FIRE

To Ducky for pushing me to be the best I can be.
(and for putting up with all my nonsense)

1

"They know what is coming."

Zelia was climbing among the upper branches of her home when she froze at the sound of Eleanor's anxious voice. She hadn't expected anyone to be up here today, and she had never heard Eleanor use that tone before. Leaves brushed her cheek as she crept closer to the high platform. Eleanor was the closest Zelia had ever known to a mother. She had been with Eleanor and Eadon for half a century, but she was not an elf as they were. Zelia was... well, she didn't know, but she'd hardly grown in all that time and still looked like a young child, barely the height of Eleanor's waist.

"Why do they not help us fight this war? The elders of all the people should be willing to stand up and fight against the Darkans. Is that not why these powers were given in the first place? The fight against the Darkans and the war against the gods to come are the only reasons—"

"Shh. They may hear you. You know what they say about the gods, especially Lumid. He can hear everything," Vainoff warned.

"Not here. You know I keep this place hidden, particularly with her here."

Who here? Zelia wondered. The things Vainoff said never made much sense to her, but he was the most frequent visitor the Elves had. Before Vainoff and Eleanor became members of the Wizard Guild, he had run messages for Eleanor in exchange for magic lessons as he had already outgrown what he could learn on his own. Zelia was always curious about his travels and loved the stories he told of the day Eadon saved him from a group of Darkans at their borders.

"I know you do. Just as you know, the elders have their reasons. It is best to leave them be. They still outnumber us if you recall."

Vainoff and Eleanor fell silent. The only sound came from leaves and limbs as they rustled in the main entrance to the high platform. Zelia took the chance to move closer. Her thoughts quieted, so Eleanor wouldn't sense her nearing as she pushed her way through the leafy limbs.

"An urgent letter from Koin."

Zelia recognized Eadon's voice, but it seemed strained as if he dreaded the news they were about to receive. She climbed closer and parted the leaves to have a clear view. Blood spotted the tiny scroll Eleanor held, and her Elven glow dimmed as she skimmed the words.

"What does it say?" Eadon asked.

Eleanor did not move as Eadon took the open scroll from her and read it aloud, "We have won, but at a grave cost. Queen O'Fell asks for *her* gift to put the King and…" his voice trailed off, and the scroll slipped from his fingers.

Eleanor's lip quivered for a moment before she spoke. "Get Zelia and Alrindel. We leave at once."

Leaving? But I never get to go anywhere.

Eleanor turned and stared straight at her.

"Zelia, I hear your thoughts. Come here. We must leave, Koin needs us."

Zelia pushed through the leaves and stepped onto woven branches that formed a platform. Eadon was so distraught by what he had read that he did not even scold her for eavesdropping.

"Eadon?" she asked.

He knelt to her level as if about to give her some tragic news, but he found no words. She hugged him tightly, returning one of the many loving hugs he had given her over the years. She could feel him quiver as he exhaled, still unable to speak.

"It will be okay," she said, not understanding what was wrong.

With a silent sigh, he leaned back from her hug and brushed the leaves from her curly hair. "Would you go find Alrindel and tell him to pack a light bag for me?"

"Where are we going?"

"To the Kingdom of The Mountains," Vainoff replied. "Now go on, dear, and pack a bag of your own."

Zelia cocked her head. She didn't fully understand, but the thought of going on a journey away from home excited her.

"Lighnif!" Zelia ran up to the older Elf child. She was a close friend of Alrindel's, as were most young Elves. "Have you seen Alrindel?"

"I just left him. He was on the other side of the pasture; I can get him for you if you like."

"No. Starjaina can take me."

Zelia hopped on the fence and let out a long and pretty whistle, something she was proud to have finally learned to do. A beautiful white horse galloped across the pasture and pranced as she slowed to a stop.

"Zelia! Hello dear. Here for a ride again?" Starjaina neighed.

"Eadon asked me to get Alrindel."

"Well, come on. I'll take you to him."

Zelia climbed onto Starjaina's back from the vine fence.

"So, what did Alrindel do this time?" Starjaina asked as she cantered across the pasture, the other horses parting for her as she went.

"Nothing, we're going somewhere."

"I hope you are taking me with you." She bobbed her head as she slowed her pace.

Alrindel was running around a tree, chasing and being chased by playful foals.

"I'm sure we are since I believe Eadon is going with us."

Alrindel stopped playing with the foals and stroked Starjaina's forelock. "What are you two talking about this time? Not stirring up trouble now, are you?"

"No. Eadon sent me to get you. We are to pack a bag."

"Pack a bag? There's a war going on. Where are we going?"

"The Kingdom of the Mountains. I think something has happened." She scrunched her eyebrows together and lowered her gaze. "I've never seen Eadon so… broken."

"Well, come on then." Alrindel swung himself onto Starjaina's back and nudged her to start back across the pasture.

"Come Zelia, you will ride with me," Eleanor said.

"But I wanted to ride Starjaina."

Eadon picked her up, his long silky black hair tickling her cheek as he lifted her onto his horse.

"Then you may ride with me until dark, but then you will have to ride with Eleanor."

He sprung on behind her, and they rode off. Eadon had called many of the healers he had taught over the years to ride with them. Some were from the trees right next to theirs, and others were from places sprinkled within the inner kingdom, but all were familiar faces, even if she did not recall their names.

One by one, they passed under the waterfall and into the outer ranges of Elyluma. A single tree root bridge connected the river island to the outer reaches of their home.

Alrindel carried his bow and rode on his own for the first time on such an occasion. The Elves were quiet as they rode, and the silence unsettled her. Even with the war going on, they were always cheerful, singing under the stars each night, but today there was no singing, and even the other Elves they had passed were silent.

"Starjaina?"

"Yes, dear?"

"Have you heard any news about what has happened?" Zelia asked her in the language of the animals, knowing the time wasn't right to ask Eadon or Eleanor.

"The King O'Fell is dead, and many Elves, including…"

"Leena?" she asked when Starjaina trailed off.

There was a catch in Starjaina's stride, and now Zelia realized the reason for Eadon's reaction. Her aunt, his sister, had died in the battle. Zelia swung her leg over Starjaina's neck and buried her face against Eadon's chest.

"Starjaina told you?"

Zelia nodded.

"Told her what?" Alrindel asked.

Eadon wrapped his arms around Zelia, almost as much to comfort himself as to comfort her. "Le—" his voice caught, "Leena has fallen."

"She fell trying to save King Skalary O'Fell. We go to release the souls of all of those fallen to the stars," Vainoff said.

Zelia turned a bit to see that Vainoff's gaze rested on her, and she wondered what her part in all this was to be.

"What will happen to Auntie Leena's soul?"

"Leena is an Elf, so her soul will rest in the stars with our elders until she chooses to be reborn."

"When will that be?"

She stared up at him and waited for his reply.

"Our souls are bound to our lovers."

"So, she will wait for Koin?" she asked.

Eadon nodded and kissed the top of her head. "You should get some rest now. We will not stop until we get there."

Soon, his humming and Starjaina's step rocked her to sleep.

Koin met them at the edge of a row of newly constructed pyres. The others continued on as Eleanor, Eadon, and Alrindel's horses slowed their pace.

"I'll go ahead with the others." Vainoff nodded towards Koin and urged his horse on.

Koin's forlorn gaze struck Zelia's heart. She had never seen him so solemn. He usually glowed brightest among the Elves, but now his glow was gone. Blood stained the tips of his long silver hair and parts of his clothes.

Zelia didn't even wait for Starjaina to stop, she slid from her back and ran to Koin. Koin knelt and caught her in his arms, holding her as if she could slip away and leave him in the dark at any moment.

"Thank you for coming so quickly." Koin's voice was quiet next to her ear.

"Koin, you are family. There is no need to thank us," Eleanor replied.

"I am so sorry."

Zelia opened her eyes, as Koin nodded, to see the young and fair Queen Orania O'Fell's approach, her daughter-in-law, Elizabeth, at her side. She had met them once before, but she remembered little of them.

"As am I sorry for your losses. I hate to ask at such a time, but Eadon, we need your help."

Koin pulled away from Zelia's hug, but he gave her one more squeeze before standing.

"She is expecting," Orania nodded to Elizabeth, "but she is losing him."

"How far along?" Eleanor asked.

"Only a month or two, maybe less. He's all I have left of..." Elizabeth glanced back at the long row of pyres.

"May I?" Eadon asked, gesturing towards her abdomen.

Princess Elizabeth cringed as Eadon's hand pressed against her. She doubled over in pain but pushed away from him.

"I... I need to get back to helping our people."

Elizabeth fled towards the gates, one hand holding her abdomen as she went.

"Elizabeth!" Queen O'Fell called after her, but Elizabeth didn't stop. "They found her on the battlefield covered in blood, cradling Skyral. She refuses to talk about it, and she won't let anyone check her out. That's the closest anyone has gotten to her."

"She was out there during the battle?" Eadon asked, shock and concern in his tone.

"I saw her myself. When she refused to return to the women and children, I tried to get her to promise to stay close. She refused, saying she would fight alongside her husband and his father. We..." A tear ran down Koin's cheek as he stared across the pyres to the ones that stood a little taller at the center.

"Koin, you and Leena did all you could to save them. We all know you did." Orania cupped his hands in hers. "And we will never forget the sacrifice you made."

"Eadon, would you go after Elizabeth? I'll get Zelia ready, but Elizabeth needs you now," Eleanor said.

"Get me ready for what?" Zelia asked once Eadon had gone.

"We would like you to do the honors of lighting the pyres, dear."

"Why me?"

There was a glance exchanged between the adults, and Koin sighed.

"Because Leena loved you as a daughter."

"And we thought there would be no one better to honor our fallen. Zelia, would you do us the honor of freeing our loved ones to take their places amongst the stars?" Queen Orania asked.

"Yes, ma'am."

"Good. Now if you will all excuse me, there are things I need to attend to before tonight." Orania leaned in and whispered something to Eleanor before walking away.

"Come, Zelia, let us see what we can help with and clean up for this evening."

Eleanor held out her hand for Zelia to take, but she couldn't help but see the distant look in Koin's eyes.

Zelia glanced between Eleanor and Koin, then took his hand in hers. His hand was clammy to the touch, and he didn't look down at her until she moved in front of him.

"Koin, would you do me the honor of helping me tonight?"

She stared up at him, waiting for his response. She wanted to help him, and this was the only thing she could think of.

"I think Aunt Leena would want you to, Koin. Come on, let's go get you cleaned up." Alrindel grabbed Koin's other hand, and together, they pulled him along.

When they came to the third-highest pyre, Koin stopped following along. He stared at the thin cloth that covered a slender figure.

"Alrindel, take Zelia and go inside. See if there is anyone the two of you can help. We will catch up with you there in a few," Eleanor said.

Alrindel nodded and took Zelia's hand. She watched Koin over her shoulder until they passed the big stone gates, and she turned to look at her surroundings. Great stone buildings rose around her, their make of Dwarven quality. She ran her hand across a smooth wall as they walked. She could not feel a single seam in the stones. Alrindel stopped the first guard they saw.

"Where are the wounded being treated?"

"Why?"

The guard stopped, but he favored his right leg.

"Because we can help. We are children of Eadon," Zelia replied.

"Vainoff and our healers have gone ahead of us, and we are to assist them," Alrindel added as he stepped in front of her.

The man looked them over for a moment before pointing down the widest path.

"Follow the path to the stairs. There will be another guard to direct you the rest of the way from there."

"Thank you." Alrindel nodded, then pulled Zelia along.

"You're not an Elf, and people will recognize this. Not everyone will be our friend here."

"I know, but I'm going to light the pyres, so won't everyone learn of me then?"

"Maybe or maybe not. I'm not sure what Eleanor is planning to do. For now, let's go see if we can put that first aid training to work."

He tapped her nose as they came to the bottom of a set of stairs. Two guards stared down at them, their hands on the hilts of their swords.

"Halt! Who goes there?"

"I am Alrindel. Queen Eleanor has sent us ahead of her to give aid to the wounded."

"And who is she?" The man nodded towards her, and she felt compelled to step closer to Alrindel.

"She's with me. Come on, you two, I could use a couple extra sets of hands." Vainoff appeared at the top of the stairs and waved them to follow.

The guard who had asked gave her a curious stare as they passed.

"Where are Eleanor and Eadon?" Vainoff asked. "The two of you shouldn't be on your own."

"Eleanor is with Koin, and Eadon is… busy. Eleanor told us to go help where we can and that she would catch up."

Vainoff nodded, his lips pursed for a moment. "Yes, Koin needs her. Well, come on, we'll find you someone where the skills of a young bowman and a Zelia can help."

Vainoff winked at her and turned down a hallway lined with doors. Moans and cries came from behind most, and whimpers came from those who sat in the halls. Women and a handful of Elves moved from place to place, doing what they could. Vainoff stopped in front of a warrior who appeared to be about eighteen, still young to be in a battle. He held a cloth to his side where blood trailed down his front. His skin was ashen and sweat beaded his forehead. When he opened his eyes, his gaze first met Zelia's.

"Here, let me look." She dropped Alrindel's hand and pulled the top of the soaked bandage from his side. "It's not deep, but it needs stitches."

She glanced back at Alrindel as he pulled off his pack. Vainoff stood behind him, a distant look in his eye as he watched.

"Well, I shall leave you to it then." Vainoff gave her a nod and walked off, swinging his staff with each of his long strides.

"He's acting weird today," Zelia said as she wiped the blood from the boy's side with a clean cloth.

"Of course, he would, he was a friend of the King, and our Aunt," Alrindel said. "Here, your stitching is better." He handed her a threaded needle.

Zelia took the needle and watched the boy's expression for a moment.

"This will hurt, but it will stop the bleeding. You'll have to be careful not to tear the stitches out though."

"Who are you?"

"Zelia. Now hold still."

She put her hand above the cut and pushed the needle through, being careful to do it as Eadon had taught her. Alrindel went on to the next person as she stitched the boy up and tied another clean cloth to his side.

"Now, keep it clean, and you can have the stitches removed in a couple of weeks. Other than that, just take it easy so you don't rip the stitches out."

"How did you learn to do this?"

The boy held his side again, but now more for comfort than out of necessity.

"They teach everyone how to do this where I am from. I learned it, hm, a hundred years ago."

"I'm sorry to pull you away, dear, but we must get ready," Eleanor said as she walked down the hall from within the castle. "Alrindel, Vainoff will fetch you when it is time."

Zelia nodded, then turned back to the boy. "You get some rest."

She could feel the boy's gaze as she followed Eleanor down the hall but didn't look back. When the latch of the heavy wooden door clicked, Zelia gained the nerve to ask Eleanor the question that had been bugging her.

"Eleanor, why do they want me to light the pyres? Shouldn't one of their men do it?"

"One day, you will understand, but for now, I want you to take this task with the grace I have seen you use as you dance in the starlight. If for no one else, do it for Koin and Eadon. I know you love them both and your Auntie Leena."

Zelia nodded and shifted her feet. *I love Auntie Leena, but why me?*

"Let us get you changed, and then I want to show you something."

Eleanor pulled a little silk black dress with edges dipped in gold from an armoire and held it up in the sunlight streaming through the open window. Its long sleeves glimmered as the breeze swept through the room.

"I remember the day Orania wore this when she was about your size. She asked that you wear it tonight."

Zelia washed the blood from her hands and slipped into the long black dress. It was tight across her shoulders as she had been working with a bow more than most women. Eleanor gave her a sad smile and plated her hair back in a long braid.

"You know, this is the first time I've ever gotten you into an actual dress."

"They're not good for climbing," Zelia said, turning to give Eleanor one of her mischievous grins. "So, what did you want to show me?"

"Something special that you need to see."

Eleanor took her hand and led her through a maze of corridors, leading deeper into the stone castle. When they came to a large set of doors, a guard nodded and pushed the door open for them. Orania stood at the edge of a platform, staring down at the water falling beneath it. A statue of a man stood staring at the open sky above them, his hand on the hilt of his sword, and the brim of his helmet shading his eyes from the setting sun.

"Do you know what this is, Zelia?" Orania asked.

Zelia shook her head, but Orania didn't need to see to know.

"It's a reminder of where the O'Fell family came from. Do you know the story?"

"They are descendants of Yargo, God of the Fallen Warriors. He hoped to unite the people by giving them someone they could follow. And this must be Lumid, guard of the bridge and keeper of the stars."

Orania turned from the edge.

"That is right, and you will release their souls to live with their ancestor, Yargo, among the stars. It is a tradition for a daughter of a fallen King to lay him to rest, and since he has no daughter, we have asked that you do it."

Zelia nodded, but she still didn't quite understand why they would ask her.

"Now, it'll be getting dark soon. We should start gathering people outside."

——————▶

Men, women, and children had gathered on the walls and in the field all around the long rows of pyres. Koin stood by her side with Orania. Whatever Eleanor had done seemed to have eased Koin's pain. Orania had just finished her long speech and excused Elizabeth for not being there, saying the grief was too much for her to bear.

Orania gave Koin a nod, and he handed Zelia a torch. As soon as she took it, the flame grew brighter, and an updraft pulled it higher into the sky.

"I'll be right beside you the entire time," Koin whispered.

She started with Skalary and Skyral's pyres but froze as she went to light Leena's. Koin squeezed her shoulder as if to say it's alright, and she stuck the torch into the kindling. When the fire took off, she stepped back and looked up at Koin. There were tears in his eyes as the soft light of the flames lit Leena's face.

"You can stay here, Koin. I'll finish."

She gave his hand a light squeeze and continued down the row. With each one she lit, she glanced back at Koin; the flames had grown, but he hadn't stepped away. With everyone entranced by the flames, she moved from pyre to pyre a little faster and circled around from one end to the other.

When she lit the last one, she threw the torch at the feet of the King as the flames of the pyres already burned high in the sky. When she did, something happened that made all the crowd gasp. The flames turned blue, and little orbs of light rose from the bodies of those fallen. As each one rose, the flames calmed back to their orange glow.

"Koin!" Zelia pulled him back from Leena's pyre as a wave of heat rolled out, and Leena's soul rose from the flames.

One by one, the blue orbs lifted into the stars, twinkling until they faded from view. Zelia glanced around at the mourners. The families crowded together, and those who stood alone held clasped hands over their hearts as they stared up at the stars. The crowd stood staring at the stars long after the souls had gone, but one by one, people trickled away, and the somber silence moved with them.

⟶

The next few days went by in a bit of a blur for Zelia. They had stayed and tended to the wounded, and Eleanor had scarcely let her out of her sight. Their trip home was much slower than their trip there as the Elves who fought in the battle returned with them; many were injured or had not slept as they tended to the wounded. When they stopped for the night, Eleanor called out to Zelia before she could run off with Alrindel.

"Stay close by, alright?"

"I believe the two of you have some archery practice to catch up on," Eadon said.

"But I don't have my bow with me."

"We can share," Alrindel offered. "Come on. I saw a board back there."

"Do not go too far," Eleanor warned again before the two of them ran off.

They weaved between the clusters of Elves that tended to each other's wounds. When they found a weathered board tangled in the grass, they wedged it between two stones and stepped back. Alrindel went first, drawing his arrow back by his ear.

"Alrindel?" Zelia asked.

"Trying to distract me?"

"No. I just... do you think Koin will be okay?"

Alrindel released, and the arrow just hit the edge of the board.

"What's this about me?" Koin's curious voice made her jump as he approached them from behind.

"Zelia here is worried about you."

Zelia twisted her foot in the long grass and fought not to look up at Koin.

"She is now, is she?"

There was a hint of the old Koin in his tone, and she glanced at him.

"How about you show Alrindel how a real archer shoots?"

Alrindel pulled an arrow from his quiver and handed it to her.

"Your turn."

She took his bow and drew it back a little past her ear. A hand touched her arm and pushed her elbow down, so it was level with her arrow.

"Remember, release with the last of your breath."

She stared down the shaft of her arrow and released as her breath steadied towards the end. The half-rotten board splintered as her arrow shot through, just off the center.

As the arrow shattered the board, it was as if the shell of dark emotion that had held her captive within since the funeral shattered, too. She spun around and gave Koin a hug, holding the bow across his back as she did so.

"Thank you, Koin."

"You're welcome." He gave her a light squeeze and leaned back from her hug. "Now, give the bow back to Alrindel before you hurt yourself with it. It's still a bit too big for you."

"But we just started."

"I will make sure you make up for the lost practice when we get back. Deal?"

Zelia couldn't help but smile as Koin looked down at her with a raised brow.

"Fine. Here you go, Alrindel." She tossed the bow to him and grabbed Koin's hand. "Let's go find Eadon."

"Sure," Alrindel said as they disappeared into the crowd. "Just leave me to pick up your arrow."

——————▶

Time seemed to glide by as she lay on Starjaina's back. They had returned to Elyluma and life resumed its normal pace, but Zelia couldn't forget the burning pyres. While she had stopped asking why they had chosen her, she could not stop her thoughts from questioning why. Riding Starjaina was the only thing that calmed her rolling thoughts.

"There you are." Koin pulled her from Starjaina's back and onto his own horse. "You are supposed to be at practice."

"So are you."

Koin squinted at her with his lips pressed together, and she giggled.

18

"Sorry, Koin." She spun around on her knees and gave him a hug.

"How is it you are so graceful on a horse and in the trees but so clumsy on the ground?"

"Guess I'm just not meant for blades."

"No, we will get you using a sword with at least a bit of skill one day. We just have to make sure you do not hurt yourself before then." He tapped her nose and turned his horse around to start back across the pasture.

"Wait, you are forgetting Alrindel."

"Thanks," Alrindel said with a sigh and stood from his hiding spot amongst the tall grass.

"Hey, you're the reason I'm out here. I came to get you, remember?"

"Well, at least you two have been paying attention to one of your teachers. Eadon must be teaching you the ancient Fairy language now."

"Why do we learn languages the Fairies don't even bother to learn anymore?" Alrindel asked.

"Why do you use contractions like the humans?" Koin asked, and he let that sink in as they crossed the pasture. "We learn the languages both to keep them alive and because we may one day need them. Just because the Fairies on the mainland no longer use the language does not mean Fairies elsewhere do not."

Koin helped Zelia from his horse and handed both her and Alrindel a bow.

"Now, you can't leave until you each hit the target across the field three times in a row."

Alrindel sighed, and Zelia laughed as she picked up a handful of arrows.

"What's wrong, Alrindel? Afraid I'll finish before you?"

"How about a wager? Last one has to retrieve all the arrows?"

"Fine."

She pulled an arrow back to her ear and released, missing by a foot. Alrindel did the same, but he barely missed. Soon they both had two arrows in the target and they lined up for another shot. They released as one, and an arrow shot from the side knocked both their arrows aside.

"Koin!" Both children complained in unison.

"What? I never said there would be no interference. Try again."

They sighed and leaned over to grab another handful of arrows.

"Rapid fire?" Alrindel asked in a hushed voice.

Zelia nodded and grabbed up a few more.

"You might need a few more, Koin!" Alrindel yelled as they began shooting arrows one after another at the target.

At first, they were in time with one another, but as they went, Zelia lagged behind. Still, they filled the target and surrounding ground with arrows.

"Alright, now go pick up your mess." Koin laughed and walked off to where the other Elf children trained with swords.

"I saw some of the elder wizards this morning. Why do you think they are here?" she asked as they picked through the grass for their arrows.

Alrindel looked as though he was about to say something, but he shook his head.

"I don't know, but they are watching us."

Zelia glanced over her shoulder. Eleanor and the wizards she had seen stood on the dining room balcony of their home, their gazes all turned towards her.

"Why do they always watch me when they come here?"

"Why don't you ask Eleanor that?" Alrindel asked. "But not until you find all those arrows."

Zelia sighed and continued picking through the grass for her arrows, more of hers had missed than hit.

2

"Gotcha!" Alrindel exclaimed.

Zelia giggled as they fell back into the tall grass. "Fine, you win again Alrindel. But I am going to beat you at archery practice today."

"Oh really? And what about swordsmanship?" he asked with a brow raised.

"Zelia! Come here, dear," Eleanor called from across the pasture.

"What did you do this time?" Alrindel asked.

"Nothing, or at least I don't think I did anything."

"Well come on, then. It's about time for practice with Koin, anyway."

"Fine, race you to the fence?" She took off.

"No fair, you got a head start."

"But you have longer legs!" She called over her shoulder.

Alrindel was about to pass her when she came to a dead stop at the pasture's edge.

"Eadon, what's wrong?"

An ashen tone replaced his usual bright, happy glow. She searched his and Eleanor's faces for the unvoiced answer. Their vacant expressions told her they were speaking telepathically, something Eleanor used occasionally, to keep conversations private.

"Come Zelia, we are going somewhere," Eadon finally answered.

"Where?" she asked, the edge in his tone gave her the urge to run.

"We will explain on the way," Eleanor assured her.

——————▶

Silence hung over their ride to the mountains and left Zelia's mind to race. She ran through recent events, fishing for a reason, any reason for them to act this way. She hadn't seen their light so faded since the day they received news that many of their kin and the old King had died in the last battle of the Daemon War many years ago.

The horses stopped and drew her from her thoughts. She looked around and saw the aged faces of many wizards, all men she had met at one point or another. She always thought the elders looked much alike, but then again, she seldom saw them, and they always wore the same grey clothing and long beards. Her favorite wizards of those who weren't Elves, were the Dwarf Multly and the human Vainoff. Multly, the eccentric lover of The Wild, would always hold a dear place in her heart as he mumbled to the animals but never truly understood them. The elders were human, but they were older than Eleanor. The power of the guild gave them far longer lives than most.

"We should camp here for the night," Eleanor's twin brother, Erolith suggested.

"No, we should continue on," countered the one who appeared to be the oldest of them all.

"Erolith is right," Asenten said, "she needs to rest before her test. Besides, it would do us well to stay within the guarded outer borders tonight."

Asenten's long unkempt eyebrows darkened the shadows across his eyes, yet she caught a gleam in them that made Zelia shrink back against Eadon. The tall and crooked wizard was always among her least favorite, but something about the others this night made him seem almost inviting.

Eadon wrapped his arms around her, his warm breath soothing against the top of her head. He took a breath as if to say something but released it in a silent sigh.

"Eadon, why are we going towards the Darkan Mountains? You have always told me never to go north of our kingdom."

"That…" his voice cracked, and she tensed. His voice had never cracked in such a way, not even when Leena died.

"He did, but now we must go there," Eleanor replied for him, the edge in her tone warning her not to push the subject.

They said little as they set up camp and ate. The food seemed dry and tasteless, but the wizards seemed content with the buzz from the elvish wine. For a moment, Zelia wondered what it was like, even when she drank more than her small cup, she never felt a thing. She looked back from where she sat almost touching the flames to Eadon. He had a distant look in his eye as he watched her.

"Eadon?" she asked, coming to sit on his lap.

"I…"

She followed his gaze to the stern stares of the older wizards burning into them. She shrank back against Eadon's chest and he stroked her long curls.

"Get some sleep." He wrapped his arms around her and leaned back against a tree. For a moment, there was silence as he let out a long slow breath, the last of it coming as a whisper, "No matter what happens, I love you."

"It'll be okay," she reassured him. She laid her head against his chest and stared at the darkness beyond the fire for what seemed like forever as Eadon hummed, wondering what silenced him and Eleanor.

The next day, they woke early and continued their journey, traveling well into the night. The wizards talked about things she didn't understand, tests and powers. After a while, she realized they were talking about her.

"Her powers will emerge on their own, we just need to give them time," Vainoff protested to the others.

"She's been getting sick has she not?"

"Well, yes, but she hasn't in a while. I'm not sure what that has to do with this."

"It's a buildup of her powers, if she doesn't have a release soon it will kill her."

"As soon as her powers emerge, she must train." Asenten nodded to Zelia.

"But I already train. What are they talking about?" Zelia turned to Eleanor for guidance since Eadon didn't seem to be able to answer her questions.

"You train with ordinary weapons; there are weapons beyond that."

"You need to know how to use a sword and a bow because your powers will drain you, but you do have powers. Possibly beyond what we have." Erolith's voice was gentle, but it did little to soften the weight of the others' gazes.

"But… I don't have powers. I can talk to the animals, but that's it." She shrank back from them, a knot of worry and fear threading its way into the pit of her stomach.

"Here, may I?" Asenten asked as they stopped at the black summit of the Darkan Mountains.

The land before her was barren, not a single sprig of vegetation in sight. *How can Darkans live here?* She thought back to Eadon's teachings about the Darkans, they were once Elves that turned away from the star light and now wished for the whole world to be in darkness. They fought the Elves, Dwarves, and humans for their love of light and connection to the gods who shine the light upon them.

Eleanor nodded so Asenten pulled her to the side, away from the others, and knelt before her. Something had always seemed off about him; he was always overly kind to her, but it seemed strained as if he had to force himself to behave this way. The other elders were so cold and distant, it pushed her to accept his kindness despite her instincts screaming that he was a threat.

"I know you don't believe that you have these powers but, trust me, you do. Here, I want you to have these." He took her hand and placed two pebble sized stones in her palm. "When the time comes, channel your powers through these and you'll be fine."

She closed her hand around the white and red stones and Asenten urged her to return to the others at the peak of the mountain ridge.

When she returned to the others, the oldest wizard stared at her even more intently than usual. She shrank back towards Eadon. The wizard looked away from her and down at the dark canyon. He said one word. "Go."

"What?" Zelia asked.

"Go on, show them what you can do," Erolith urged her forward when Eleanor couldn't bring herself to say a word.

"Down there? Eadon, Eleanor, what are they talking about? What am I supposed to do?" she cried. They had always taught her to never go near here, and everything about this terrified her.

Asenten knelt and whispered in her ear, "You must go down into the canyon. You will know what to do when you get there. Do it for Eadon, be strong for him. Go on now."

She descended the steep slope and could hear Eadon break down and plead behind her, "She's not ready. You can't make her do this."

"It is out of my hands and it has been decided." There was an audible crack in Eleanor's voice. "She must do it or we risk everything."

Zelia could feel the edge in the air as she descended the side of the mountain. She had only been past the river a handful of times and now they expected her to do what even the Elves dared not do… walk unarmed into the land of the Darkan Mountains. Even armed the Elves avoided this place, only coming near to guard the farthest reaches of the kingdom from the Darkans whose hatred of light seemed to desolate forests with their mere presence.

She clenched her hands tightly, each hand holding one of the little pebbles Asenten had given her. The hair on her nape stood on end when she reached a set of stone gates that led into the side of the mountain. Hordes of dark and hunched figures flooded out from behind the twisted stone pillars. The largest of them were far taller than the Elves, even with their hunched backs. They grabbed and pulled her in different directions as they fought over her. One, in particular, towered over her and licked his leathery lips. His dark wrinkled skin stretching as he snapped at the other Darkans and in her face. She screamed and frantically scanned for a familiar figure. The strange creatures were everywhere she looked. They reeked of rotten flesh and the smell alone threatened to steal her breath.

The Darkans shoved each other as a little one elbowed his way to the front where others argued over her. Their words came out in a rush and mingled together, making them impossible for her to understand more than a word or two. The little one pressed a blade into her side, the cold and jagged metal biting into her skin, and her nails dug into her palms as her warm blood ran down her side. As fear burned through her, one arm erupted in flames, her other turning to ice. The Darkans holding her shrieked and scrambled away, some flaming and others clasping ice covered limbs.

A surge of pain ripped through her as her bones cracked, and her blood boiled where ice met fire. The two halves ate at each other, tearing her apart. She gave a blood-curdling scream and collapsed to her knees. Even though the flames and ice were a part of her she still felt the searing heat and the bite of the cold penetrate to her core as the two shredded her very being.

With one last surge of energy, the pain disappeared, and everything went black.

For what seemed like years she lingered in a void, feeling something move her, shift her, and pull her back together; the pain was agonizing as her broken body lay on the cold, uneven ground.

"Oh, thank goodness, you've come back! Do you know who I am?" The man's long beard appeared to be blue in the light of his staff, but the shadow of his hat shrouded his eyes.

She propped herself up on one arm and surveyed her dimly lit surroundings. The air was stale and had a metallic tang to it, no light shone in from the outside world. The damp chill of the cave cut right through her and sent her into an uncontrollable shiver. She looked down at her shaking hands.

"What happened?"

"What can you recall?"

"Darkans and darkness. I... I died. I should be dead."

"Do you know who I am?"

"Asenten."

She shot to her feet in a sudden panic, recalling bits and pieces of her final day. She remembered the pain, the faces of the Darkans, the blade, and the horrid stench.

"Where's Eadon?"

Her legs buckled beneath her and sent her crashing to the ground, pins and needles jabbing through her every muscle. It was almost a welcome pain as the memory of her body exploding and trying to reform lingered. She could almost feel how the ashes and crystals of ice were swept up, and how each piece struggled to reform what she was now.

"My poor dear, have no fear. Eadon can't hurt you anymore." Asenten wrapped a blanket around her to shield her from the cold.

"What do you mean hurt me anymore? He never hurt me."

"Tsk, tsk, Eleanor must have meddled with your mind more than I feared."

"No! Eleanor would never do that!" She pulled away.

"Careful, it'll take you a while to get used to being back in your body."

"What? So, I did die... but I never left it. Where are we?"

"We're in the only place that I can shield you from the others. There's something else I must tend to. Whatever you do, do not follow me, and stay in the cave or Eleanor will find you."

"Wait, you're leaving me?"

"Yes, but only for a short while. Rest assured I'll be back. Here's some food." He placed a leather pack at her feet. "Remember, whatever you do, do not leave this place."

With a blinding flash of his staff, he disappeared, only the echoes of his magic lingered in the cave.

For the next several hours she didn't move and didn't eat. She just sat and stared into the darkness, all the while she fought to understand Asenten's words. She knew that Eleanor could sway people's minds, but could she change someone's memories? Had Eadon hurt her? She had so many questions and so few answers, but she knew one thing for sure. She shouldn't be alive.

Zelia's exhausted body and mind gave in to sleep, but it wasn't long before she stirred to something tapping her foot.

"Zelia, wake up."

Even still half asleep, she could hear how forced his tone seemed, as if he were on the verge of screaming at her.

"Hmmm, Asenten? Did I do something wrong?" She rubbed the sleep from her eyes.

"No, no, my dear. You didn't do anything. Come, on your feet."

She squinted against the glow of his staff and steadied herself on the damp wall.

"Here, I have something for you." He held a sword out to her. "This is for you. Do you see that stone in the hilt?" She took the short sword and brought it closer to her face for a closer look. "That's a fire stone, just like the one I gave you that day on the side of the mountain."

With a jolt, she threw the sword away and cowered in the corner. The echoes of the sword chattering against the cave floor pounded in her ears, like great war drums.

"Heavens, child, it won't hurt you. Well, not so long as you don't use ice at the same time. Come on out of the corner," he coaxed. She edged from the corner but stayed clear of the sword. "Well go on, pick it up." When she shook her head, he strode towards her and shoved her towards the sword. "I said pick it up!"

Her heart wrenched in surprise as she dropped and, in that moment, her fear of Asenten was greater than her fear of the stone. She grabbed the sword from the cave floor, instinct and Koin's training took over, she flipped around and kept the point of the sword between her and Asenten.

"So, Koin did teach you a bit about the sword after all! Very good, now get up."

She stood with her back to the wall.

"Now light the sword, like you did the pebble on the mountain. Do it, or I'll leave you in the dark." He let the glow of his staff fade.

Something whirled around and smashed against her side. There was another swish of air and she lit the sword, but it didn't give more than a flicker of light before she fell to her knees. Her muscles already burned as if she had trained for hours when all she had done was light a simple flame.

"This won't do," Asenten muttered to himself and kicked a bag at her before mumbling on his way out of the cave.

As soon as he had gone, she fell over and closed her eyes, welcoming the rest that called her. Some part of her knew she should eat, but she couldn't bring herself to fumble around with the bag.

3

Distorted voices echoed through the cave and stirred her from her slumber. She rubbed the sleep from her eyes and stumbled towards the voices. With each bend of the cave their chants grew louder.

Before she reached them, they quieted until they were speaking rather than chanting. Their voices blended together as if there were a single person with Asenten, but the shadows from around the last bend in the cave showed otherwise.

"Does she know?"

"No, she doesn't know that we are her creators. It appears the Elves kept her in the dark on a lot of things, as if they could hide what she is."

"Like anyone could hide such a beast from the world. Eleanor may be powerful, but even she can't do that."

"You're right on that, Zelia may look human, but she's just a wolf in sheep's clothing."

"You're still calling her by the name Eadon gave her?"

"What else am I supposed to call her? It's not like I could even just call her by her species since she crosses so many races."

An inaudible grumble echoed through the cave.

"Fine! Just don't go getting attached to her like Eadon and Eleanor; she's a weapon, nothing more and nothing less."

Zelia turned to run from their words and tripped on the cave's uneven floor. Her cry when she hit the floor sent echoes through the cave.

A hand, grasping a chunk of her hair, yanked her around the last bend in the cave tunnel before she could push herself back to her feet. She grabbed at the hand, trying to stop the searing pain in her scalp. They thrust her into the center of the wizards' circle. She squinted her eyes against the blinding light that lit the cave. The butt of one of their staffs drove into her chest and pushed her harder against the cave floor with every breath, the uneven floor digging into her back.

"What do we have here? Someone is putting their nose where it doesn't belong. So, what shall we do with it?"

"We should teach it a lesson, eavesdropping is very, very bad," sneered one wizard, amusement at the idea played across his face.

"Yes, then we can use her blood to bind her soul here."

"That's enough, we don't want her knowing too much."

The gleam of steel flying towards her caught her eye a moment before the cold blade cut through her neck. What happened next didn't hit her until the last of her breath gurgled out and the blackness overcame her once more. She could feel her blood pool around her, turning cold, long after her last breath. She could no longer hear the wizards, but she could feel her muscles, skin, and veins pull back together at an agonizing pace.

⟶

"That's enough rest. Get up!" Asenten demanded.

Zelia dragged herself to her feet, her sword already in hand. She didn't take the time to think of her actions while in his presence. Instead, she let her instincts take over as if she were a wild animal in a never-ending struggle to preserve her existence. In her weakened and starved state, she couldn't help but shake under the weight of the small sword. Part of her wondered how long she had been there, but then it didn't matter much anymore.

"Hm, this will never do. Put the blade down, child." Zelia gave a slight shake of her head. "I said put it down!" he commanded and slashed the sword from her hands.

She fell back against the cave wall in surprise and clasped her bloodied hands. "P... please don't hurt me... I'll be good," she pleaded through muffled sobs.

"Good," he replied with a rather pleased and amused tone. "Now, first things first, no more crying." His staff raked across her ribs as he pried her away from the cave wall.

When she moved, the gleam of the sword caught her eye. She lunged for it but stopped short when something hard slammed into her side. Even the echoes of her own ribs cracking didn't stop her. Her hand clasped around the cold leather hilt of her sword, but it didn't budge. She looked up to see Asenten's foot planted atop her only weapon and the butt of his staff flying towards her.

It slammed into her stomach, forcing her to release the sword.

"Now, we won't be doing anything like that again, will we?" Asenten asked with a wrench of his staff deeper into her side.

The rags she wore pulled tight around her, threads popping under the tension. She gasped through tears and pain and shook her head. With one last thrust for good measure, Asenten left the cave.

Again, she found herself left to grapple with her new reality in the pitch black of the cave. Darkness, that's all she had left now.

→

Huddled in the corner, Zelia watched Asenten lay the wood for a small fire. While she would be glad for a change from the blue light of his staff, she couldn't help but feel that the fire wasn't for her comfort.

"Go on, start it," he demanded, the corner of his mouth curled up in a wicked sneer. She saw no harm in starting the fire and plucked her red and black speckled fire stone from the floor. The logs crackled to life. With a smirk, Asenten scurried from the cave, and Zelia wondered what he was up to now.

She wasn't at a loss for long. Asenten returned with a young boy. The boy was pale and his light-colored hair shimmered in the firelight as the wizard slammed him to his knees with a sickening thud. Asenten held the boy so close to the fire that the flames would lick the boy's skin with the slightest change of position. The boy winced at the heat and stared at the flames with wide eyes.

"Do it! Or I'll do it for you, and it won't be as quick." He held the struggling boy's head closer to the flames.

"What? No, I won't. I won't kill him! He's just a boy!"

"You won't do it? Fine."

The boy screamed as Asenten shoved his head into the fire.

She clenched her fists so tight blood dripped from her palms. She bent the flames around the boy's head, and into Asenten's chest.

Asenten shoved the bound boy into the hot coals and struggled to rip the flaming tunic from his chest.

She bolted towards the screaming boy, but just as she reached him her chest burned. She looked to Asenten as he ripped the tunic from his chest, revealing blistered flesh where her own pain came from.

Asenten muttered some chant, and a blast from his staff slammed her against the cave wall. She struggled to break free, but his magic held her tight.

"Never forget, you did this to him! You caused this! All because you refused to do as I asked." He pushed the boy further into the hot coals. "Remember, he died this way because you were too weak to do it yourself!"

Her head snapped to the side, and a loud CRACK echoed through the cave. The last thing she heard was the faint screams of the boy as the world went black. Once again, she faced this other darkness and pain filled every agonizing second as her body struggled to repair itself.

>———>

"No! Please! I'll never do it again! Just please let me go!" a girl's voice cried from the tunnel outside her cell and shocked her from her slumber.

Zelia drew a deep breath and stood to meet her captor, the lashing from his last visit still burned as a reminder. Sometimes she wondered why they didn't heal like the blows that killed her, but part of her was thankful for it. At least the scars were proof that what she was going through was real.

"Good you're awake. Get your stone," he said when he rounded the corner.

"Oh, great Asenten, the mightiest of the wizards, which would you wish for me to use on this glorious day?" she asked with a grand bow. Over the years she had learned that he liked flattery and he would sometimes leave without hurting her if she did as he asked.

"Hm, what do you think? Fire or ice?"

"Uh… I… ice?" the red-haired girl stammered.

Zelia fought back the urge to save the girl. She knew all too well she'd only make matters worse. At least if she did it, she could spare her some pain and make it quick.

Asenten's face looked even more evil when he grinned with wicked delight. "Fire it is!"

Zelia's gut wrenched at the sight of his glee, never would she get used to that sight. She spun around and snatched the red and black speckled stone from the cavern floor. With a deep breath, she withdrew behind a wall in her mind and it left a dead look in her eyes. She numbed herself to the world, it was the only way she could cope with what she was about to do.

Asenten flung the girl to the floor, and the girl pleaded from her knees. "Please, please don't do this. I just stole food for my little si—" the girl saw the look in Zelia's eye, her plea cut short.

Zelia held back the tears that threatened to spill over and clenched her fist around the stone as her open hand raised towards the girl.

In a flurry of panic and fear, the girl leaped at her. She knocked Zelia to the ground and landed on top. Zelia's breath whooshed out, and the stone rolled from her grasp. The girl jumped up and ran. Before Zelia had even caught her breath, Asenten dragged her to her feet by the hair of her head.

"Go get her, kill her!" Asenten demanded with a shove towards the cave entrance.

She caught the girl stumbling around near the dark entrance of the cave and lit her ablaze. When Zelia realized something was different, her gaze dropped to her empty palm. She staggered back. With the cold cave wall at her back she looked back to the girl, who gave one last scream and collapsed.

"But… but, how? I didn't have the stone."

She raised her gaze to Asenten's as he towered over her.

"You've lied all these years, decades."

She raised her hand towards him. She didn't care if burning him killed her, she wanted him dead. But his staff connected with the side of her head before she could burn him, and she collapsed in a heap. In that still moment before unconsciousness all she wanted was to get away, to be free of this place.

→

A warm light shined through her eyelids as she stirred. *"Where am I?"* she wondered. A shadow moved across her still closed eyes and dimmed the warm light.

"Do you feel that?"

"Feel what?"

"The presence of someone else." It sounded as though it came from her, only it wasn't her voice.

"Steffon, I think Rog has lost it."

Rog? Who's Rog? Where am I?

Her eyes flicked open, and she glared at the strange, yet familiar, boy, the urge to loathe him fell over her. She tried to look away, but her gaze was unmoving.

"Who's there?" the unfamiliar voice sounded through her head as if it were her own. She tried to reply but he didn't seem to hear her.

Am I dreaming? But why would I dream this? Where am I? An arena? She pulled as much of her surroundings in as she could, blurred forms dotted the huge stone stairs that led up to the blue sky. Sky, oh how she missed seeing the blue of the sky, even if all she could see now was from the corner of her vision, as she continued to stare at the strange boy.

"Rogath, sword up!" yet another voice interrupted her train of thought. Her head shook. "No more games, come on."

"I'm not playing, I feel someone else's presence!" There was that voice again, the one in her head. She felt her irritation with the blond-haired man rise, only it didn't seem to be her own irritation.

"Maybe if you didn't play tricks on everyone all the time someone might believe you. Now, raise your sword." The tip of the sword gleamed in the midday sun before her. "Well go on, back to the pells. Good job Terik, go again."

Rage swelled up and splinters of wood flew away with each hack at the post.

So I, or whoever's head I'm in, must be Rogath, the other boy must be Terik, and the boy, Terik, called the man Steffon. Why and how am I here, and where is here?

Steffon's coaching faded into the background, she wasn't sure if it was her doing or Rog's. With each turn, she focused on as much of her new surroundings as she could, the chipped and splintered posts, the wooden racks of weapons, the large wood targets, and the glorious white stone seats that sprawled in all directions.

They were on the verge of exhaustion when Steffon released them. "That's enough for today boys. Try to be a little more focused tomorrow, Rog."

With a roll of his eyes, Rog slid the sword into the wooden rack. It amazed her how he seemed to glide up the stadium stairs even when exhausted. They skirted the edge of a strange, yet familiar city and she marveled over the beauty of the stone buildings and enormous carvings of god-like men.

Rog glanced down the river and traced the line of a bridge. A pang of joy fell over them, a mix of emotions from her and Rog. A round building seemed to float at the end of the bridge that jutted out past the edge of a waterfall. Something about it drew her to it, but they continued to move towards the golden building. Guards dressed in gold armor gave a curt nod as they passed and she, or rather Rog, returned the gesture.

She couldn't help but feel odd, and out of place in such a building, yet it felt as though it was home. They passed column after column. Hallways led in every direction. Each one appeared the same as the last. Soon she wondered less about where she was and more about how much Rog could feel of her, as she felt his every emotion.

They sat through a dinner with barbaric men who spoke of wars long since passed. She found how they spoke of death as this glorious thing to be off-putting. Part of her wished she could see death as they did, but she knew better.

Halfway through his meal, Rog pushed back from the table.

"Where are you going?" Terik asked.

"To speak with Mother."

"Okay… have fun with that."

Their eyes rolled again, and they returned to the hallway. They soon came upon a brown-haired woman wrapped in rippling waves of silvery cloth.

"Mother?"

"Yes, Rogath? What's the matter?" she asked.

"Mother, I feel someone else's presence as if they are a part of me, yet not."

"Oh, Rogath, you and your overactive imagination. How about you just go get some rest, I'm sure the feeling will go away soon enough."

"Alright, Mother."

The kind and gentle women leaned over and kissed them on the forehead, a warm feeling fell over Rog. Zelia longed to revel in the feeling, but her heart felt heavy with memories of a time she once felt love directed towards her.

Rog laid down in his plush bed and she stirred awake, back in the cave.

➤

Was that real? Her head spun with a hollow ache.

She rubbed the back of her head and her vision focused, only to fall on the charred remains of the girl she had just killed. She recoiled at the sight, looking down at her own hands and recalling what had happened.

She swallowed back the knot in her throat and raised her hand towards the girl's charred remains. The chill of the cave had long since stolen the heat from the fire and yet the flames sparked to life to eat the last of the girl's body until nothing but her charred teeth remained in the darkened spot.

A single tear ran down her cheek. It wasn't just a nightmare. She was the sole reason behind their deaths. No longer could she blame their deaths on these objects the wizard had led to believe were the source of her powers. She knew she was always to blame, but she needed something, anything, to ease the guilt.

She recalled her past in search of any shred of information that could explain her powers. Time and time again all she could recall was the screams of those she'd killed, like the chorus of the dead screaming from the depths of Fregnar's realm. For hours, maybe even days, she sat and stared at her shaking hands, sick of her actions, yet knowing that the wizards would make her kill more in the future.

4

Click, click, click. What used to be her fire stone made a weird hollow noise as she made a new mark for her height. She couldn't track the days, or even the years, so her growth had become the tale of time. She was now maybe a foot or so shorter than Asenten, about the same height Alrindel had been the last she had seen him.

With a sigh, she sat and picked through the rest of the food Asenten had left her. When she heard a yelp and the crack of a tree just outside the mouth of the cave she jumped, it was rare to hear something so close. A little black pup stumbled at her feet as she rounded the last bend of the cave.

"I've got you now!" a deep and garbled voice boomed.

A thick hand as big as her waist pushed through the vines.

"Why do you even bother with such a little thing?" an almost feminine voice asked.

"Pack leader's pup, leave no one to get revenge."

"Enough!" Zelia yelled.

The wolf pup cowered behind her. As the hand pulled back, she stepped closer to the entrance, being careful not to get too close to the barrier that held her there.

"Who's there?" The ogre separated the vines so he could see. "Oh look, the main course."

"Oh, shut up." The other ogre shoved him aside. "It's just a little girl. Come here darling, we'll keep you safe."

"Or you could wait, and there will be more. Someone bigger, more flesh to eat."

Zelia thought of Asenten, she couldn't hurt him, but the ogres could.

"We don't have time to wait, get out of the way."

A hand reached in again and this time grasped her waist before she could move away.

"No!" she screamed as she hit the barrier and the parts of her that touched it burned to ash.

She let a wall of flames erupt in front of her and the ogre threw her away as he drew back.

"Why you little…" the feminine voice half growled as another hand reached in and swatted at her.

It too she lit ablaze as she pressed her burnt shoulder against the cold stone and waited for all to be still outside the cave.

"Wha... what are you?" the little pup asked as he backed away from her.

"It's okay." She drew a deep breath and suppressed her pain. "I'm not going to hurt you."

"Wait, you understand me?"

"Yes. Are you hurt?"

The little pup shook his head, and his stomach growled.

"You're hungry I take it. Well, give me just a second."

She pushed herself to her feet and held a flame out in front of her as she went back around a bend in the cave to retrieve the last of her food.

"It's not much, but you can have it."

The pup sniffed it before gobbling it up.

"What's your name?" she asked.

"Dain and yours?"

"Zelia. How far off is your pack?"

As if on cue, a faint howl sounded in the distance and the pup's ears perked forward.

"I have to go, mum's calling. I'll be back though. Thank you for saving me."

The pup squirmed through the vines and left her alone once again.

➤━━━━━━━➤

"Look, ogre tracks. There must be a cave around here somewhere," a deep voice spoke with a tinge of disdain in the dwarven tongue, not far from the mouth of the cave.

"More like a pile of ashes."

Something stirred the ashes of the ogres and she coughed as the breeze blew them into the cave.

"Shh, did you hear that?"

Zelia grabbed the leather bag at her feet and moved deeper into the cave as metal scraped on metal, the telltale sound of a sword being drawn. If someone found her Asenten would make her kill them, even if he had to track them down first. The vines parted, and she froze in the blinding light.

"You there."

"Shh, you'll scare her." The young Dwarf pushed past his grey-haired companion. "It's alright, we won't hurt you. I'm Prince Connan, what's your name?"

"Prince Connan?"

She shook her head. The young Prince gasped when she turned, revealing her ash covered burn. For a moment she thought of lying, but what could the truth do to her now.

"I'm Zelia."

"Why are you in here?"

"I..." Her shoulder burned and reminded her why she couldn't leave. "I like the cave," she lied.

"The ogres are gone. You needn't hide here. Come, where's your family?"

"I know they are. I killed them." She glanced at the charred remains of another she had killed and lowered her head. "And my family is dead, they have been for a long time."

"You could come with us."

She shook her head. She knew she couldn't pass the mouth of the cave. She had tried, and the ogres were just a reminder. Prince Connan reached for her and she bolted deeper into the cave.

"Leave her." There was a bit of a struggle behind her. "I've never seen this cave before, and we have no light. We'll come back."

"She's just a little girl."

"There's something more to her, she's not from The Trading Town, her accent doesn't match. We'll come back with light."

"Fine."

She could hear their footsteps fade and the rustle of the vines as they passed outside. She waited in silence for a long while before retrieving the pack. If Asenten saw it, he would lock her deeper in the tunnels again. The barrier kept her from leaving, but with access to the cave mouth, she could at least breathe the fresh air when the wind blew up from the south.

When she snatched the pack from the floor, she noticed something by the vines. With a flame lit in her palm, she scooped up a leather pouch. She let the flame creep up her arm so she could use both hands to untie it. As she pulled it open the smell of fresh seasoned meat hit her. It wasn't something she had liked when she was little, but now the jerky was the best thing she had. She ripped off a little piece of the tough tangy meat and settled down next to the vines. A storm had rolled in, and the wind was misting the mouth of the cave.

What am I going to do when they come back? Asenten will make me kill them if he learns they saw me. He'll make me kill them all when he finds out.

She stared down at the shriveled piece of meat in her hand. The jerky burned a little as she swallowed, the Dwarves always liked spicy things. She stuffed the rest back in the pouch. *Who knows how long it will be before I'm given food again?*

I'll just have to hide when Connan comes back, just like I'll have to hide this.

Lightning crackled outside, lighting up the dark hole for just a moment. She covered her ears as the thunder boomed, amplified by the acoustics of the cave. Then she waited for the echoes of the thunder to settle before continuing deeper into the cave.

She tucked the jerky into a little hole low and out of sight, then she curled up with the rough leather pack tucked under her head as a pillow.

I have to keep Asenten from finding out, she thought and drifted asleep.

"Rog!" Terik half growled.

Rogath laughed and darted between the wooden posts that served as training pells in the arena.

What did you do now? Zelia thought.

"Rogath." Steffon sighed and rubbed his temples.

Rog stopped behind Steffon and peered around at Terik. Terik stomped towards them, his hair dripping, and clothes plastered to him.

"No magic at practice!" Terik threw himself at Rog.

Rog didn't even bother to dodge him, getting caught was all part of his plan. He rolled with Terik in the sandy dirt, thoroughly coating the other boy. Rog jumped to his feet and ran for the stairs as he dusted the few particles of sand from himself.

"That's enough for the day. Go clean up, Terik," Steffon conceded.

Rog slowed as he neared the bridge over the water.

"Hello again. You've been visiting a lot, I may not be able to see or hear you, but I can feel you," Rog said.

Zelia sighed, Rog had become more perceptive of her presence over time and she had found she could sometimes sway his decisions when he was in the best of moods.

"I don't think Terik is quite done with you, Rog. What did you do this time?" a guard asked.

She could almost feel Rog's grin as he looked over his shoulder at Terik and picked up his pace.

"Want to watch the sunset? It won't be long," Rog said as he climbed a tall staircase.

Even a brief mention of the sunset or the stars was enough to stir Zelia's longing to see them again with her own eyes.

"I'll take that as a yes."

He skirted a few long halls and came to a balcony where he sat on its edge.

"You know, one day I will find a way to hear you, to free you."

He sighed and leaned back against a column. They watched as the sky turned from blue to gold and then darkened until the stars twinkled on the horizon.

⟶

"There you are. Zelia."

A wet nose nudged her cheek, and she rubbed the sleep from her eyes.

"Dain?"

"I need your help, there's a hatchling, I found it stuck under one of the trees the ogres knocked over while chasing me," the pup rambled on.

"Wait, slow down." Zelia took a deep breath. "Where is it?"

"I left it at the mouth of the cave. I was hoping you would know what to do with it. Mom wanted to eat it, but it's my fault it's tree got knocked over."

She scratched Dain's head and stared towards the mouth of the cave. *What can I do? I don't have any food.* Then she thought of the jerky. *Prince Connan will be back, I can leave it out for them if I can keep it alive that long.*

"Do you care if I pick you up?"

"Why?"

"You ran into things walking back here, didn't you?"

"Y... yeah," the pup conceded.

She couldn't help but snuggle him to her chest when she scooped him up. She breathed in the musky smell of his coat and rubbed her cheek against his soft fuzzy fur as she walked. She loved the gentle warmth that radiated from him and the steady thud of his heart.

"I wish you could stay." She shook her head, shifting her thoughts to the reality of her existence. "No. No one should stay here. Especially not a fine future leader as handsome and kind as you."

She gave him a little squeeze and set him down.

"Zelia, why don't you leave? Why have I never seen you in the woods?"

"I can't leave, but don't worry about me. Where's this hatchling of yours?"

He sniffed the air, and the vines rustled as he pushed through them. A startled screech came from the little bird, and Dain dropped it at her feet. She knelt and picked it up before it could run off again.

"Thank you, Dain." She scratched him right behind the ear and he leaned into it. "You should get back to your mother, she's probably worried about you."

Dain sighed and shook out his coat. "You're right, but I'll be back."

"No, it's not safe for you to come here again. Maybe one day I'll be able to visit you."

"Alright, I'll keep a watch out for you."

The soft glow of morning light shimmered through the vines as Dain passed through them.

She sat back against the cave wall and sighed. "Now what am I going to do with you?"

She stroked the little bird's head.

"Do you have a name?"

"Flyx."

"Really? Well… alright."

"Zelia?" Connan's voice called from just outside the mouth of the cave.

Her first instinct was to hide, but Flyx screeched and she settled back again. *Have to take care of you first, then I'll deal with Asenten.*

"Here?" another voice asked. "But there's no cave here!"

"What's that? James, wrong for once?" Connan spoke again.

"He's not lying, there is a cave here," Zelia replied.

"An elf?"

"No, a girl."

The vines parted and Connan and James ducked inside, holding a torch out in front of him so he could see.

"Awe, there you are. You weren't waiting on me, were ya?" Connan asked.

"No. I have something for you," the dwarven language felt strange and clunky on her tongue after so long. She rocked to her feet and put Flyx in his hand. "Will you take care of her for me? Her name is Flyx. The ogres knocked down her tree."

"Where did you learn our language?"

James reached to brush her hair behind her ear. Her heart jumped in her throat and she backed away.

"I'm not an elf if that's what you're asking. I've known your language for many years, though it's been a while since I've used it."

"Your grandfather will want to meet her."

"Please no." Zelia backed further into the cave and her jaw quivered as she fought to think of some way to convince them to go. "Please just go. I wasn't going to let you find me again, but Flyx needs someone else. Please, just take care of her."

Zelia turned and darted into the cave, lighting a flame in her palm so she could see enough to run.

"Zelia!"

She could hear his footsteps as he followed, but she smothered her flame as she ducked behind a stalagmite and hoped he wouldn't see.

"Connan. I don't think she wants to be found."

"Did you even take a good look at her?"

"Of course, I did." James took a deep breath. "I know she needs help, but you can't help someone who doesn't want help."

I do want help, but I'm tired of killing. Her eyes watered, but she refused to let a tear fall. If Asenten saw she'd been crying, he'd punish her.

"Well, I'm not giving up. Zelia, I know you can hear me. Please come out, I only want to help."

Zelia struggled to steady her breath as she waited, hoping Connan would give up before Asenten returned. Her back ached from sitting still in the awkward position by the time Connan sighed.

"I'll be back."

The footsteps receded, and she waited a while before moving from her hiding place. She found a larger leather bag waiting for her this time.

She was about to throw it through the vines when Asenten pushed his way through. She stepped back and dropped the bag behind her.

"What are you doing this far up?"

He scowled at her and then noticed the bag. He shoved her to the side and snatched it up.

"What is this? Where did you get this?" he demanded.

"I… It was left in the cave. The storm, someone took shelter here."

"Who? Did they see you?"

"No." She shook her head and edged closer to the back of the cave.

Asenten flipped the bag open and dumped its contents.

"No? Then what's all this?"

"I… I don't…"

Asenten mumbled in an ancient tongue and she stumbled back.

"Please no. I didn't say anything. They didn't see me."

Asenten strode towards her and slammed her against the wall, knocking her senseless.

⟶

She blacked out to find Rog asleep, and they were caught in a black void between minds but could both feel each other's presence.

"Who's there?" Rog's voice echoed through their heads.

"Y... you hear me?" her internal voice caught as her head throbbed.

"Who are you and why are you in my head?"

"Zelia and if I find out, you'll be the second to know."

"Are you okay? You don't feel like you usually do."

"Wait... how do you know anything about me?"

"The same as how you know so much about me. So, where are you?"

"Then why did you never say that you saw through my eyes while you sleep?"

"I didn't want to make things harder for you, but now... where are you?"

"The Forgotten Lands."

"Where?" Rog asked, downright puzzled.

"South of the Mountains of The Old Ones, a home of Dwarves on Mineria."

"So, I was right!"

At that moment, if Zelia had possessed a physical form, she would have rolled her eyes.

"So, now that we can talk, why are you being held in a cave?"

"Can we talk about something else, please?" she begged. *"Anything else, horses, wolves, birds, the stars…"* An overwhelming sense of longing washed over them.

"You really miss seeing the stars, don't you? Wait, no, don't hide your feelings. I'm sorry, it's just…"

"It's okay Rog, I… I just can't."

"Can't what?" Rog prodded through her feelings. *"Wait… you weren't always held by Asenten were you? He took something from you, more than just your life and innocence. You had a family before…"*

"Stop!" she demanded and locked her emotions away from him, just as he sometimes did to her.

"Zelia, I could ask fath… Yargo… he could save you."

"No. He'll make me hurt him. I don't want anyone else to get hurt because of me…"

"You know he'll make you kill Connan as soon as he finds out."

"I… I know." Another spike of pain hit her as someone was trying to nudge her awake.

"Just hold on a little longer, alright." There was a sweet and concerned tone to Rog's voice that she had never heard before as their connection severed.

5

"Get up! We're going somewhere," Asenten demanded with a jab from the butt of his staff.

"Where?"

"You forced our hand. This is Prince Connan's bag. We can't just let him and everyone he has told live."

What? He doesn't mean... She shrank back at the sight of his twisted grin. *He does!*

"No, I won't kill all of those people!" She pushed back against the cave wall and wedged herself in place. *"Rog, if you're there, please hurry."*

"Would you rather die, again?" He asked.

"Why does it matter? I'd die doing what you want, anyway. You know I can't do that big a blast."

He ignored her words and bashed the end of his staff into her gut. She pulled away from the cave wall as she clutched her stomach.

"Disobedience again?" He threw her around so her back faced him.

Her fingers dug into the wall. *Just take it, you can't go back there, not again.* Another lashing across her back ripped open old and new scars. The taste of iron nipped at the tip of her tongue as she bit her lip, she knew what punishment would ensue if she let out so much as a pained gasp.

"Now, are you going to come?" he asked.

She still faced away from him when she shook her head. She couldn't make out his chant, but she knew him well enough and braced herself. With the tap of his staff beside her, she went hurtling towards the far cave wall. Ribs cracked with the force driven into her chest by Asenten's staff. She gasped in pain and hugged her chest.

46

"I'll be back, and you better be ready to be obedient when I get here!"

⯈

"Father! Father!" Rog yelled as he ran across the massive throne room, ignoring the magnificence of Yargo's throne, having seen it so many times before.

"Yes Rog?"

"I... Zelia needs your help..."

"That girl you dreamt of all those years ago? Not this again, Rog," Yargo said.

"But she's real! She lives on Mineria, and he's going to kill her! Please Father," Rog reached his father. His eyes were frantic and he was breathless as he grabbed the foot of the throne. "I'm begging you, at least ask Lumid if she's real."

"Why are you so interested in this human girl?" Yargo sat forward to look down on his son, not understanding why Rog was so insistent on helping this girl.

"She's not human... she's... well, the wizards claim she's my sister... she's the same age as Terik and me." He pulled back from Yargo to watch his reaction.

"Very well Rog, I will ask Lumid." He sat back in his throne.

"Now," Rog demanded when he saw Yargo was in no hurry to see to his request.

"This isn't another one of your games is it?" Yargo asked, an eyebrow raised.

Rog's shoulders rolled back as he spun around. "If it was, it would be my worst one yet." He turned back to his Father and continued, "Please, go ask Lumid, now."

Yargo heaved a sigh, stood, and swung his staff with each step. "Very well, Rogath."

⯈

Lumid, the God of Passage, was in his home, the sacred place of passage to Mineria, when Yargo found him.

"Why do you ask?" he demanded, but he was already turning the magnifying lenses towards Mineria.

Yargo sat on a nearby chair and waited for Lumid to finish fine-tuning the lenses. "Rog says he is connected to this girl and sees her in his dreams.

He claims that a wizard that holds her is about to kill her… and that this wizard claims that she is Terik and Rogath's sister."

"Could she be from the line of Kings?"

"Perhaps, but that wouldn't explain her connection to Rog."

Lumid stiffened as the lenses stopped moving. "Well, I do not know whose daughter she is, but she is real. It appears the wizard has bound her using his life force." Lumid winced as he studied her and continued, "And she undeniably needs saving from him before he kills her."

"So at least part of Rog's story is true, there's only one way to find the truth behind the rest of his story." He sighed and turned towards the bridge entrance. "Barg, Gaeru!"

"Yargo?" They both turned from where they stood guard.

"We're going to Mineria."

"Look for the thick vines and tree roots, the cave is well concealed."

Lumid gave Yargo a nod and sank his sword into the initiation switch centered in the room. All the colors of the rainbow exploded around the trio. When the light faded Yargo and his warriors had disappeared.

"May I watch through your eyes, please?" Rogath asked.

Lumid studied him for a moment before nodding. Rogath drew a symbol in the air that glowed and pulsed once before they were watching through Lumid's eyes.

On Mineria, Yargo appeared outside a cave veiled in vines. The entrance didn't look like much, but the draft that drifted through as they moved told otherwise. They found a young girl near the entrance, her ripped and tattered clothing soaked in blood. Cautious not to startle her, Yargo laid a gentle hand on her shoulder.

She flinched at the touch, her connection to Rogath snapping away. She raised her teary eyed gaze. "Yargo?" She rocked to her knees and buried her face in the crook of his shoulder. "Thank you, Rog," she whispered.

"Shh, I have you now," Yargo assured her with a stroke of her tangled mess of curly hair.

"You are not welcome here! Leave now or face your deaths!" an old man's voice boomed through the cave.

Zelia shook her head and shrank back from the voice.

Yargo turned to face the aged wizard but was sure to keep himself between her and the threatening stranger. "Zelia is coming with us, release her now."

"Never," Asenten spat as he raised his staff and chanted in the Wizard Tongue, "Fe father en dais lath en thesinos."

"No!" Zelia screamed and jumped from behind Yargo, throwing a wall of ice between Asenten and the others.

Asenten's staff slammed on the ground and a blast of fire, metal, and rock shook the cave. It caught Zelia in its path, the shockwave hitting her like a stone wall, throwing her through the air. She landed with a sickening crunch like ice shattering against the far wall, her chest caving in on itself. The pain was so great she nearly screamed, but she couldn't. She could never express her pain. Her heart thudded against the freezing stone of the cave floor as she slipped back to Rogath's mind, the echoes of the blast still rattling her teeth.

With his magic spent, Asenten pulled a sword. Caught in a rage, he slashed at the warriors but they stepped clear of his swing. His rage out of control in a way she had never seen, he launched himself at Yargo.

Yargo knocked Asenten to the side and Barg, unfazed by the attack, cut off Asenten's head with one clean swipe of his sword.

The weight of power that hung in the cave seemed to shift as Asenten's death released Zelia from his spells. Yargo knew the magic of wizards well, Rogath's mother had gifted them the power. The dead wizard's powers were tainted, they couldn't be allowed to pass on to another, so Yargo trapped them in his own staff.

"My lord Yargo…" Gaeru stared at Zelia's motionless body as she lay face down on the cave floor, surrounded by rubble and scorch marks.

When Yargo turned her over, the color drained from his face. Her half-frozen beating heart showed through the gaping hole in her ribcage. There was little blood as the flames of Asenten's spell had cauterized most of the wound.

Yargo scooped her limp body from the ground and cradled her close. She slipped back into her own mind, the pain of being moved ripping her back and a sense of terror coursed through her at the thought that he could leave her in this place for the others to find.

"Plea... please, don't leave me," she begged, through ragged and choked breaths. With one last flutter of her eyes, she fell unconscious and her mind slipped back to Rogath's.

"Lumid!" Yargo called as he strode from the cave. He didn't even slow his pace as Lumid pulled them back to Hyperia.

Lumid snatched Rog when he ran across the threshold of the chamber.

"Let me go! Let me see her!" Rog yelled and struggled to break free.

"No," Lumid said as he struggled to hold him. But Lumid's attempt to keep Rog from her ended in vain as he wriggled free.

Rog leapt into Yargo's path and stared right at Zelia's mangled chest. "Is— is she going to be okay? Pl... please tell me we can save her," Rog begged. His shaking hand brushing against her hair.

"I don't know Rog, but please stay with Lumid for now."

Rog didn't move a muscle when Yargo hurried down the bridge. Once they were gone, he just stood there, staring at the drop of blood he had brushed from her cheek. He clenched his fist then ran after his father. He feared Yargo would turn him away, so he wrapped himself in mist, using it to refract light to hide himself.

"Yalif!" Yargo called as he neared the infirmary, her body still draped in his arms.

"Yes sir? How is she still alive?" Yalif gasped when Yargo laid Zelia on his table.

"I don't know but do what you can."

Yalif caught the concern on Yargo's face and gave a reserved nod, then set to work. He pulled the first few hunks of shrapnel from her chest and stopped as he neared her heart.

"How is her heart frozen yet still beating?" He asked, astonished at the sight.

"I'm not sure but learn what you may once you save her."

With a glance at Yargo, Yalif brushed his fingers over the exposed ends of her bare ribs.

"I will need a metal plate to replace the ribs that are missing." Yalif didn't even have to look to know that Yargo had left the room.

"Why does he care so much about you? What is it that interests him?" Yalif asked himself as he pulled metal, rock, and fragments of bone from her chest. "Rogath, if you are going to hide you need to learn to hide your concern. Well, do not just stand there, hold this." He held out the bowl he was putting the pieces of shrapnel in.

Rogath took the bowl without looking away from Zelia's face. She could feel more than hear his thoughts as he stared at her. He had never seen her face before, now he had one to go with the sorrowful presence in his mind. She was pretty, even with the hint of a faded scar on her temple.

How Terik would tease him once he saw her, even if she felt like a sibling to him as much as Terik did. He glanced at her chest and blanched, forcing himself to turn away. He couldn't stand the thought of losing her, not when he should have pushed father to save her sooner. Asenten had said her soul was bound to the cave. What if he meant she would always reappear there when she died?

"Is there anything more I can do?" Rogath asked.

Yalif paused to glance at him. "No, but you can take a break if you need to."

Rogath shook his head. "I'm the only one she knows. I don't want her to freak out if she wakes."

Yalif nodded and continued the tedious task of removing the shrapnel.

Zelia wished she could reach out and tell Rogath she would be okay, but she had no way to do so with his emotions such a mess. He didn't even seem to feel her presence as he usually did, though it may have been her own body's exhaustion pushing her to be a silent presence in the back of his mind. Besides, she wasn't sure if this was real or just some mind trick the wizards were playing on her. But for the first time in centuries, she held a sliver of hope in her heart, no matter how mangled it was.

⟶

It was several hours later when Yargo returned.

"The blast that caused this, do you know what spell he used?" Yalif asked.

"No, why?" Yargo asked, then seeing Rogath he glared. "So, this is where you have been, your mother has been looking all over for you."

"Do not mind him, he has been helping," Yalif said. "I need to know what spell he used. Some shrapnel has bonded to her heart and lungs. I cannot remove all of it. I have been trying for hours."

Rogath's gaze dropped to the bowl full of shrapnel that they had removed, it was the size of a dinner plate and was almost full. "Mother may be able to pull residual magic from these and figure out what spell he used," Rogath said and handed the bowl to Yargo.

"He is right. Now do not come back until you have an answer or the metal plate," Yalif said, shooing Yargo from the room.

"What now?" Rogath asked, needing to help.

"Now we stitch what we can. There is some thread that will dissolve with time in the cabinet, in the blue jar."

51

Rogath went to the wood cabinet and pulled a little blue jar from a shelf at eye level. He watched as Yalif pulled a length of thin white thread from the jar and threaded a needle. He needed something, anything to do. Watching Yalif move with the slow tediousness of a master while Zelia's life hung in the balance was about to drive him mad.

"Would you work on cleaning the dirt and blood from her while I do this?" Yalif asked. "Just make sure you dump the water often, so she does not get an infection. There is sterilized water in the barrel behind you."

Rogath turned, finding a bowl and sponge sitting on top of the barrel. He drew water from the tap, the slow stream driving him to use his powers. When he stood, he stared at the sponge.

"Do I have to use the sponge, or can I—"

"Yes, you may use your powers. While you are at it, warm the water. She's losing too much heat."

Rogath nodded, letting a flame lick up the sides of the bowl, warming it like he would his bathwater. They had created mechanisms to heat their water, but sometimes he found it faster to warm it himself. Besides, he seldom had a reason to use fire. His mother always pushed the use of air and water above all else.

He pushed the water across her skin, scrubbing years of dirt from her inch by inch. Each time the water clouded with dirt or blood, he would pause and push the particles from the water and into a bucket Yalif kept by the door. The drain of using his powers felt nice, it made him feel as though he was helping. As he cleaned, he found that her skin was paler than it had seemed. Between the lack of light and loss of blood, her skin was the lightest he had ever seen, its color standing in stark contrast to even his own pale skin. Terik was always the one graced with a stunning tan, but Zelia made him feel downright sun kissed.

➔

The plate for her ribcage came with word that Zivu couldn't pull anything from the shrapnel. So Yalif finished and slathered his special healing salve across her open wounds. Half of the front of her ribcage was missing and each time he tried to bond the metal to her ribs with magic the connection fell apart. At last, he wiped his hands and conceded.

"You may want to leave for this," Yalif said.

"No. I'll help hold her still."

Rog moved to her shoulders and was shocked at how cold and clammy her skin had become, even with his water warmed. He forced himself to look away as Yalif drove small screws through the plate and into her ribs. With each twist she fought her body's call for her to return, but when Yalif began to bend her sprung ribs back into place, she slipped back. She couldn't help but arch her back as she battled the urge to lash out and stop him, her body screaming for him to stop.

"Shh, you'll be okay. You're doing very well," Yalif comforted her with a soft tone.

She shuddered as she forced herself to return to Rogath, where she clung to his mind as her body went back to its limp state.

It seemed like it took an eternity, but Yalif was finally done. He tied off the last of her bandages and stepped out to speak with Yargo. "I've done all I can, only time will tell now. But to tell the truth… I wouldn't count on her making it."

"Thank you Yalif."

Rogath's heart sank at the words, she had to make it, he wouldn't be able to forgive himself if he had been too late.

6

"Rog, I need you to tell me everything you know about Zelia." Yargo said, guiding Rogath to take a seat on a long couch in the study down the hall.

In a flash of Rog's memories, Zelia found herself trapped in images of her own past, unable to pull herself from Rog's mind. Their back ablaze in pain as they crumpled to the damp cave floor, only to be jerked back to their feet for the next lashing. He didn't feel the pain as she did, but it still blazed through her own mind.

Chants of unseen men echoed through the cave, Zelia knew the voices well enough, but Rog didn't place faces with the voices. The chants stopped, replaced by arguments over what to do with their failed creation. Horror ran rampant through Rog's mind as a man before him burned alive, the searing heat of flames lapped at their outstretched hand, yet they remained unburned. An old man with a long beard leered at them as they struggled to raise their sweat drenched body from the cave floor. Lectures from the same old man over and over of control and destiny and war and how she was the biggest disappointment they'd ever had.

"Rog?"

Yargo's voice snapped them back to the present and for the first time, Rog spilled all the horrors he'd seen through his connection with Zelia. Caught up in Rog's feelings and memories, she didn't think of what Rog was saying. What little she caught; she couldn't believe was coming from his lips. He told Yargo everything, everything from the powers she held to how she tortured and killed people, even children, leaving out only the worst of what she had been through as he couldn't bring himself to recall them in detail. But she did notice one thing, not once did he think of the true reason for her creation and it made her wonder if he knew?

Her mind moved and tugged away from Rog's finding warmth as she returned to her body. *Where am I?* she thought, her mind spinning as the pain hit her. *I was...* She rolled from the bed and scanned the room. When her feet hit the ground, she crumpled. Her lungs burned, and she hugged her sides, rocking in a desperate struggle for air.

"Yargo?" she breathed.

She pulled the sheet around her shoulders as she staggered to her feet and into the hallway.

She scanned the corridor, white marble columns capped in gold ran in either direction, with doors standing in the alcoves between them. *I really am on Hyperia? Why did Yargo bring me here? Wait... that was real. That's why Rog was telling Yargo about me, but that means he didn't know what I am and what I've done before he brought me here. What will happen when they find out? What will Rog think when he learns the wizards created me to kill them, everyone he cares about?* She forced herself from her rampaging thoughts and looked around. She stood at the open edge of a balcony and her breath caught at the sight of the clear, blue sky. Easing down against a giant column until her back rested against it, she scanned the horizon and saw Hyperia with her own eyes for the first and maybe last time. *It's even more beautiful in person.* People bustled in the busy streets, horses moved to and from the stables, and water rushed beneath the bridge that led to the passage to Mineria. She watched the water flow over the edge of what seemed to be the world itself and allowed herself to drift from her pain and questions, to enjoy this little slice of peace before it could come crashing down around her.

"She's missing!" Yalif's voice echoed from the hall and pulled her conscious mind back to the present.

"She's missing? Where could she have gone? It's not like she could have just gotten up and walked off," Yargo said.

"Yes, she could have." Zelia's attention perked at the sound of Rog's voice, it seemed sweeter to the ear than in her head.

"I doubt that, she shouldn't have even woken up for days, let alone walked off!" Yalif said.

"How would you know? You know nothing about her." Zelia imagined Rog shaking his head as his gliding step drew closer.

"And just where do you think you are going?" Yargo asked.

The tap of Rog's feet ceased. "I'm going to find Zelia." He didn't wait for his Father's reply before his pace quickened until he came to the balcony. He crept around the column, as if scared of what he might find.

"Rog, I…" her voice trailed off. She hugged the lower half of her chest, her breathing strained as she sucked in shallow breaths.

"It's okay, we don't need to talk, let's just sit."

She edged away, her mind begging her to run and never look back. *What if he ends up like all the others? What if this is all just part of the wizards' plan? No, that won't happen, I won't let myself…*

"Zelia, you… you're safe here."

But you're not, not as long as I'm here. She turned her head away.

"Asenten can't control you anymore. Yargo and his warriors killed him."

She could feel the warmth of his hand grow closer and she fought with herself, part of her yearned to connect with him, but she just couldn't bring herself to close the gap.

"So, this is who you've been seeing in your dreams." Rog's hand shot back at the sound of his brother's voice right behind him. "I didn't really believe you. So… how did you know she'd be here?"

"She's always been drawn here. I could feel her pulling me here every time I passed. She loves the stars and is fascinated by the passage to her realm."

"Feel her pulling you here?" Terik asked, confused.

"We each see what the other did that day, or are doing, whenever we sleep. At least, I think that's how it works."

A shadow fell across her and she looked up to see Rog's mother, Zivu, kneel beside her.

"Zelia, you are welcome to stay here with us."

"I… thank you, Lady Zivu."

"You'll love it here, I promise," Rog assured her.

"Yeah, welcome to the family, sis," Terik said as he leaned against Rog's shoulder.

"Perhaps we should let Zelia rest, she has been through a great deal."

"I don't think she wants to go lie down," Rogath said.

She glanced at him, then turned back to the view outside. He was right, rest was the last thing she wanted when her time here could be cut short at any second.

"Hm, well, Rog, how about you and Terik show Zelia around after you grab her some clothes," Zivu suggested as she rocked onto her feet. "That is, if you are up to it."

Zelia nodded. While her pain was nearly overwhelming, her longing to be outdoors again was stronger.

"Come on, we'll give you the official tour, right Terik?"

Rog stepped into her line of sight, a mischievous grin on his face and offered her his hand. It was the first time she'd seen his face when it wasn't a reflection she saw through his eyes. His wide grin captivated her attention and drew her to reach for his hand and made her question how long it had been since she had given a genuine smile. The thought reminded her of what was happening, and she looked away from his face, pulling her hand back.

"It's okay, there's nothing to fear here Zelia," Rog said, his shoulders dropped, and he pushed his hand closer to her. "Please?"

The need to pull away still gripped at her, but she forced herself to take his hand. Even if it was just an illusion created by Asenten, she needed this.

They were about to pass the infirmary when Yalif stopped them. "You should not be up and walking."

"It is okay Yalif, the boys will keep an eye on her," Zivu said, yet there was something about her tone that implied that they wouldn't be the only ones watching.

The chance to make a break for it before him, Rog led Zelia down the hallway and Terik trailed close behind.

7

"Watch this!" Rog dropped Zelia's hand and ran towards the pond. When he reached the water's edge it erupted in movement with a wave of Rog's hand.

"Awesome, you'll have to show me how sometime," Zelia said. *I wish I could be more like you, Rog. So carefree, viewing the world with curiosity, but then I'd risk hurting or even killing everyone…*

Caught up in his own feelings of excitement, Rog flashed a broad smile. "You know, we could learn together!"

"And I can teach you to fight, well, once you're healed," said Terik from his stone perch above the rocky shore.

Zelia forced a smile and looked back and forth between them. "I'd love that." She drew a deep breath, steeling herself, and sat against Terik's rocky perch.

"Are you okay?" Rog asked.

Her fingers dug into her side as she let out the breath she held. "I'll be fine, it just hurts."

She could feel Terik's gaze as his blurred form climbed down the side of the rock.

"She doesn't look so well. We should get her back inside."

No. She shook her head. She didn't want to go back inside, but the lid she kept on her pain slipped, the steady trickle that leaked out swelling to a torrent. All the pain she had suppressed swelled to the surface, and she leaned forward, gasping.

"Guard! Help! Come quickly!" was the last thing she heard as she fell into Rog's arms.

⟶

She opened her eyes to find Yalif checking her temperature, as sweat dripped from her brow.

"Zelia, how are you feeling?"

"F... fine."

"You should be dead," he said with a puzzled look.

"You're right, I should be."

She sighed and refused to meet his gaze.

"Zelia, I can't help you if you don't tell me."

"I don't think Asenten was trying to kill Yargo, though the spell could have if he was any of the other wizards. No, he was trying to kill me. I just don't know why."

"Why would he use a spell strong enough to kill a god to kill you?"

"Because I can't die, at least not really. I still remember how it felt as they swept up my ashes and the pain as my body took years to reconstruct the first time. It's strange how I can heal from that, yet normal injuries linger."

"How? You're not a phoenix," Yalif said, his eyebrows knit in confusion.

"It doesn't matter anymore. I... I just can't let myself or my powers hurt anyone else."

"What do you mean?"

"My powers are only meant to hurt people, even me." She sat up, her chest screaming in protest, but she ignored it.

"Magic is not meant to hurt. I'm sure Yargo and the others will do all they can to help you."

"If they don't find out…" she muttered to herself.

"Find out what?"

She shook her head and a silent moment passed before Yargo appeared in the doorway.

"Thank you Yalif, I will take her from here," Yargo said.

I never should have told him. I never should have told anyone, she thought as Yalif withdrew from the room.

Yargo sat beside her and waited until she shifted under his gaze.

"You know, if you feel the need to talk, you can always talk to Lumid or myself. There is nothing you need to hide from us."

Caught in thoughts of the past an image rose before her eyes, one of a pleading man's face with blood dripping from the little boy he held tight in his arms. She swallowed hard, shivered, and shook herself back to the present.

"Why do you trust me? You don't know me. How do you… how do

you know I won't hurt you or your family?" Tears brimmed in her eyes, but she refused to let them spill over.

Yargo gave a small, sad smile. "I don't know for certain, but I know you wouldn't do anything to hurt us on purpose. You proved that when you were willing to sacrifice yourself to protect me and my men. Rogath told me how your powers react to one another. I know your ribs shattered like that because you used ice to protect us when you shouldn't have."

"That's just it, I did it for selfish reasons. I wanted you to kill Asenten. But…" She pulled away, unable to do anything but loathe herself and what she had become.

Yargo swept her hair out of her face.

"Zelia, there is no shame in wanting to be free of an abusive captor. Even if it means that the captor must die in order for you to do so."

"It wasn't abuse I sought to escape. He... he forced me to kill people for him. THAT is why I had to get free of his control. I just can't. I can't keep doing that. And yet I'm here."

Caught up in the webs of her past, her chest tightened and pressed against the metal plate. She clenched her teeth against the pain. She couldn't help but feel as though this might have been part of the wizards' plans all along. A flicker of movement from the hallway drew her attention to Rog and Terik's approach and she shifted away from Yargo, pulling herself back together as she did.

"Perfect timing, you all need to get to dinner, and I need to go tend to my official duties."

"She's seen through my eyes. She knows you're the keeper of fallen warriors and must see to them each night. You don't need to hide it," Rog said. "Come on, let's go get you something warm to eat. That'll be a first in a while."

He grabbed her hand and turned on his heels to lead her away.

8

"Praise the gods, she lives!" Barg elbowed Gaeru and pointed to her as she entered the dining hall.

"Nice to see you're still kicking," Gaeru said.

She just glanced at him and took her seat beside Rog, at the far end of the table.

"I thought you said she lost half of her rib cage, and you could see her heart."

With a laugh, another warrior continued, "I wonder how many other times you've over exaggerated things!"

"He wasn't exaggerating," Zelia nearly whispered it, yet they all heard.

Everyone at the table turned towards her, food fell from their forks as they sat in silence. None of them even made a move to regain the fallen pork from their stew. She wasn't sure if it was what she said or the fact she knew their language. *Language,* she mused. It was one of the few things Asenten never took from her, he would even come in speaking different languages from time to time, as though he wanted her to keep the knowledge of each of them.

"Then... then how are you alive, let alone already up and moving?" one of them broke the uneasy silence.

She stared out at the stars to avoid their gaze. "I... I've grown accustomed to being in pain."

"So, Gaeru, tell us how you defeated the wizard," Rog interposed to take the warriors' focus off Zelia.

"Actually, she made a wall of ice in front of us before we even realized what he was doing. After his attempt to attack us, it was easy to defeat him.

Zelia, why didn't you kill him yourself?"

"Because, he cast a spell so that anything I did to him would happen to me. I would have gladly killed him long ago. Still, I tried on occasion." Her gaze fell from the stars, and a veil of hair shielded her face from their stares.

Caught up in the past and her inability to stop Asenten herself, ice crept across her chair. Without so much as a word, Rog pried her hand from the arm of the chair. She dug her nails into her palm and pulled from Rog's grasp. *Why did you do that? I trained you better than that!* Asenten's voice boomed in her mind. She shook her head. *No, he's gone now. He can't control you anymore.*

"So, who wants to tell me about the war with the old gods tonight?" Terik interjected.

With a grin spread ear to ear, Barg rambled off about how he fought giant creatures and the old gods. Her mind running with thoughts of how she could have hurt Rog, Zelia didn't listen to Barg.

"Rogath, I'm going for a walk."

"Would you like me to come?"

"No, finish eating."

With that, she stood and slipped from the room. She wasn't going anywhere in particular but found herself back on the balcony. It wasn't long before the shush of a gliding step approached.

"It's amazing how different the stars appear from here." When Rog sat, she continued, "Thank you for stopping me back there."

He flashed that little trickster grin of his, the one she had only ever felt him give, never seen and said, "Don't mention it. Would... would you show me how to do the ice thing? The little sculptures you used to make."

"You saw those?" It had been years since she had risked making one.

"They were beautiful. You can do things like that again, you're free."

Nodding, she cupped her hands together. As she pulled them apart a glass, or rather ice, figure of a howling wolf grew in her hand. Without even a pause to admire her own work she dropped the ice figure into Rog's hand.

"It's beautiful," he gasped.

Unsure of how to reply to the compliment, Zelia watched Rog admire the detail in her work. Without being in his head, she wasn't sure if he meant it or was merely trying to make her feel better.

"There you are! I've been searching all over for you two," Terik's voice rang through the hall.

"You didn't search too hard, brother, as we have been here the entire time."

He ignored Rog's snide comment and plopped down on the balcony. "So, what's it like having all this awesome power you are supposed to have?"

Rog gave Terik a look that could kill and Zelia retreated from them, leaving the balcony.

"Terik doesn't mean anything by it," Rog said when he caught up to her. "He doesn't know."

She stopped mid-stride. "I know Rog, it's just, I don't want to talk about it. I never should have mentioned anything about it earlier, I just…"

"I know, I saw what happened." Rog pulled her into a gentle hug. "It haunts me too, and I'm not the one who did it. I can't imagine being… You know, you look exhausted. How about we go get some rest?"

She nodded and Rog took her hand, leading her towards their chambers, a place her connection to Rog had taken her many times. She didn't even feel the urge to pull away from his touch as she was lost in her thoughts, numb to the world around her.

They came upon an open door and Rog announced, "This is your room. My room is right next door, and Terik's room is just across the hallway. Mother and Father's room is two doors down on the right."

"Thank you," she replied, though she didn't feel her own words.

"You're welcome. Good night Zelia," Rog said. She could feel him glance back one more time before he pulled the door closed behind him.

For hours she tossed and turned, the insistent pain from the metal plate that hung and pushed on her ribs made sleep impossible. Even the strange comfort of the bed pushed her to move to the cool stone floor. It was the early hours of the next day before exhaustion overcame her and she dozed off on her side.

9

As sleep came, she was thrust into the past.

A chill ran down her spine not a second before the crack of a whip and searing pain hit her. The warmth of blood washed across her back, almost tickling as it spilled onto the cave floor. Tears dripped down her face as she clenched her teeth to bite back a yelp of pain. She squinted through her tears at blue light reflecting off the stone. She had to stop crying.

Sharp pain ripped through her cutting her dream short as she convulsed. Her eyes flashed open in time to see the last of the sparks fly from her chest, the end of Yargo's staff pressed against her. The mass of the convulsions passed, and she gasped for air like a fish out of water.

"Your heart stopped. I... I couldn't feel your presence," the familiar voice cracked in her ear then his face came into view as he scooped her into a hug.

With each painful gasp for air, she recalled more of the events of the past few days. Then she realized that what she had just seen was a dream, a piece of the past that would forever stay with her.

Yargo excused a guard as Terik, and Zivu came in the room. Zelia could see the concern in his face and her mind raced to piece the puzzle of all that had happened back together.

"What's all the commotion about?" Terik asked as he stretched with his arms raised high above his head.

No one replied, they just stood in silence. When Rog released Zelia from his hug, she sat back against the side of the bed and shook. A dull pain still emanated from her heart and she watched those around her through a haze of exhaustion and pain.

"We will talk about it in the morning. You boys should go back to bed," Yargo said.

"I'm staying here." Rog shook his head in protest.

Oblivious to what had just happened, Terik yawned and turned towards the door. "I for one am going back to bed."

Yargo held Rog's stare for a moment before relenting.

"Okay Rog, you keep watch over her then. Yalif will be here soon."

"Do I need to keep her awake?"

She was aware of Yargo watching her as she fought to keep her eyes open, the electric shock and all the events of the days past had zapped her energy.

"No, just keep a close eye on her until Yalif gets here."

Zelia edged away as Rog scooted over next to her, her thoughts were scrambled but her fear of hurting others drove her to push away. It wasn't long before she couldn't fight it any longer and her eyes closed. She relaxed and a warmth spread through her as her head rested against Rogath's shoulder.

It seemed as though she had only just shut her eyes when she woke to Terik crouching over her.

"Talk about bed head! Or rather floor head. And I thought mine was bad." Terik raised a matted piece of Rog's hair.

"Oh yeah? Taste some pillow!" Rog whacked the back of Terik's head.

Terik pulled a pillow from the bed to counter and Zelia moved from their path before she could get caught in the middle of their mighty pillow war. As she watched the boys fight, she found that she was glad they didn't tiptoe around her like she was some fragile little thing.

"Good morning to you too, Terik." She ran her fingers through her tangled mess of hair.

At the sound of her voice, Terik stopped mid swing and Rog's whack sprawled him out on the floor.

"Now you're going to get it!" Terik threw himself into Rog and they both tumbled over the bed.

Before they could escalate their bickering any further, Zelia stepped between them.

"That's enough. Why must you two take a nice pillow fight into an all-out wrestling match?" she said, half-teasing. It felt nice to tease and joke after so long in the cave, but part of her still glanced around for the hand that would strike her.

"I did no such thing." Rog brushed little white feathers from his pajamas.

She gave him a 'really, you're going to go there?' look and shook her head, hoping the banter would help ease his worry.

It was at that moment that Yargo, and Zivu appeared in the doorway.

"Good to see you made it through the night. I see the boys have already set you to work keeping the peace," Yargo said with a hint of a grin.

Zivu ushered her husband and sons out.

"Well go on now, it is time for breakfast. Zelia, I would like to speak with you for a moment."

Once Yargo and the boys left, Zivu continued. "How would you like to have some dresses? We wouldn't want anyone making fun of you for your attire now, would we? Besides, we can't have you running around in Rogath's pajamas all day."

"Lady Zivu, that would be lovely," she rushed the words out so as not to offend her. "Will they hide my scars?"

She knew they would fade in time, but for now she wished to keep them hidden. It wasn't the scars themselves that bothered her, rather the pity she saw and felt in the gazes of the warriors.

"I am sure we can arrange that. Come dear I want you to meet Dain, our fashion designer extraordinaire."

Something brushed against her back, and she reared away from the unexpected touch. The moment she turned, her stomach dropped. Zivu was staring at her with wide eyes, shock clear on her face.

"I'm sorry," she said, turning away from her.

"No," Zivu took a shaky breath, "I'm sorry."

Zelia was staring at the floor when a slender shadow stretched across the room and drew her attention. A regal man entered with a measuring tape draped across his shoulders, the smooth trim of his black beard complimented his wide grin.

"At your service your highness," he began, with a grand bow. "This is the girl? My, I have my work cut out for me! Such a beautiful young lady."

Zelia shifted her feet, unsettled by the complement.

"I see you know not of your own beauty," he said as he measured her height. "Tell me Zelia, has no one ever complimented you before?"

"Not in a very long time." She turned her face from his gaze.

She winced when he raised her arms and wrapped his cloth tape measure around her chest. As quickly as the expression came, she forced it from her features, though every connection of the metal plate to her ribs still pulsed with each breath.

"Oh, I see." The glimmer in Dain's eyes faded. "Well, I am here to tell you that you are beautiful, now let's make you feel like it. So, what is your favorite color?"

She stared out at the sky. "Blue," she said wistfully. It had been so long since she had seen the sky with her own eyes that it was all she could think about when her memories didn't plague her.

"Then blue it shall be," he said as he turned to walk out of the room.

"So, how long has it been since you gave your hair a proper brushing?" Zivu asked as she grabbed a brush from the vanity at the far end of the room.

How long has it been?

"You don't know how long you were in that cave, do you?"

No, it was easier not to think about it, to let the decades blend together. She shook her head. *It must have been centuries. Dwarves live too long for it to have been less with how old the last prince was and having never heard of Connan before.*

Her shoulders sagged with the thought of how many years she had spent in that cave. Centuries spent killing and torturing people. Years without seeing the sky, the stars, and only fractions of sunlight. Years spent alone.

"Zelia?" Zivu's voice cracked. "My poor—"

"Please, please, just don't. I don't deserve your pity, not with what I've done." She pulled away from Zivu's nearing touch and sagged against the wall on the far side of the bed, back turned to Zivu.

"Zelia, that's enough self-pity, you have to snap out of this!" Zivu snapped at her.

Zelia reeled at Zivu's sudden change in demeanor.

"You think this is self-pity? I hate myself and everything that I've done and what I've become. I'd kill myself if I actually *could* die! I deserve all the torture and pain Fregnar sees fit to offer for what I've done. I've tortured people, even children in front of their parents. I should have destroyed myself over and over again instead of hurting all those other people, but I was weak. I couldn't make myself do it. No, I don't deserve anyone's pity. I only deserve hatred, even from myself."

Her lungs burned from her rant and she clasped her chest, leaning against the post of the bed as she struggled to suck in air.

"Oh Zelia, you don't deserve that, no matter what you may think. Now look at me. You will put this behind you and you will thank Dain when he comes back in here with a dress. You understand me?"

Zelia nodded, orders were one thing she could take, even if she didn't believe she could follow through with them.

"Now, let's get these knots out of your hair."

The stiff bristled brush caught and tugged on her hair. Every few strokes Zivu stopped and picked knots out by hand before brushing over them again.

"My, what beautiful hair you have," Dain's voice rang as he entered the room.

He held a sky-blue dress draped across his arms. Zelia gave a faint smile. "Thank you."

She took the dress behind a dressing screen and pulled it over her head before stepping back out.

"See? You are beautiful. May I?" Dain asked as he tied the back of the dress.

The dress was long-sleeved and came up around her neck with gold lace trim. The material was silky and smooth with an almost metallic feel to it. It was so lightweight that it didn't hurt as it pressed against her more recent wounds.

When she looked in the mirror, she couldn't quite believe that the girl looking back at her was her own reflection. She had never worn such a lovely article of clothing before, not even when she lived with Eleanor and Eadon.

"It's beautiful," Zelia whispered and glanced at Dain's reflection in the mirror.

With a soft grin, Zivu pulled part of Zelia's hair up in a little blue ribbon. Zelia felt it was unnecessary but didn't dare voice her opinion of it.

"There's that beautiful young lady. Thank you, Dain, spectacular work as usual. Now, let's go join the boys for breakfast."

➤

Terik and Yargo were first to see them enter the royal dining hall. When Rog noticed their awed faces, he turned to see what they were staring at. He did a double take but finally managed to force words out of his mouth.

"Wow! Zelia you look, um, fantastic."

Yargo gave Zivu a nod of approval before addressing Zelia. "What would you like for breakfast young lady?"

Zelia seated herself at the massive dining table and glanced to Rog's plate.

"The same thing as Rog," she said.

She found the amount of food people ate here astounding compared to what she had been allowed in the cave, though it never seemed to be so much through Rogath's eyes.

"Ah good choice, beignets are delicious," Yargo replied as a cook brought in a fresh plate.

Zelia soon discovered why Rog liked beignets so much. They were delicious; their little dash of powdered sugar adding just a hint of sweetness to the exquisite flavor as they melted across her tongue like the bread she had as a small child. She scanned the table and found the delectable little pieces to be out of place against the others' plain breads and meats. Part of her wanted to question their origin, but she found she couldn't as the first sweet thing she had eaten in what seemed like forever pulled her in.

When they stood from the table, Yargo said, "Zelia, if you feel up to it, I want you to go to magic practice with Rog and when you are finished you and Rog will join Terik for combat training. You two must not be relying solely on your magical abilities, but I would rather you just watch for now."

Rog looked to his mother.

"You two go ahead. I'll be right out."

Zelia and Rog gave a quick nod and headed off down the hallway.

"Rog, what do you think Zivu wanted to talk to Yargo about?"

"Hm? Oh, you know, I don't know."

"The great Rogath doesn't know? Well that's a first."

"Hey! So, you do have a sense of humor."

He moved to elbow her playfully but stopped short and stared. She could see the joy fade as his thoughts churned.

"I know you so well, yet I feel there are things you have yet to tell."

She shifted her feet and lowered her gaze to the stone path leading out the open doorway.

"Rogath, I…" She stopped and let out a shaky sigh.

"It's alright. You'll share when you're ready."

He offered her a reserved smile and took her hand.

"Come on, we need to get to the pavilion before Mother."

10

"You should have started practicing without me Rogath," Zivu said as she entered the little open-aired, pillared building.

"I wasn't sure what we would work on today since Zelia is here."

"She can practice with you."

"Um, I can't use water magic," Zelia said.

"You can control ice, it's not all that much different from water."

"I know I should be able to, but I can't. I'm not like Rog, fire and ice are the only two I can control."

Zivu studied her for a moment, then sighed.

"Alright, well, I'd still like to see what you can do."

"Mother, maybe we should wait," Rog said.

"No, I can show her. What would you like me to do?"

"Let's start by freezing the water in the podium. Show me how fast you can make it freeze."

Zelia walked over and stood at the edge of the water-filled stone podium. She touched the top of the water and it froze in an instant. Instead of expanding up, the ice expanded out and cracked the stone podium.

She glanced down at the floor as it turned a frosty white.

"Stop." Rog lifted her hand from the ice. "You'll heal slower if you're not careful."

"Rog." She jerked her hand from his.

"How? Very few can freeze water like that." Zivu pried her gaze away from the cracked podium to Zelia. "Heal slower?" she asked as what Rog had said registered.

"Like she said, her powers are not like ours."

"Rogath, you don't understand," Zelia almost spoke under her breath.

"What? I know how your powers work."

"I'm not talking about that. The spell Asenten used, I think he was trying to kill me, not stop your father."

"What? Why would he do that?"

"He knew he couldn't beat Yargo, and the wizards weren't about to let me fall into your hands. That's why Yalif couldn't remove some of the shrapnel in my heart and lungs. Most of the damage from that blast won't be undone. There is no point in waiting for me to heal."

"Why didn't you say something about all this before? What about all of your other injuries?" Zivu asked.

"Because it doesn't change anything. Yalif didn't know of my ability to heal, but that's just as well since I won't heal from this. The scars from the other injuries will fade, it just takes time."

"Alright," Zivu paused, "let's work on improving your skills for then, Rogath."

Zivu looked at the podium and heaved a sigh.

"We'll practice at the pond today. Zelia, you can watch."

Zelia sat and leaned back against a column as Rog practiced at the pond where he had so proudly shown her his abilities. At first, he struggled as he kept glancing back at her.

"Remember to let your emotions flow like the water, use them to shape what you want," Zivu instructed.

Finally, he made a snake rise from the water. It was weird to watch him practice from such a strange angle, as she had grown used to seeing through his eyes. She saw the snake twist and turn and weave through the air with each change of Rog's expression and wave of his hand. With creases raised across his brow, he forced the water to evaporate into a mist that hovered over the pond.

"Very good, now make the mist condense back into water," Zivu encouraged him.

His forehead scrunched even further in concentration and water droplets formed from the mist. They dropped back into the water like rain. Their pitter patter reminded her of the sound of rain hitting the lake of her childhood home.

It was hours later when Zivu stopped him. "Very good, Rog. I think that's enough for today; off to the arena with you."

The chill of the marble stairs bit through the thin soles of Zelia's shoes and reminded her of the cave, yet it highlighted the stark contrast of the sun's gleam off the white stone. Like any day she had seen through Rog's eyes, Terik trained in the center of the gigantic oval stadium. She watched Steffon's posture, his movement, and recalled everything she knew about him, down to the expression he made when he was about to lunge.

When they reached the dirt floor of the stadium, all eyes turned to Zelia, and her confidence shrank back. *What if I mess up with all these people watching? No, snap out of it. This isn't a place you can afford to fail. Do it for Koin. Asenten may have sharpened your skills, but it was Koin who laid the foundation.*

Steffon stopped and turned towards them, he bowed with a swing of his sword.

"Steffon, at your service, my lady. How may I be of service?" His slicked back hair gleamed in the midday sun.

"Yargo has requested that I train with Rog and Terik."

"I see. Well, you came to the right place my dear. So how much experience do you have?" His little mustache turned up with his smile.

Terik had jumped at the chance to take a break and leaned against one of the wooden pells, where he watched her with eager eyes.

"A little." She pulled a sword from the rack and checked its balance before trying another. "I've always preferred working with a bow, but I haven't used one in ages." With a sword that seemed somewhat balanced in her hand, she turned back towards Steffon.

"Really? Why a bow?"

"That's just what I am best at, but in its absence, I've gotten better at using a sword."

"Okay, show me what you got. Terik, would you help me out? Start off easy."

Terik lifted the point of his sword at her.

"Maybe that's not such a good idea." Rog moved to step between them.

"It's okay Rog," Zelia assured.

At first, she took it slow, being careful not to strain her ribs, but soon, Terik pushed her a little further. He swung his sword down from the right. Zelia raised the hilt of her sword with the blade stretched across her front to deflect Terik's strike.

She caught his upward strike and faltered, the stretch of her ribs stole her breath in a spike of pain. Black dots invaded her vision, and she grabbed her side with her free hand, but she was still unwilling to release her sword.

"Terik," Steffon's tone warned that Terik had pushed it too far.

She wavered in agony, about to collapse, when Terik grabbed her. Zelia tensed at his touch, but her body faltered and forced her to allow Terik to keep her upright. She drew in a long slow breath and the skipping beat of her heart pounded against the metal plate.

After what felt like ages, the spots and pain receded. She let out the breath and shoved herself away from Terik, taking his sword with her. She still held her side with one arm as she warned Terik, "You should never let your guard down for anyone, especially me."

"I think that's enough for today. Zelia, are you okay?" Steffon's tone softened when he addressed her.

"I'm fine. I just need to get used to the metal plate."

"What plate?" Steffon eyed her with suspicion. "Wait, you're the one everyone has been talking about. The one that has shrapnel in her chest and a metal plate holding her rib cage together?"

She nodded.

"But that was just a few days ago. You shouldn't be up and around, let alone performing that kind of swordplay!" Steffon took a deep breath and rubbed a hand down his face. "Well, I think that's enough practice for today."

"No, Rog just got here. Don't stop on my account. I'll be fine." She slid the sword back into the wooden rack, the sound of metal gliding across wood causing her pause.

"Zelia?" With her name called, she released the sword.

"I'm fine Rog. I'm... I'm just going to go for a walk," she faltered, unused to the freedom to do anything other than hide in the corner and bide her time. She turned away from him and climbed the stairs. She could feel the pitying stares of the men as she passed. She froze, images of those who had shown her pity and kindness in their final moments flooded through her mind. It was those people that made her hate being pitied even more than feared, as their faces and last screams haunted her more than all the cursing men and women combined. She forced her mind from her thoughts and continued up the stairs in a shroud of eerie silence.

11

Faced with the backs of men, she halted at the top of the stairs. "Did you hear about that girl from Mineria?"

"I heard she had a gaping hole in her chest, doubt she'll make it."

"No, I heard she ate dinner with the warriors last night."

"Impossible! Even if she did live, she shouldn't be up and moving anytime soon."

Please don't let them see me, she thought as she skirted around the group.

"Wait, that's her!" one man shouted over the banter of the others.

"What?" They turned towards her and their stares spurred her to pick up the pace.

She darted inside the nearby stables and slid down the post just inside the door. A nervous bleat rang from the goats mashed in the corner of the nearest stall. For a moment she stared back at the goats, struggling to catch her breath.

"Shh, it's okay. I won't harm you," Zelia assured them in the language of the animals.

A scruffy black and white buck perked his ears forward as he approached and smelled her with an upturned lip. He turned to the others. "I don't know about this one, she speaks our language, but she smells funny."

With their language spoken by an unknown voice, all the horses peered over their stall doors. There was a wide range of horse-like creatures, everything from a pegasus and a gold-maned stallion to a simple bay horse.

"What language was that you were speaking just now?" a voice asked from behind her. She spun around, facing the rather scrawny stable hand.

"Um, truthfully, I don't know what it's called. But all animals seem to speak it."

"I've never heard that language, where did you learn it? And who are you?" His blue eyes searched her up and down as if regarding a thief.

"Oh, I'm Zelia." She bowed her head, a custom of what had become a past life. "And I don't know where I learned it, I suppose from the animals since I'd spent a lot of time listening to them."

He still eyed her with suspicion, unable to place her.

"I'm a guest of Yargo," she informed him, but that did not make him any more sure of her. "I'm staying with Rog and Terik." She realized he was still unsure of her and sighed before continuing, "I'm the one everyone is talking about from Mineria."

"Oh, yeah, I *have* heard about you. But what are you doing in the stables?"

"Getting away for a while." She stroked a big bay horse.

The stable hand nodded, a knowing look spreading across his face as if running to the stables was the natural thing for a person to do when they needed to get away from the world for a while.

"I see, well just be careful of that one, he bites."

She stared into the horse's eyes. She could feel his tromp below the surface. He longed to be as free as the wind to go wherever the current took him, whether that be through mountains or over sea.

"He only bites because he doesn't like being cooped up in here. May I take him out for a ride?" She fought the smile that crept across her lips.

"I'm not sure about that. No one has been able to ride him."

"I can, would you give me a lift?" She gave into a grin, and her soul fluttered. It had been so long that she had forgotten what it felt like to give a genuine smile.

"Just be careful," he agreed, a hint of reservation in his voice.

"I will," she assured him as she swung her leg over the horse's back.

Leaving the stables, she let the horse pick his own path through the woods. Zelia locked her thoughts out and just absorbed the peace and tranquility of the world around her.

"So, what's your name?" she asked when the horse stopped for a drink from a small secluded pond.

"Thunder. Thank you for getting me out of there," the animal said when he lifted his head from his drink.

"You're welcome; I could tell you hate it in there. I'll talk to Yargo and see if the stable boy can put you out to pasture from now on." She played with the coarse hairs of his mane.

Thunder shook as he raised his head a little higher. Zelia smiled and regained her balanced seat, she had forgotten how good it felt to ride. Her smile faded, and she turned in thought. *What else have I forgotten? Things, little things I hadn't pushed away...*

"That'd be nice, so where do you want to go?" he asked.

"It won't be long before someone starts looking for me, we'd better head back."

"Help! Help! My hatchlings, tree, kids! Oh, please help me!" tweeted the little blue bird as she swooped down onto Thunder's neck.

"Thunder?" Zelia inquired.

Without a word he turned and started towards the edge of the woods. Zelia steadied herself with a wad of his mane and kept a smooth seat with his steady canter down the wood's winding path.

"Stop!" she yelled, as Thunder came to a halt and she jumped from his back, landing in front of two young boys.

"Oh yeah? Why should we?" one of them taunted, one hand already raised with a rock.

"Because it's wrong to hurt innocent creatures for no reason. You, of all people, should know that as a Hyperian."

They almost rolled with laughter, and one of them threw a rock square at the nest. Zelia flicked her hand at it and a shard of ice knocked it from its path just before it hit.

The boys staggered back. "Who are you?"

"Zelia. And I don't want to catch you messing with innocents of any species ever again. Got it?"

The flash of fear in their faces and how they trembled struck her back as they ran away. *What am I doing frightening little boys? No, they were going to kill the fledglings, I did a good thing. I didn't hurt them.*

The bird flew into her nest, and Zelia climbed onto a stump to remount.

"Are your babies okay?" she asked.

"Yes, thank you, thank you, thank you!" the bird happily tweeted as she hopped onto the edge of her nest.

Zelia nodded and nudged Thunder to head back towards the stable.

12

When she returned to the stable, she met the stable boy again.

"Good, you're still in one piece. I was beginning to wonder if he dumped you and ran off."

"Thunder wouldn't do that without good reason. So, what's your name?" She fed Thunder a handful of grain and led him into the stall.

"Oh, I didn't introduce myself earlier, did I? My name is Donequen."

"Well, nice to have met you Donequen. See you later."

On her walk back to the palace, Zelia absorbed the sights and smells of Hyperia. Her own emotions and senses gave new meaning to the world around her, painting a deeper, crisper image than anything she had ever seen through Rog's eyes. She studied people as they came and went from one shop or home to another. She came across the boys she had just stopped when she passed along the edge of the town. They were in an animated conversation with two older boys, their arms swung about their heads. Captivated by their excited flailing, she stopped. When they noticed her standing in the path, they pointed and jumped up and down.

This won't be good. She turned down an alley, trying to avoid a confrontation.

The older boys followed her and called out, "All talk and no game! No one messes with our little brothers and gets away with it! Come here, you little brat!"

You'll have to come up with something better than that. When she came to the end of the alley, she entered a street lined with stores. *Great, now where am I? Well, the palace should be that way, so left it is.*

Zelia scanned the shops as she passed. All sorts of weapons and magic supplies she had never seen before lined the walls. The area seemed a little darker than what she remembered seeing through Rog's eyes, but then again, Rog saw everything in a different light. He always seemed to walk on air, as if nothing could touch him.

When she passed a mirror set out in front of a shop, she glimpsed the two boys and drew her focus back to the predicament at hand. *Don't let them catch up with you, you can't afford to hurt them. No, you can't hurt them, you won't. I... I just can't do that anymore.* She picked up her pace.

As if fate laughed in her face, someone walked out in front of her and she flat ran into them. By the time she recovered her step, the boys were near striking distance.

"So, what are you going to do now little witch?" one of them called out.

"I'm not a witch, a witch can do so much more." She straightened her dress as she faced them. She thought Hyperians were better educated than this, but perhaps not all of them were.

With the stir of commotion, shop owners and shoppers trickled to the openings of the stores.

"We don't take kindly to witches messing with our little brothers," one of the boys warned.

"Well, if your brothers wouldn't pick on innocent creatures, I wouldn't have a reason to bother them. Besides, all I did was stop them from knocking a nest full of hatchlings out of a tree. I did nothing to them," she said.

"Oh, yeah, well that's not what our little brothers said!" the more robust of the two boys yelled and gripped his sword so hard his knuckles turned white.

"Then I am sorry for anything I've supposedly done. If you don't mind, I have someplace to be." She waved her hand as she started down the street once more, scanning her surroundings for something to defend herself with.

"Oh yeah?" One of them bellowed, "Well, I do mind. I'm not done with you!" He charged at her before his words had finished leaving his mouth.

Really? Charging while yelling? So much for not fighting. She sidestepped behind a post into the open fronted weapons shop.

"So, you're willing to attack an unarmed girl, now are you?" she challenged. She looked up at the shop owner and picked up a sword. "May I borrow this?"

The round little man nodded and waved his hand upward.

She turned just in time to catch the strike of the bigger boy before it could hit her. Cringing as she held against his blow, she willed herself to focus. She glanced around. *Too many pointy objects in here.* She ducked out and slipped between them.

The boys slammed into each other when they turned to follow her, and she stopped in the middle of the street.

"I don't want to fight you, but I won't stand by."

"You're just afraid to get beaten!" cried one of the boys.

Oy, I bet that one sounded better in his head. Great, now I'm starting to sound like...

"That's enough!" a voice rang out from the opening of the next shop.

"Oh yeah?" the burlier boy called and charged the unarmed shop owner.

Without so much as a thought of her own safety, Zelia leapt in front of the shop owner and let her instinct and training take over. She struck the boy in the side, but the boy's sword cut across her chest. With the force of his charge drilled into her, she fell into the shop owner.

The boy sprawled across the ground and blood oozed between his fingers.

Caught in the heat of the moment, Zelia hardly felt the gash across her front or the new cracks in her brittle ribs. The boy's friend charged, and she sidestepped to avoid his blade. As he passed, she grabbed his sword arm and threw her weight backward, he flew headfirst into the side of a shop knocked cold by his own momentum.

She turned to the shopkeeper and checked that he was unharmed with a quick glance.

"Would you return this?"

She held out her borrowed sword to him, her free hand across the gash in her chest. The shop owner's mouth gaped with his nod. *Don't look back,* she thought as she headed down the street.

She had not gotten far when she heard a familiar voice, "Hey, what are you doing here, little lady?"

She turned to see the warrior Barg's eyes widen at the sight of the blood that seeped down the fabric of her dress.

"Zelia, are you okay?"

"I will be. The plate blocked most of the blow."

"You shouldn't be around these parts by yourself. This is not the best part of town. Here, I'll take you to Yalif. Want me to carry you?"

"No, I can walk." Her words were a little strained as she started in the direction Barg had indicated.

"You just can't stay out of trouble, can you? So, what happened?" he asked.

"Some boys were trying to kill some hatchlings earlier, and I stopped them. So, they convinced their older brothers to go after me."

"And?" he pried.

"I avoided hurting them until they went after an unarmed shop owner. I jumped in front of him and had to strike the boy." She stopped walking. "I... I should go back. His friend I just knocked out, but he was bleeding pretty badly. I should go help him."

"Do what? Uh, no, you should go get checked out. Besides, they're probably not there anymore, people get tended to pretty quickly here."

With a reluctant nod, she chewed her lip against the pain and started down the path again.

"You know, Zelia, you are wise beyond your years. That boy got what he deserved for going after a little girl," Barg said.

She slowed to a stop, as if lead weights dragged her down.

"No child deserves to be hurt," she spoke under her breath. She struggled to hide her emotions and Barg's shift in demeanor told her she was failing.

"Maybe I should carry you."

She gave a slight shake of her head and continued down the path in a daze, stumbling now and then.

Yalif paled at least two shades when he saw her approach the infirmary. He shook himself as he opened the door.

"What happened this time? And it better not become a regular thing." He patted the bed for her to sit.

She glanced to Barg, pleading for him to explain so she wouldn't have to before she sat. She clenched the side of the bed and closed her eyes as the world seemed to spin around her. Yalif spread his special healing salve across her open wound.

"It's a clean cut and you should heal quickly with this, but I will wrap you up to keep it clean in the meantime."

Yalif's hand bumped against her back and she gasped as a wave a pain rushed across the back of her ribs.

"You broke a rib too, didn't you?"

She nodded as she forced a breath.

"You can't pop it back into place yet, it'll just break in another place."

"What do you mean? How?"

"I... I'm not really sure. It seems my bones turn brittle, like ice, if I use fire and ice too soon after one another." Her jaw quivered as she paused. "I think that's why my ribcage shattered like it did."

"Does Yargo know this?"

"No. At least, I don't think so."

"Alright." He sighed and continued wrapping her up, this time being careful of her broken rib. "You know you need to tell Yargo. I will tell him if you don't, but it would be better if you did."

She looked down at the cut in her blood-stained dress and sighed.

"Dain is just going to love this…"

"Oh, don't worry about him; it just gives him an excuse to make another dress. He's just two doors down on the right. Go see if he can make something else up for you," Yalif assured, giving her a faint smile.

"Thank you." She forced a pained smile and headed down the hallway.

Zelia gave a light knock on the door.

"Come in," Dain's voice rang from the other side.

He stood over a strange metal contraption, busy at work on his latest project. When he looked up, he dropped his tape measure.

"Are you okay? What happened to my dress?"

"I'm fine, and I'm so sorry about your dress. Could… could you make me another?" Zelia asked, shifting her feet in embarrassment at the damage to her dress.

"Oh, my dear, that is not a problem. As it happens, I just finished making you another!" He spun around and pulled something from a rack. "Here, see how this fits, but that doesn't mean you should go out seeking to mess them up."

It's not like I tried to, she thought as she handed the torn dress to Dain from behind the changing screen.

"So, what happened and why does it look like you got into a sword fight?" he asked, holding up the mangled outfit.

"Because I did," her muffled voice replied through the fabric of the new white and silver dress as she pulled it up around her shoulders.

He mumbled a noise she could not quite make out.

"You should probably avoid doing that, at least until you get better at it."

"I don't want to fight at all. But I only got hurt because I stepped in front of an unarmed man after he stood up for me."

"Well, in that case, I will gladly make replacement dresses for you. Just promise me you will take care of yourself. Never mind the clothing."

Zelia appeared from behind the changing screen, attired in her new dress.

"I'll do my best, but no promises."

"That is all anyone could ever ask for my dear," Dain assured her as he tied up the back.

"There you are!" Yargo exclaimed as he entered the room. "I have been looking all over for you, ever since I caught wind of a little girl getting into a sword fight with the Jophlin boys."

"I'm fine. Sorry to have worried you." Zelia looked down at the floor, her attention everywhere but on Yargo.

"Oh come, dear, Barg told me what happened." There was a long pause, and she could feel Yargo sought answers to some questions, but he didn't voice them. His jaw set for a moment before he continued, "I am just glad you are alright. It is about time for dinner, you should go join your brothers."

Zelia flinched at the word *brothers*, the laugh of the elf child she had once played with long ago rang through her ears. She shook the memories and drifted past Yargo going off towards the dining hall.

"There's our little sword fighter!" Barg called out when she entered.

Terik sat up in his seat. "I wish I could've been the one to knock the Jophlin boys down a notch. They've been causing issues for years, but father won't let me."

"And I wish I wasn't the one who did," she said from her seat.

"That's just because you're a girl." Terik sat back in his seat a little further.

"Oh really?" Her eyebrows raised at his assumption. "So, if you had it your way, you would beat everyone into submission?"

Everyone at the table fell silent.

"I didn't think so. Now if you'll excuse me, I've lost my appetite," she shoved herself back from the table and left. No one made a move to stop her.

If you feel the need to talk, you can always talk to Lumid or myself, Yargo's words came to her. When she neared the end of the bridge, she found herself unable to speak of the things that weighed on her mind, but the views offered beckoned her to enter.

"Lumid, do you mind if I sit and look out at the stars with you?"

"I do not mind at all my dear, come, sit. But why are you not eating dinner?" he peered at her from beneath the brim of his golden helmet.

"I just don't feel like eating right now," she confessed. She wanted to plop herself carelessly next to him, but sat gingerly, favoring her still-hurting chest.

"It would not have anything to do with that fight you had earlier, would it?"

"Word sure travels fast here."

"Actually, I saw it happen. I heard the commotion and turned to see what was going on."

"May I ask you then, is there anything I could've done to stop them without hurting them?"

She faced him and watched his expressions as he replied, "Zelia, you just cannot reason with some people and those boys are a perfect example. They think they are the rulers of that part of town and have no respect for anyone, other than Yargo. If you had not handled it the way you did, they would have escalated, especially if you had used your powers."

When he finished, she turned back to the stars.

"Tell me, why did you not use your powers?"

"Something told me I shouldn't, not against them. Besides, I didn't want to hurt them. Of course, I never really wanted to hurt anyone." She could feel it as a tangible weight as her past bore down on her. She shoved it back and used the stars to distract herself. "That star over there, it's dying isn't it?"

"Yes, it is. Wait, you can see that? But how?" Lumid's eyebrows went further into his helmet, surprised at her abilities to see so far.

"I've always been able to see far out into space. The bridge just makes it easier. It's amazing how different the constellations look from here and how much farther I can see."

"Well, you are just full of surprises. Not many see the stars as I do."

"What's your favorite thing to look at, Lumid?"

"Ah, well, there is just so much. You see that mass of purple, pink, and blue gas over there?"

Zelia followed the direction of his hand and nodded.

"That is called a nebula. I would have to say that is my favorite thing to watch, and, some day, that collection of gas will turn into a whole new galaxy."

"Hopefully, it'll happen in your lifetime, so you may see it happen."

"I can only hope."

They sat in silence and looked out at the stars for a while until Yargo walked in.

"There you are. I was coming to see if Lumid could see you. Rog and Terik said you left dinner without eating."

"I'm sorry Yargo, I just hate the way they talk about death."

Yargo eased down beside her and looked out at the stars. "I am sure you know that the only way I can accept them into the hall of fallen warriors is for them to die honorably in battle. So, battle is glorified here for the sake of honor and the right to dine in my halls upon death. It has been this way since the old gods and is something that cannot be changed."

"I realize this, but that doesn't mean we should encourage fighting. Every step should be taken to avoid a fight and keep the peace. I know I'm not one who should speak of it given the things I've done, but that is how it should be."

The focus of the bridge shifted to Mineria as it aligned with Hyperia and she found she could see the planet's surface.

Seeing something moving below them, Zelia asked, "Lumid, what is that moving between islands on Mineria?"

"A dragon." Lumid replied after looking down at the islands.

Yargo peered down at her, a question on the tip of his tongue. "You can see as Lumid does?"

"My hearing isn't as good as his, but yes I can see much like he does."

There was a long pause of silence and she could feel the tension between her and Yargo rise.

Finally, he asked, "Zelia, is there something else you need to tell me?"

"I... you talked to Yalif, didn't you?"

She caught his nod on the edge of her vision.

"Rog told you how my powers don't get along well together. Thankfully, he doesn't feel my physical pain, at least not the same way." She couldn't help but dig her fingers into her side as she spoke, the pain keeping her grounded and her emotions from flooding from the box she so desperately tried to keep them in.

"Zelia, where did you get your powers from?"

She shook her head and avoided eye contact.

"Rogath already told you." She forced the words and fought against the urge to move away from him. Her fear of being turned away still bound her not to tell all she knew, though she knew it was only a matter of time.

"How—"

"I was there, I relived the memories just as he did. I didn't know he could see through me as I did him."

"Come, you need to eat. We will stop by the kitchen and get you something."

She nodded and reluctantly rose to her feet. She paused before she passed Lumid.

"Thank you for allowing me to keep you company."

"Anytime, Zelia." He gave her another toothy grin before Yargo led her away.

13

Thunder, she thought with a great yawn.

"What are you doing up so early?" Rog rubbed sleep from his eye with the heel of his hand.

"Just remembered something."

Rog shook as he held back a laugh, and she gave him a sidelong stare.

"And that woke you up?"

"No." She held her side as she stood. "I need to talk to Yargo about Thunder."

"Thunder? What are you talking about?"

"Thunder is a horse in the stables. I promised him I'd talk to Yargo about having him put in a paddock instead of locked up in a stall," she replied from behind the changing screen.

"So that's where you were yesterday. I should have known you'd go to the stables."

Rog had flung himself across the bed, half under, half on top of the bedding when she came back out from behind the changing screen.

"Would you tie this for me?"

He swung his legs over the side of the bed and secured her dress.

"There you go. Go ahead, I'll catch up with you in a bit."

She ducked into the bathroom and then a few minutes later, she walked into the throne room.

"Yargo, are you busy at the moment?"

"No, why?" He raised a single eyebrow.

"I wanted to ask you about putting one of the horses, Thunder, in a paddock. The stable hand said he's not allowed to, and that no one can ride him. The only reason he doesn't let anyone ride him is that he hates being locked up inside. I promised him I'd talk to you about it," she rambled on.

"So, you have been talking to the horses now have you? Well, I am sure we can arrange that," Yargo responded, scratching his dark beard. "Actually, you can go turn him out before breakfast if you like."

Zelia grinned as she bowed her head and headed off to the stables to do just that.

———————▶

"So, did you talk to him? What did he say?" Thunder neighed when she entered the stables.

"He gave me permission to turn you out. So, come on, I need to get back in time for breakfast." She opened the stall door and waved him to follow.

"Back already? What are you doing with him?" Donequen asked as he entered the barn.

"Yargo gave permission for me to put him out in the pasture, where he'll stay from now on."

"Good. Less work for me," Donequen replied with a shrug of his shoulders, but his hint of a smile showed he cared more than he let on.

After she let Thunder into the fenced meadow, where he bounded across the lush green field, she hurried across town to get back in time for breakfast.

"So, is Thunder happy now?" Yargo asked when she entered the dining hall.

"Yes, and he might let someone ride him besides me for a change." She took her seat by Rog at the long table.

"Wait, you rode that wild bay horse?" Zivu asked, eyes widened with concern.

"He's not wild, but yes, we went for a walk through the woods yesterday."

"You should never get on a horse you don't know," Zivu scolded.

"I asked Thunder first. He was happy to get out of the stall and stretch a bit."

"You asked him?"

"My dear, Zelia can talk to animals." Yargo took Zivu's hand and her jaw tightened for a moment.

"Still you should be careful. He is a large stallion and even if he does not intend to hurt you, you could get injured accidentally."

"I've been riding since before I could walk."

They all stopped and stared at her, and she shrank back in her seat. *I shouldn't have said that, they still don't know who raised me.* She closed her eyes, and a white mane rose before her. *Starjaina.* Memories of riding alongside Alrindel played through her mind and renewed her longing to be there alongside him again. She shook her head. *No, I can't go back there, not while Eleanor's alive.*

She forced herself to look back at those around her and Rog clasped his hands together.

"Well, let's eat."

Once Rog slowed down and ate like a civilized Hyperian, he and Terik told Yargo about what they had done on the previous day and their progress in their studies. Rog even gushed about Zelia's ice magic. Yargo just nodded his encouragement to the boys, but Zelia could feel his gaze fall on her with every pause while her mind continued to wander back to her time with Alrindel.

"Glad to hear you had a good day. Now, off to your studies." Yargo turned to her. "Zelia, may I have a word with you?"

She continued to pick around at her food in silence and the others left the table.

Yargo took Rog's seat beside her. "Zelia, is something wrong?"

She set her fork down, her plate hardly touched.

"Just thinking."

"About what?"

"The past and the people on Mineria who once considered me kin. They'd hardly remember me anymore." Her shoulders sagged, laden with the weight of her past.

"You mean Asenten did not always hold you captive?"

Her jaw quivered for a moment before she answered, "It doesn't matter," and shoved back from the table.

Yargo grabbed her wrist to stop her. "Obviously, it does matter, or you would not be so lost thinking about it. Why did riding remind you of them?"

"No, please don't. They think I'm dead and it's best that way." She ripped her wrist from his loose grip and headed out of the room.

"Best for who? You, them, or Asenten's cronies?" his voice echoed down the hallway after her, but she slipped out a door to the grounds outside.

Her heart hurt as her core froze, her power swelling with her anger at her past, at herself. When she skirted around the edge of the pond, she couldn't hold it in any longer. She flung a tense open hand at the water.

All the water leapt from the pond in a wave of ice, and much of her anger went with it. When she realized what she was doing, she snapped her hand into a fist and held it back, parts of the water still trying to expand as it froze.

She stood frozen as the ice before her when a hand touched her arm.

"Just let it go," Zivu assured her.

She unclenched her fist, and the ice shattered into a rain of tiny crystals.

"Come on, you will need to sit after a burst like that."

She wavered for a moment, then followed Zivu in a daze.

"Are you okay, Zelia?" Rog asked.

"I shouldn't have done that."

"Zelia, Asenten is dead, you won't get punished for something like that. It's not good to hold everything in like you do."

"Please just go back to practicing Rog. I don't want to talk about it."

"Fine, but if you ever decide to, I'll be here."

She nodded, acknowledging his offer even if she never intended to take it. She sat and watched them practice the water magic lessons, the first being how to turn ice crystals to fog.

After a few hours, Zivu decided Rog had practiced enough for the day and sent them on their way. When they reached the turn in the path, Zelia stopped.

"I'll pass on the swordplay today. Would you let Steffon know for me?"

"Sure. But why don't you come watch? That's all father wanted you to do until you've healed, anyway."

"I... I want to go for a walk. I might come watch later."

Rog's shoulders slumped. "Fine, please just be careful."

She could feel his disappointment as she walked down the hill, but she needed time to think. So much had changed in a matter of days, she needed some time to step back from it all.

On her way to the woods, she passed Thunder's pasture. Excited to see her, he jumped the fence and trotted up.

"Are you ready for a ride again today?"

"Sure."

She climbed on the fence as if it were a ladder and eased onto his back. Her mind already lingering in the past, with stirred memories.

———————▶

She was lying across Starjaina's bare back as she grazed and went racing across fields only to be stopped by Eadon.

"Just what do you think you are doing?" he would ask.

"Riding."

"Zelia," his short reply was accompanied by his stern stare.

"I'm sorry Eadon. I couldn't sleep and Starjaina was up, so I went for a ride."

He heaved a heavy sigh and pulled her from his horse's back. "Come on, it's time for breakfast."

The trickle of water pulled her from her memories. When she reached the edge of the pond in the woods, she slid from Thunder's back and sat against a log near the water. She leaned back and listened to the voices of the woods. Birds sang as they darted back and forth between trees. Snakes slithered across the ground and leaves rustled as they went. Bugs buzzed and hopped around. A dragonfly neared the water, and a fish jumped out and caught it with a big gulp. A few frogs croaked from their lily pads and then she noticed it... the sounds of the trees themselves.

She had never spent time being still in the woods before, so she hadn't ever noticed the sounds that emanated from the trees. An audible raspy voice, or rather the sounds of many voices, vibrated through the forest as the trees called out to each other.

She sat and listened for a long while.

"What's your name?" She looked at a huge tree across from her.

The trees quieted to a murmur. "She can hear us? But how?"

"Yes, I can hear you. Please, what's your name? I take it you're the oldest of the trees in the area, you are certainly the loudest and the largest."

"Trees do not keep names, that's an animal thing. But yes, I'm the oldest amongst the trees here. Why do you ask?"

She scanned the trees. "Just curious. I hadn't heard the trees until just now. I didn't know that trees had voices. Out of curiosity, how old are you?"

"I'm nearing forty thousand years old, and you my dear?"

"I'm almost five hundred years old. Can others hear you?"

"The animals can when they take the time, but your kind doesn't. Or if they do, they don't show it."

The trees talked amongst themselves and the slow chatter picked back up to a steady hum. She nodded off to the sounds of the forest and of Thunder munching grass at the edge of the pond.

"Zelia!" She woke to the sound of Rog, Terik, and Donequen's calls,

"Zelia! Zeeeellliiiaaaa!"

She blinked and propped herself up, the faint sound of chanting still ringing through her mind. The back of her arm brushed against something furry and she shot around, now face-to-face with a wolf as he stood.

"Good, you're awake. People call for you."

She rubbed her eyes in disbelief and realized it was already dark out.

"Over here!" she called.

When she turned to speak to the wolf, she found that he had disappeared back into the woods. *There are wolves on Hyperia?* She shook her head. *Why is it always wolves? A wolf in the mouth of the cave and now a wolf while I'm sleeping on Hyperia. I didn't even know there were wolves on Hyperia.*

"Thunder, why didn't you wake me?"

Thunder looked up from his grass chewing.

"You looked so peaceful, I didn't want to disturb you. Besides, I was not going near that wolf."

She rolled her eyes at Thunder. "That wolf wouldn't hurt you, you big lug. He was protecting you as well as me." *Even if I don't know why.*

Rog tackled her with a hug. "Oh, thank heavens you're okay. We were worried about you!"

"I just dozed off listening to the trees talking." She gasped as the pain of the sudden embrace took her breath.

"Just dozed off? You've been gone for hours. Wait, listening to the trees talking? Trees can talk, too?" Terik asked.

She looked over at the huge tree.

"They can. I hadn't heard them until today, so it must be another thing the wizards blocked from me. How did you find me anyhow?"

Donequen raised his hand. "Um, I told them you went into the woods when I noticed them looking for you. The guards won't be far behind us, so maybe we should head back." He gave a sharp look at Thunder. "Would you mind getting him? He doesn't seem to like me too much."

Zelia knew the horse's mind well enough to know Donequen was right.

"Thunder, back to the pasture."

"You want a ride back?"

"No, you go ahead. I'll walk with them. Try not to scare any of the guards on the way."

Thunder nickered as if to laugh and took off towards the pasture with a flick of his tail.

Zelia started after him. "We'd best get going then."

"So, how did you sleep without your heart stopping this time?" Rog asked and walked alongside her.

"A wolf kept watch over me while I slept. He disappeared right before you got there."

"So now you have a wolf watching over you, and you can talk to trees and animals?" Donequen chimed in with his own thoughts.

"Well, now I just sound like a lunatic, but yes, that's correct."

Rog stepped in front of them and walked backwards. "Aw, you are my sister after all. We can be crazy together."

He flashed a grin and fell over an exposed root before he could turn around.

The laughs of the trees popped through the air in loud creaks and cracks, drowning out the chanting that ate at the edge of her consciousness.

"It seems the trees have a sense of humor," she said.

Terik laughed at Rog and a branch popped out in his face. He stumbled backward and exclaimed, "Hey! That's not cool! I didn't say anything!"

Not to let Donequen feel left out, a tree goosed him and caused him to fall into Rog and Zelia. For a moment, the chanting in her head grew louder, then stopped as all three of them sprawled across the forest floor.

Donequen and Rog laughed and sat up, but Zelia kept her place as she struggled to breathe. *The chanting, had that been real?* She closed her eyes and forced herself to take a deep breath. *No, it was just a memory. It had to be.*

Donequen choked back a laugh. "I'm so sorry, I didn't mean to…"

She sat back against a tree.

"It's fine. I know the trees pushed you."

"Little one, are you okay?" a tree murmured in a slow drawl.

Zelia nodded in reply and the tree helped her to her feet. The blood drained from her face and pulled away from her head as she stood. She paused and leaned against the tree as her vision went fuzzy and disappeared. *No.* She frantically searched, looking for some speck of light.

The soft tips of Rog's fingers brushed her cheek.

"Zelia, are you okay?"

She struggled for each breath and shook her head. *I can't see,* she thought but couldn't get the words to form.

"Terik come here," Rog called, as he suspected something was wrong.

She put her hand over Rog's and ran it down Rog's arm.

"It's fine. I… I don't need to see." She forced the words and rested her forehead against Rog's shoulder. "I just… I want to go to bed."

"What do you mean you don't need to see?" Rog asked.

Her breath was shaky as he stroked her hair and she felt him struggling to open the connection he usually only felt when they slept.

"Zelia…" She could hear panic in his voice.

"I can't see," she whispered.

"What? You mean you're blind? How? We have to get Yalif." Rog was in full panic mode and she shook her head.

"Please, Rog just get me back to my room."

She didn't want to talk, and turned to continue down the path. With a sigh, Rogath led her, leaves crunching under their feet.

They said not another word until they were met by some guards. Rog and Zelia continued on as she stumbled on rocks here and there, while Terik told the guards what happened.

When they reached her room, Rog turned about to leave when Zelia's voice cracked, "Rog, would you stay with me? I... I can't stand being in complete darkness, not anymore."

"Shh, it's okay," he whispered and pulled her against him. "I was just going to Yalif, but they'll send him soon enough." She clamped her eyes against the dark and fell asleep to the steady beat of his heart, hoping beyond hope that this was just a dream.

14

"Zelia, I need to have a look at your eyes, dear."

The bed shifted as Yalif sat on the edge. She clenched a wad of Rog's silky tunic in her fist as she opened her eyes to find there was nothing for her to see.

"I'm right here."

He touched her shoulder and waited for her to sit up on her own. He guided her to drape her legs over the edge of the bed. She could feel his body heat beside her.

"Keep your eyes open for me, alright?"

She cringed as her eyes burned for a moment.

"Your eyes are fine. I will have to run more tests to find out what is wrong."

"Yalif," Yargo's voice sounded from the doorway behind her.

"I'll be right back, Rogath will be right here."

The bed moved as Yalif stood and Rog took his place. "You'll be fine, Zelia, I promise." He told her, leaning against her in a gentle hug.

"How can you know that, Rog?"

"I just do." His fingers intertwined with hers, and she turned her head towards the door.

"Wizards" was the only word she could make out from Yalif and Yargo's conversation.

"Do you think this could be the elders?" Zelia asked.

"Elders?" Rog asked, "Wait, you mean the other wizards? I thought Asenten was the only one that knew you were alive."

Zelia opened her mouth to say something, but she stopped herself.

"What haven't you told me?"

"I... please don't leave me."

He can't find out now, he won't understand. She laid her head on his shoulder, his hand clenched in hers. *I can't lose him, not now.*

"Zelia, I need to run some scans on you."

"Here, I'll come with you," Rog volunteered.

"No, you stay here Rog. Zelia, I'm going to carry you, is that alright?"

She nodded and Yalif scooped her up. His footsteps trailed down the hall and when a door closed behind them, he set her down on a hard surface.

"I need you to sleep. When you wake up, you'll be back in bed, but I'll be there."

Something soft and damp wiped across her face and she fell asleep.

▶——————▶

"Did you find anything?" Yargo's voice drifted to her as consciousness returned.

"Nothing that should have caused her blindness."

"But you found something?"

"She's related to the old gods. She should be much more powerful than she claims to be." There was a weird edge in Yalif's voice, as if he knew that the wizards had planned to kill them, and it was a while before Yargo spoke again.

"Does anyone else know?"

"No. Why?"

"Let's keep this between us for now and Rog certainly can't find out about it."

"May I run more tests? By all the laws of life, she shouldn't exist."

"Not yet, but soon. Let her rest. Being thrust back into the dark will weigh on her more now that the sun has risen, and her own flames can't help her."

"Will you stay with her, or shall I?"

"You told her you would be here, so it should be you. Take good care of her."

The door creaked open and closed as Yargo left. The silence weighed on her, and she slipped back to sleep. In this state, she dreamed about the wizards.

▶——————▶

"What do you mean fire and ice are the only powers she has?" one of the other wizards yelled.

"I've tried everything, no other powers will emerge," Asenten replied.

"All that work to get the blood of the old gods and it doesn't even work?" one of them grumbled.

"Perhaps we should cut our losses and kill her now? She can't kill Yargo and Zivu with the powers she holds, much less get near Fregnar."

"And waste everything we have done? No, we'll find a use for her. For now, use her as you wish."

Asenten grumbled.

"You have a problem with that?"

"No," Asenten's tone made it clear he wasn't happy that they left him to take care of their disappointment.

⟶

"Yalif?" she asked as she felt the warmth of a bed rather than the chill of the cave.

"Shh. It's okay, I'm here."

She could feel the bed shift beside her as she opened her eyes. The world was dark, and she fought to ignore it.

"What was that you gave me?"

"Just something to put you to sleep."

"Why didn't you give it to me before?"

"Many have a poor reaction to it. It was too risky to give to you when you were in such a state. How do you feel?"

She started to take a deep breath and remembered the rib that had yet to be popped back in place.

"Yalif," she clenched her teeth for a moment, "Can you pop my rib back into place for me? I think it's been long enough."

"Are you sure? If what you said is true, it could cause more damage than good to try too soon. Perhaps we should wait a few more days, just to be sure."

She nodded, then tears welled up.

"Yalif, will I ever see again?"

A warm and soft hand touched hers, and she jerked away, clenching her fist.

"I wish I knew, but I will not lie to you. I have no idea if you will ever see again, though I do not think your fall caused this."

"Why didn't you tell Yargo that earlier?"

"You did not think your fall was the cause either, did you?"

She shook her head and gingerly rolled to her side, away from him, if he didn't know, she wasn't going to say. Besides, she wasn't sure if the chanting in her head was real or just her mind playing tricks on her. The bed shifted as Yalif stood.

"There will be a guard just outside your door, just call for him if you need something."

Soon his warmth left the spot where he had sat on the bed and the familiar cold touch of the stone called to her. She rolled from the bed, keeping one hand on the wall at all times, and slid down until she was half curled up against the cool stone wall.

Time passed, and she could hear someone speaking near the door.

"That time already?"

"Sure is. So why are we guarding the girl's room?"

"They didn't tell you?"

"Tell me what?"

"The poor girl has lost her vision. It's a shame really. You should have heard how Lumid described her looking at the stars with him. It sounded like they might be two peas in a pod, but now…"

"That is a shame."

She could hear the pity in their words and the long sigh one of them let out.

"Just take good care of her and don't forget to report to Yalif and Yargo before you leave."

Footsteps faded, and the hallway was silent again. The pity in the guards' tone still rang in her ears and a face floated to the surface in her memories, her lack of vision making it all the easier to picture him. She'd never forget the look one gives right before they die, but some were harder to forget than others.

➤

"I forgive you, just do as he says, but never forget who you are."

The man's face was twisted in pain, but his words couldn't have been more genuine and the sorrowful look in his eyes would never leave her.

➤

"Evening Rogath. Come to get Zelia for dinner?"

"Yes. Zelia?"

His gliding step halted as he rounded the side of the bed, then he continued with a catch in his step.

"I'm sorry I left you."

She shook her head and tried to pull away as his hand touched her back, but he hugged her anyway. He pulled her away from the cold wall, and she rested her cheek against his soft tunic.

"Everything alright?" the guard asked.

Rog's chin brushed her hair as he nodded.

"You know you need to eat something. Will you please join me for dinner?"

She shook her head and pressed herself closer against him. For a moment he reminded her of Eadon, how he used to hold her on his lap and comfort her.

"Kerm, would you have the cooks bring us something to eat in here and let the others know we won't be joining them?"

"What would you like me to have them bring?"

Rog took a slow deep breath and pressed a hand against her head. She could feel him reaching for her thoughts and suddenly his presence was stronger, as if a door had swung open between them.

"How about some fruit? It'll be easier to eat here."

"I'll be right back."

The guard's heavy steps faded away and left her with nothing but the beat of Rogath's heart to hear.

"When did you eat fruit? I don't remember you having any in the cave."

She ignored his question, not even letting her thoughts wander to the answer as she still wasn't ready to share everything with him.

The familiar clang of metal on stone made her jump.

"It's alright; it's just the food."

Though Rog tried to hide how he struggled with her keeping things from him, it still showed in his tone.

"Here, I believe this is a favorite of yours."

Rog placed a smooth roundish object in her hand. She rolled it in her hands for a moment, feeling how it dipped in around the stem and the three bumps at the other end. She could almost see the apple as it sat in her hand, the red skin and how the light reflected off its surface, but it was just a faded memory.

"You recognize it, don't you?" he asked, his pitch going up the slightest bit.

She pressed it to her lips before opening her mouth to take a bite. It crunched as her teeth bit through the skin. She couldn't help but picture herself eating apples with Alrindel as the sweet and sour flavor brought back memories.

"Thank you, Rogath."

She took a couple more bites, then set it down.

"Full already?"

"I'm just not hungry."

"Alright, ready to go to bed then?"

She nodded and put her hand behind her to feel for the bed, but jammed her fingers on its wood frame.

"Here, let me help."

He took her hand and guided it to the top of the bed.

"I'll be right back, I have to take care of the leftovers and change."

She nodded again and crawled into the bed, hitting her knee on the frame as she went. *Fregnar,* she cursed to herself. After fumbling to cover herself up, she curled up on her side. Without Rogath there, she could almost hear the screams that haunted her dreams and were once her reality.

She jumped when something pulled the wad of blanket from her clenched hands.

"It's just me." The bed shifted as Rogath sat beside her. "Go to sleep, I'll stay up so you can see for just a little while."

Her hands shook as she grabbed another wad of the blanket.

"Rogath, I... I can hear their screams."

"I know you can. I hear them too sometimes. Do you want me to go see if Yalif can give you something to help you sleep?"

She shook her head and felt for his hand. She could feel it pressing into the bed beside her.

"No, just, please stay here."

"Alright, I'm not going anywhere, but you need to sleep."

She felt Rogath slump over asleep before exhaustion finally took her.

→

Zelia woke just in time to catch herself as she fell from the bed to the cold stone floor. She shivered as she lay there, an image of an old man burned before her. He didn't scream, his gaze held compassion, acceptance, and something that almost seemed like sorrow for leaving her there to suffer. She sat and leaned against the wall. She thought she heard Rog say something, but it was faint as if far away.

"Zelia, would you please come out with us for breakfast? I promise I won't let you fall," Rog said.

She shook her head and pressed herself against the wall, her arms wrapped around herself.

"Alright, I'll have someone bring you something to eat." His steps faded away down the hallway.

Morning came again and images continued to haunt her, but this time Rog grabbed her hand.

"I know what you're going to say, but too bad. You're coming to breakfast."

He pulled her to her feet and steered her down the hall.

"Quit fighting, you're coming to breakfast."

With his hands on her shoulders, she gave in and let him guide her.

"Now sit down."

She eased into her seat and he pushed her in.

"I see you coaxed her from her room," Zivu's voice was warm and welcoming.

"More like dragged her, but she's here." There was a hint of humor in Rog's voice and he nudged her.

Zelia picked at her food as the boys told Yargo about the previous day.

"Zelia, I want you to go with Rog to magic practice today. Zivu has something she wants to teach you," Yargo's voice was gentle, as if he talked to a broken dove.

"Okay, Yargo," she replied. *What does she think she knows that can help me? I don't even know why I'm blind.*

"You'll see, Mother always has a plan. Come on, let's go," Rog grabbed her hand and led her away, and this time she followed him with more ease.

"You've figured out how to hear my thoughts while we're awake haven't you?"

"How else am I supposed to know what you're thinking? But it would be nice if you would quit thinking in Elvish, it's such a complicated language."

"Guess I'll have to start thinking in the language of the animals since it seems to be the only one you can't speak."

He stopped and his footsteps spun in front of her, his hand still holding hers. "You so would, wouldn't you?" He heaved a sigh. "Fine, I'll stop."

She stifled a laugh. "Yeah, right."

"Hey! There's that smile of yours. Come on, we're wasting time." He dragged her outside and down the path.

"Rog, you go practice for a while. I will have a talk with Zelia," Zivu touched Zelia's arm to let her know where she wanted her to go.

"I'll be right here if you need me." Rog squeezed her hand a little before he dropped it.

"Zelia, I want you to learn to use magic as your eyes. Now, you said you only have control over fire and ice, correct?"

She nodded.

"Let frost grow around your feet."

She shivered and could feel the ground freezing beneath her.

"Open your senses to your magic, feel where the ice goes as it reaches out."

Grass crunched as Zivu stepped back. Zelia could feel the ice reaching up as it came to a column.

"Can you feel it?"

Zelia nodded.

"Good. Now, try to weave between the columns."

She passed between two of them, but gave them both a wide berth, with each column she grew closer. Her shoulder collided with a column and she could feel the ice spread as she leaned against it.

"Very good! It will take you a little time to refine and you must be careful not to freeze things you touch like that."

She pulled the ice back as she pushed away from the column.

"I think you have a handle on this, so I am going to go see how Rogath is doing. I will be nearby if you need anything."

"Zivu, thank you."

"You are welcome, now go on."

Zivu's steps receded and left Zelia to spend the rest of the day running into things. *Where ice grows up, there is an inanimate object. Where ice is reluctant to go, is either water or a person.* She repeated her findings over and over to herself as she walked along the training fields.

That night she tossed and turned until she gave up on sleep and got out of bed, being careful not to disturb Rog. A chill ran up her as her feet hit the smooth surface of the stone floor. All was quiet, and she edged onto the balcony, hands held out in front of her. The smooth surface of a column brushed her arm, she froze and tried to remember how far out the ledge was. The howl of a wolf called for her to follow. *I shouldn't, but I can't stay locked up in here forever.* She ran into column after column on her way, but the nearing call of the wolf kept her going.

"And just where do you think you're going at this hour?" a man's voice asked as she neared the front gates.

"For a walk."

"I don't think so young lady. I'm not in the mood to go searching for you in the dark again."

His voice sounded in her path and she slowed to a stop as she didn't want to run into someone yet again.

"It shouldn't matter what time I choose to go for a walk, it's not like I can see either way."

"I don't care, back to bed." He grabbed her and spun her around.

Her broken rib shifted, and the pain made the world spin, even after she stopped.

"Zelia?" the guard asked as she fell to her hands and knees. "I'm sorry, I didn't mean to... Do you need Yalif?"

She shook her head.

"Then here, let me help you up."

"Get away from her," a wolf's voice came in a snarl.

She could hear the sword on the guard's belt loosen and she grasped a wad of his clothing.

"No, don't. He's a friend."

"What!?!"

"Please don't hurt him," she pleaded with the guard before turning towards the wolf, "You know, I never asked for your name."

"Lobo. You alright?"

She nodded.

"Good, let's go for a walk."

The guard reached to stop her, his fingers brushing her shoulder, but Lobo snarled, and the man backed away.

She ran her fingers through the course hair across Lobo's shoulders and followed him away from the palace.

"We won't have long before they'll come searching for you, but I have something in mind for you to do," said Lobo.

"What's that?"

"I think you'll figure it out on your own."

She followed Lobo for a long time until the comforting voices of the trees enticed her to follow their winding paths. Their murmurs and Lobo's body guided her through their rough and leaf-covered paths. The loud croaks of frogs and the slight trickle of water told her she was nearing the pond. Lobo stopped, and she continued despite not knowing what was in front of her.

When she came to the water's edge something overcame her and she tapped her foot to the water's surface. A thick layer of ice spread across the pond. She swiped her foot over the smooth surface and stepped onto it.

The chill bit through her and memories she had long forgotten took over. She glided across the water's surface and her mind took her back to the first time she wasn't the clumsiest of the elf children. They had a hard winter that year, and it almost froze the lake in Elyluma solid. Most penned themselves up indoors, but the Elves took the chance to teach the elf children and Zelia how to skate across the ice. Even Alrindel fell a few times, and she giggled as they slid across the ice together.

Unable to see where she was going, she caught a rough patch where cattails grew through the ice and stumbled. She fell on the back of a large furry animal instead of the cold hard surface of the frozen pond.

"Whoa there, careful," the rough voice of Lobo sounded from under her arm.

"Thanks, Lobo."

"So, when are you going to stop hiding away in that room of yours and get back to training?"

"I can't anticipate their moves if I can't see what they're doing."

"You'd be surprised what you can do. I want you to at least try. But not here. Do you think that horse of yours will let us use his pasture? It wouldn't do you any good to practice here with the trees guiding your every step."

"I'm not sure, but we can always ask."

She placed her hand across his shoulders and let him guide her.

"Zelia!" A voice rang from the edge of the woods.

Lobo tensed beneath her hand.

"They're getting quicker. Sorry, but the trees will have to guide you from here. Meet me by the pasture when you can, I'll be waiting."

"Alright."

She let her hand drop from Lobo's back and lifted her hand to the low leafy branches of the trees.

→

"There you are! Where's that wolf?" an unknown voice scolded when she reached the edge of the trees.

She stopped dead in her tracks. *Who are you? I don't know you.* She stepped back.

"Don't!" Gaeru warned.

"Don't what? I was just going to lead her back."

One of Gaeru's inaudible grumbles sounded under his breath. "Just go back to your post, I'll get her. Zelia, you know who I am right?"

Of course, I know who you are, it'd be hard not to. She nodded.

"Good, come on. Let's get you back inside." She could feel the Fallen Warrior coming to her side to help her get back to her room.

"I don't want to go back inside. I... I can't sleep."

"And what would you have me do?" he asked.

"Leave me, I'll come back in time for breakfast."

"You know I can't do that, Yargo would have my head."

"I thought you were technically already dead."

"I am, but Yargo could still send me to Fregnar and I still have a head," his tone making him sound exasperated.

Something brushed her shoulder, and she shot back. The echoes of the cave bounced in her ears and she shook herself back to her senses.

"Please, I... I just need some time alone, outside of stone walls," her voice cracked.

There was a heavy sigh. "Yargo will be pissed, but fine. If you need me, I'll be in the stables. Try not to get into any trouble."

She forced a flicker of a smile. "Thank you."

He grumbled again, "Don't mention it."

When he had gone, she waited for her thoughts to slow so she could once again understand the trees.

"Lead me to the pasture?"

"Of course, to your right dear."

"That was easy; I figured you wouldn't slip away for at least a day," Lobo spoke as he retook his spot at her side.

Thunder met them at the pasture fence.

"Oh no you don't, I don't care if he *is* friendly! That thing is *not* coming in here!"

"You didn't even let me ask."

Zelia could hear Thunder's tail whip through the air with a snap and the stamp of his feet in the packed dirt that skirted the pasture.

"Ha! You think I can't tell by the look on your face?"

"So, you'll let a wolf approach me while I'm sleeping, but you won't let him in your pasture when I say it's okay?"

"It's fine," Lobo said with resignation. "I'm not too fond of getting trampled by hooves. Come on, we can do it over here." Lobo guided her away from the fence.

When they once again came to a stop, she caught a whiff of dung.

"Really? By the compost pile, that's the best you can come up with?" she asked, a hint of amusement in her voice.

"Would you rather do it on the road?"

"Alright, what now?"

"See if you can sense me coming."

His movements were eerily silent, only the rustle of grass in the wind with the occasional sound from the barn drifted to her ears. Frost spread from beneath her feet but even then, she couldn't feel or hear his movements. She was about to give up when his cold wet nose nudged her from behind.

"You're not using your senses. Quit trying to see as you once did, you need to feel your surroundings. Your powers might help with some things, but they won't help with a light-footed moving target."

Each time he disappeared he'd nudged her from another direction with no hint of where he was.

Zelia plopped down in the rough grass.

"I give up. I can't do it. I think you might be even sneakier than an elf and I should know, I spent enough time with them!"

The hair on the back of her neck stood on end when there was no reply. She spun around and grabbed Lobo's snout. With her hand still on his snout he leaned forward and touched his cold wet nose to hers to emphasize just how close he had gotten once again.

"Not bad but try to keep your face away from the business end of the wolf next time. I have to wonder, why aren't you afraid of me? You're not even nervous around me." He circled her once more, but this time Zelia followed his movements.

"I've never had a reason not to trust a wolf. It's humans and the other so-called intelligent beings that I have cause not to trust."

She didn't lose a step when Lobo changed directions.

"Just be careful, not all wolves will be friendly. This time see if you can knock me off my feet, with no powers."

Lobo pulled back a little further and made it harder for her to sense where he was. Again, the hair on the back of her neck stood on end, but this time a sense of urgency overcame her. She stepped to the side, lunged forward, and rammed her knee into Lobo's side.

Lobo let out a loud puff of air. "I'm still on my feet, but not bad. Well, if you're up for it I think you should go practice in the arena some before the sun comes up. I'll catch up with you later."

"Okay… see you later then."

She called for Gaeru once Lobo had gone.

"Yes?"

"I'm going to the arena."

"What for?" He started down the path, and she followed the fall of his steps and the sound of his voice.

"I want to try something."

"Really? Okay. Right this way, me lady."

He turned down the path and led her down to the main floor of the arena. Then he leaned back in a chair and dozed off.

She tuned out his snores and focused on her surroundings, frost growing out beneath her feet. When she had finished her second pass at the pells, she heard the steady step of a single person descending the marble steps into the arena.

"Very good. But I must ask, what are you doing here so early?" She recognized the voice of Steffon.

"Lobo encouraged me to open up my senses, to prove that I could fight without my sight."

"And who's Lobo?"

"A wolf."

"I see," he said with more than a bit of skepticism. "Well from what I saw, he was right. Even blind you use a sword better than most men."

She knew he only said it to encourage her, but she couldn't help but smile just a little.

"But you know that it's about time for breakfast and they'll be looking for you. And you too Gaeru."

There was a thud and she could tell Steffon had kicked Gaeru's chair.

"Hm? What? Oh, we best get going, Zelia."

"Really? That's going to be the worst thing about not being able to see. It's so hard to tell what time it is."

She tossed the sword to Steffon hilt first. Steffon chuckled as she followed Gaeru up the stairs.

➡

At the front entrance, she met Terik.

"There you are, I was just about to come get you. What were you doing outside?" Terik's voice echoed down the hall.

"I was just practicing my swordsmanship. Well, I went for a walk in the woods first…"

"Wait, you went for a walk through the woods in the middle of the night?" Terik stopped mid-stride, causing Zelia to walk into him.

"Yeah, it's easier to walk through the woods than here."

"How?"

"The trees and all the animals guide me. That and trees don't stop mid-stride like you do." She might not be able to see, but she could still glare in his general direction.

When they entered the dining hall, Rog greeted them, "There you are. At first, I thought it was just a strange dream and then I realized it was our connection."

"How much did you see?"

"Let's just eat."

Part of her wished she could see his expression, but she knew she wouldn't be able to look him in the eye even if she could.

15

Breakfast and magic practice came, and went, then Rog and Zelia went to the arena. She could hear the solid thuds of metal against wood as Terik worked away at the pells.

"Terik, left foot back, right foot forward when striking," Steffon coached, a hint of annoyance in his voice as he repeated what he'd been saying for months. "Good to see you back again this morning, Zelia. You and Rog grab your swords. Terik, you can take a break for a few."

"Back? But you said you were in the woods," Terik said.

"I was." She said, shrugging.

"Zelia, you first."

She ran her fingers across one of the pells and they caught on nicks and splinters left from years of being whacked with a sword. For a moment Koin's voice came to her, *"Pretend you are moving from tree to tree and your sword is just a part of you. It's a dance and you can be graceful, I've seen it."*

Why did they have to take me from them? Why didn't they protect me? Her anger swelled, and she pushed it away. *No, it's a dance, anger won't help.* With a long slow breath, she spun around and struck the pell. There was a pause in her movement as the sword stuck in the wood. When she continued, she hit the other eight without a pause. She moved between the unevenly spaced posts with ease as the frost grew up them and told her where they were, though there were some she barely caught with the sword.

"Close your mouth brother. We wouldn't want you catching flies now, would we?" Rog said with a snicker.

"Very good. Terik, you and Rog can work on form. Zelia, come here my dear. Let's see if you can sense someone's approach."

107

Rog gave a slight moan of protest as he headed for the pells.

She heard wood scrape on wood as Steffon pulled a wooden sword from the rack.

"You don't have to use a wooden sword."

"It's a precaution, just in case," Steffon assured her as he approached.

She caught his first move but missed his second. The wood sword caught her left arm, the force of the unexpected blow knocked her from her feet. When she hit the ground, pain stabbed through her chest, but she drew a deep breath and swung her feet at Steffon's. She jumped to her feet and made a strike. Steffon struggled to regain his balance and barely managed to block it.

With their swords locked against each other Zelia coughed up a bit of blood. "Zelia, are you okay?"

"Don't stop; others wouldn't give me a breather. Don't worry, I'll be fine."

Steffon's wood sword scraped against hers as it dropped to his side.

"Zelia, just because you don't die doesn't mean you should push yourself to the brink of death. You're done training with me today. I won't be responsible for pushing you that hard."

"Fine, I'll go train on my own. Rog, Terik, don't wait up for me." She flung her sword into the rack and snatched up a bow and a handful of arrows.

"Great, now you've done it. You know, she can't handle being seen as weak. Her captor punished her for so much as a yelp of pain," Rog said.

"Back to your footwork," Steffon grunted as she climbed the stairs.

⟶

In her haste, she stumbled over some loose boards. *Really!?!* She kicked at them, and one chattered across the ground. *Wait, I can use those.* She set them up against the pasture fence and walked across the field. She notched an arrow. As she turned, she drew and stopped. The air chilled as she felt for her target and all other movements in the area. With a long slow breath, she let it fly and missed.

She walked back across the field in search of the arrow, and Lobo padded out of the woods.

"Looking for this?" he spoke through clenched teeth. "I picked it up on my way."

He dropped the arrow in her outstretched hand.

"The trees say you weren't very far off. Is this your first time with that bow?"

"Unless this is an elvish bow from Mineria, yes."

"Well then, try again." Lobo headed to where she had stood.

When she reached her spot, she tried again, and this time, she hit it, but just barely.

"See, you did it. Whoever said blind people can't shoot hasn't met you. So, go on, shoot the next one."

She shot three in a row, each time she got closer to her mark, until she hit dead on. When she pulled back a fourth time, she winced in pain as her broken rib shifted but she continued through.

"You know, if that hurts you, you really shouldn't do that. But um, how are you doing that? I thought you haven't been able to see, um, since that night and what's with the frost?" Donequen's voice carried from across the fence.

"I haven't. If I stopped doing everything that hurt me, I would never do anything."

"What do you mean by that?" He approached her side.

"You try having shrapnel in your heart and lungs and see how you feel."

"Do what, wait, those rumors are true? I figured they were just made up. You can't tell by looking at you."

"That's kind of the point. I don't want people's pity… or to be feared for that matter."

"Why would anyone fear you? You're the kindest person I know and just a little girl."

"Do people not fear someone who can control fire and ice, who can speak to animals and trees, and comes back from the dead without being bound to Yargo." She rolled her eyes at his ignorance. "Sure, no reason to fear me whatsoever."

"Anyone can see that there's a price for the powers you have, a great price at that. There's pain and suffering in your eyes. More than anyone else I've ever met. Yet you care about others, even when others don't care for you." The grass crunched as Donequen plopped down and continued. "That says something about who you are."

Surprised by Donequen's little spiel she sat in the grass beside him.

"Thanks, but you don't really know me. I've done things that can never be forgiven."

"No need to thank me and anything can be forgiven, no matter how horrible you think it is."

"Don't you have animals to tend to?" she asked, flustered.

"Nah, I already finished for the morning and since you talked to Thunder my job has been easy. So, were you the one who froze the pond back in the woods?"

"Yeah, I suppose I didn't unfreeze it, did I?"

"No there's still some ice floating in it." A laugh broke beneath his words.

"I should go melt that."

Lobo shifted beside her and Donequen flipped out.

"Wolf!" he yelled and tried to drag her away.

"Let me go!" She pried herself from his grasp.

"There's a wolf! We have to get away from here and get a guard."

He grabbed her again, but this time she was ready for it and stood her ground.

"You will do no such thing. He is my friend."

"He's your what? You can't be friends with a wolf!"

"And what do you know about wolves besides what others have told you? Now, I'm going for a walk."

"Uh… may I join you?" Donequen asked, his concern and reservation showed in his tone.

Lobo grunted, but she ignored him.

"I don't see why not." She switched languages and continued, "Lobo, why did you let me walk off without melting the ice?"

"Because, I figured what better time to teach my pups about the dangers of ice than in the summer when they won't get frostbite."

"You have pups?"

For a moment, she thought of Dain, the little black pup in the mouth of the cave. "May I meet them?"

"If Yla is okay with it, then yes."

"Yla is your mate?"

Zelia could feel Lobo as he shook his coat out, "Yes."

"What are you two talking about?" Donequen asked.

"The ice and Lobo's pups," she explained.

"His name is Lobo?"

"Got a problem with that, kid?" asked Lobo.

With a smile, Zelia replied, "Yes, his name is Lobo, and I wouldn't make fun if I were you."

"I wasn't making fun, only making sure I heard that right."

"Sure kid," Lobo grunted.

16

Zelia sat on the log by the shore after melting the last of the ice from the pond with a wave of her hand.

"I'll go see what Yla says about bringing the pups to meet you." Lobo slipped off into the woods.

Donequen sat down by her feet. "I take it this must be your favorite spot since I keep finding you here."

"Yeah, it's nice to get away from everyone for a while. I lived in a cave most of my life and I'm not used to being around so many people. And since I can't see, I can no longer enjoy the stars." She let out a long sigh. "I miss seeing the stars."

"I've heard rumors that Yalif says you might regain your vision. Is that true?"

"It's true, Yalif says I may see again, but he only says that because he's not sure what's causing it in the first place. My eyes are perfectly fine. So, how's your mother doing? I hear she's been sick as of late."

"Oh, she's, she's… Well, this morning she was doing better than usual." She nodded, even without her vision little gestures still felt natural.

"I hope it lasts. I think it's noble of you to work as a stable hand to support her and your little brother."

"That's just what any man of the house would do."

"You call yourself a man, yet you call me a little girl. Why?"

"Well, um, you have other people to care for you. I don't. I care for my mother and my little brother. That makes me the responsible one in my family. And that makes me the man, no matter my age."

She sighed. She didn't like the double standard he was applying. Besides, he knew nothing about her.

"I see your point, but Yargo only took me in because of what my existence means. And I only stayed to get to know Rog and Terik in person, and to learn," she lied, knowing full well it was because she had nowhere else to go. "Well, that and I wanted to see if all the stories about the view from the bridge were real."

"And are they?" he asked, excitement in his voice.

"Yes, and more. The stories didn't do it justice. I only wish I could enjoy that view with Lumid again."

She couldn't help but long to look out at the stars. *Maybe I could look for Alrindel?* She shook her head. *No, they think I'm dead. They led me there. Alrindel probably tried to forget me just as I did him.* Zelia felt guilty for trying to forget them, but it was how she had survived. She had shut everything out as if she hadn't once danced and sung among the children of Elves. Compared to them, she was a wolf in sheep's clothing, only a withered shadow of what she had once been.

"These two woke up early and were driving her crazy, so Yla sent them with me." Lobo said as he padded out of the woods.

Two crazy little pups ran past Lobo, one jumped into Donequen's lap and the other into Zelia's. Donequen fell backward off the log, trying to avoid being licked to death. That attempt failed, so he just ended up on the ground with the pup on his chest, where he endured more licks than if he'd stayed put.

The puppy kisses tickled and made Donequen giggle like a little girl.

"Aw really, okay, okay, that's enough. Zelia, a little help here?"

"Now who's the responsible adult?"

Lobo let out a weird sound that resembled a chuckle as he sat.

She petted the pup on her lap and directed her comment to the other wolf pup. "Little one, settle down. Give poor Donequen a break."

The pup settled, and sat on Donequen's lap as he sat up.

"Uh, thanks."

He petted the pup a few more times before he got up off the ground and retook his former seat on the log.

"Are all of your pups this way?" Donequen asked.

"No, I have one calm pup." Zelia translated for Donequen.

"Wait, you didn't translate for him. He understands me?"

"Yes, the animals understand you. You just don't understand them. Most animals are more intelligent than those who consider themselves the only intelligent ones. They just don't exploit things as some do."

Mystified, Donequen asked, "Then why do some animals work for us?"

"Free food, protection, and sometimes being trapped." Zelia felt the temperature drop. It was much chillier than it had been a few moments ago. "It's getting dark, isn't it?"

"Yeah, I guess we should head back."

"We have to go. You be good for your parents okay?" She ran her hand over the pup's back one last time. When she stood from the log, she switched languages. "You're right, we should go."

The trees led her to the edge of the woods and retracted their protruding roots so she wouldn't stumble on them as she went.

"Well, I have to go do the evening feeding. See you tomorrow?" Donequen asked.

"Maybe, depends on whether Yargo has other plans for the day. Goodbye." The two separated, he to the stables and she to the palace.

17

Still can't sleep. She threw back the covers. *Fine, might as well go train.* The guards paced near the front door and she slipped by when their steps turned away. She hurried across to the arena and worked hard at the pells, until sweat drenched her clothes and the breeze changed directions, bringing with it the warmth of morning. *I should head back before they notice I'm gone.* She snuck back in and got rid of the evidence of her actions with a quick wash.

Breakfast and magic practice went well that day and the next few, but when they came to the arena, Steffon refused her each time.

"I'm not training you. I'm not letting you use a sword, not here." She could feel the concern and desperation in his voice, but she couldn't give it up.

"Fine." She'd snatch up a bow and arrows and disappear from the arena. Each day she'd regain more and more of her confidence with a bow. *Not as good as I used to be, but it'll do.*

She yanked her arrows from the board now riddled with holes and Donequen called from over the fence. "Ready to go?"

"Just a second."

"Lobo and the pups will be waiting."

"Awe, someone has taken a liking to Lobo's pups," she teased.

"What? They're cute."

She laughed, feeling for once that perhaps the wizards had forgotten about her and that she could live here in peace. "Sure. Now remember, we have to leave in time for me to catch Rog and Terik leaving the arena."

"I know."

➤——————

She had just made it to the top of the arena's stairs when Rog started up. "Where do you keep disappearing to? Even this morning you were up and about when I got up."

"Just going for a walk."

"Every morning before the sun is up and every afternoon after training against Steffon's wishes? With a bow? If I didn't know any better, I would say you were up to something."

"Says the one with all the tricks and plans up his sleeve."

"Hey! We were talking about you, not me."

A sudden spike of pain hit her, like an ice pick being hammered through her skull, and she doubled over. Her knees slammed against the paved walkway as she clutched at her head. There was a faint chant ringing through her mind with each drop of the hammer. This time tears ran down her face as she fought back a scream.

She could feel the warmth of Rog's palms on her back as he yelled, "Help! Guards come quickly!"

The guard reached her as the pain overwhelmed her, and she passed out. Her mind slipped to Rogath, but the chanting kept her from being able to connect fully. Together, the guard and Rog rushed her to Yalif.

Rog nearly busted the door down.

"Help her!" Rog demanded.

Yalif searched her, looking her over head to toe. "I can't find anything wrong with her Rog. We'll have to wait until she wakes."

Rog sat on the counter with his chin in his hand as he stared at Zelia's unconscious body. Terik paced the room, his fists clenched and unclenched with each step.

Hours passed before the chanting faded, and she slipped back to her own body. She rubbed her head as she sat up with her eyes closed.

"Easy there." Yalif moved to lay her back down.

She blinked a few times before it registered that she could see again. She blinked a couple more times to make sure she wasn't just imagining it.

"I can see," she ran her fingers through her hair and groaned, "but I think I'd rather be blind."

"You have a headache?"

"Compared to earlier, yes."

She closed her eyes. She knew it was more than a headache, but it was nothing compared to the pain that made her pass out.

"You rest and I'll have a cook bring you something to eat. You need nourishment and sleep, in that order," Yalif instructed.

She slid from the examination table. "Only if they bring it to me on the bridge. The view of the stars is better there."

"Fine, if that's okay with Lumid you may go to the bridge. Just don't overexert yourself. I'm not sure what happened and I'm not sure if it will happen again. And Rog or Terik, or better yet, both boys, must escort you. I don't want you alone until we know your sight will remain."

Rog and Terik agreed, and she forced a smile.

"In that case, I'll stay away from the edge of the bridge. Thank you Yalif."

→

As she walked down the bridge Lumid called out, "Finally coming to visit again I see. I heard that your vision is back."

"How does news travel so quickly in Hyperia?" She gave him a knowing grin and continued, "Nice to see you too, Lumid. Care if I join you in looking at the universe?"

He waved his hand in an over-exaggerated gesture of welcoming. "Not at all, my dear. Come, sit. The two of you may also come."

Zelia sighed and sat on the raised portion of the floor around the switch. She stared out at the stars. She knew she should tell them about the chanting, but the prospect of being sent away terrified her. So instead she distracted herself with the stars so Rogath wouldn't suspect anything.

"The nebula is nearing star formation. You might get to see it become a galaxy after all," she smiled while looking back at Lumid.

"You're right; it is nearing the final stages of development."

She nodded and turned back to the stars. The throb in her head made her vision fuzzy from time to time but she still enjoyed the view.

They sat there in silence until a cook started down the bridge.

"Good evening, Lumid, I've been instructed to bring dinner out here for Miss Zelia. And some for Terik and Rog since they also skipped dinner," she said with a stern glance at the boys.

Lumid just smiled and nodded.

Zelia thanked the cook as she took the food. On the menu that night was turkey, mashed potatoes, gravy, and multiple rolls. As the cook left, Zelia offered, "Lumid, would you like some? I couldn't possibly eat all of this."

With his one of a kind golden toothed grin, he sat down between her and Terik.

"Do not mind if I do." He picked up a roll and took a bite. "So, I have heard that with or without your sight you are a force to be reckoned with on the battlefield. Even if your vision stays from now on, you learned a valuable skill."

"It will come in handy if I ever face someone who can see in the dark." She sighed and continued, "I really hope I don't lose my vision again."

"I do wonder what caused your loss of vision, but we have never seen something like this happen." Lumid took another bite of the roll as he pondered that. When he finished the roll, he took a swig of mead and changed the subject. "So, just how far can you see?"

"It's hard to describe since I don't know what you call most of the realms and galaxies."

He pointed to a faint little star far out in the distance. "Do you see that star right there? That's the farthest reach of my vision."

"Yes, I see that star and the planets around it. I can see past it, but not by much. And my head throbbing doesn't make it any easier."

Lumid's expression lightened in curiosity. "How many planets circle that star?"

"Five planets circle it. Why?"

"At that distance, my vision is not the most accurate. I was wondering if my count was correct."

Rog and Terik paused from stuffing their faces to exchange a surprised glance.

Curious if he had gotten it correct Zelia asked, "So, was it?"

"Yes, but only because I have watched for the star to dim as the planets pass in front of it."

She paused in thought. "The guards of the bridge before you, could they see as far as you?"

"I cannot speak of all of the past guards of the bridge, but I know the one before me fell short of that sun by a few hundred leagues."

I might be able to see farther than anyone of the realms has ever seen, yet I've only scratched the surface of the vastness that is the universe. With that thought she yawned.

"Hm, I think it's time the three of you got some much needed rest," Lumid suggested, ushering them from his home.

Together they headed down the bridge as he called out after them, "Sleep well, Zelia. You too, Terik and Rog!"

She yawned in reply, "And may the views be ever beautiful."

18

"No. Please no," she muttered in her sleep.

The bedding crunched as she rolled and her eyes flashed open, the chants of wizards still ringing in her head. She could feel the ice creeping out from her core. She tried to pull it back as she had always done, but all she could do was slow its growth. The stone froze under her feet as she climbed out of bed.

She could hardly hear Rogath's snores through the chanting that seemed to grow louder as she walked. The door froze in place before she opened it all the way.

"What are you doing up?" Kerm, the guard who seemed to always be nearby, reached for the door.

"No, don't touch it."

She pried her fingers from the door as the ice grew thicker.

"Zelia, what's going on?"

"I don't know." She squeezed through the doorway, glancing back at Rogath as she went.

"I'll go get Zivu."

Kerm's boots stuck a little as he moved away. She gasped as a spike of pain shot through her head and a wave of cold air rolled away from her.

"Yalif," she gasped and turned down the hallway.

She didn't make it far before footsteps echoed behind her. The chanting in her head grew louder, she recognized the voices but not the words. Her hands had turned to ice, she lifted them to the light of the moon shining between columns and spikes of ice shot up from the stone.

"Zelia, stop this at once!" Zivu commanded, the pace of the footsteps having quickened.

"No!" Zelia meant it as a warning, but ice impaled Kerm as she turned.

Frost crackled across the floor as Yargo pulled Zivu back, putting himself between her and the ice.

"No," this time Zelia breathed the word.

Her hand shook as she reached to touch Kerm, but she turned and ran instead. Guards froze as she ran by, and it seemed to her that the longer she ran the louder the chanting became. She bolted down the steps to the bridge, and the water froze where it lapped at the bottom of the bridge.

"Zelia, halt!" Lumid called.

She slowed to a stop and Lumid stepped back as his breath fogged in the cold. His sword was out, and his palms rested atop its hilt, but he didn't brandish it at her.

"Lumid, I can't control it. Please, just send me somewhere I can't hurt anyone before I kill you."

"You know I can't do that."

"I'm sorry."

She lunged, took his sword, and ran past him. As she sank the sword into the initiation switch, she could only hope it would carry her away before Lumid froze.

She landed in water and felt it freeze around her as her fingertips touched sand. The chanting that boomed in her ears faded until the voices fell silent, and her eyes drifted closed.

——————▶

"Mother!"

Barg caught Rog before he could reach her. As he struggled, she could see Yalif tending to Zivu and Yargo's frozen forms. When Rog stopped struggling, his thoughts turned inward.

"You did this!"

"Rogath, I couldn't control it."

"Couldn't control it? I've never seen you freeze things like this. This isn't like frost growing on a chair, Zelia."

"Rogath, I'm sorry."

"No, you're not. You may have run away, but I'll follow you no matter where you go for what you've done."

"Please Rogath, I didn't mean to. I left so I wouldn't hurt anyone else. I couldn't control it, I couldn't even hold it back," she pleaded with him, but she knew he wasn't listening to her words or feelings.

"No, I'm done listening to you."

She felt the connection slip away as he closed her out. His absence left her alone with the reality of what had happened and questions of whether they would be all right.

19

She shivered as the gusts of wind slowed and the warmth of someone's presence creeped against her. She could feel the water drip across her face and the grit of sand against her skin as someone shifted her in their arms.

"Father!" a young voice cracked.

An islander, she thought, judging from the language he used. "Where, where am I?" she breathed the words, and the breeze swept them away.

The piercing cut of wind through her wet clothes ebbed and the person holding her slid off something. Her hand slipped from her side as they jolted to a stop, her fingers brushing the dew-covered tips of grass.

"She was in the water… I think she might be a survivor of the dragon Trapper raids," the boy seemed breathless as he gasped for air.

The breath of some animal warmed her for just a moment, only to make her shiver even more as she slipped away again.

———▶

"Where did you say you found her?" a voice drifted to her as she stirred.

"A couple islands over. There was some frozen wreckage floating near-by, they must have had an ice breather this time."

"You keep an eye on her and let me know if anything changes." She heard the thud of a closing door.

She could feel a rough warm pelt against her cheek and shifted towards it, enjoying its comfort.

"Easy, you were in the water for a while," a young voice cracked beside her.

She opened her eyes and shot away from his towering form leaning over her.

"Careful, I won't hurt you. My name is Dotchavitch." He reached for her, but she edged away. "Do you understand me?"

121

She nodded, grasping for yet another language she and Alrindel loved to use.

"So, you understand me. I pulled you from the water, remember?"

She stared at him blankly, she didn't remember anything the blond-haired boy had just said, but she was still damp.

"What were you doing way out there?"

She leaned back and glanced at the large-grained door.

"You can go if you want, but there's no way off the island right now." He removed something from a chest of drawers on the left side of the room. "Here, how about you change into something dry? It'll be big on you, but it'll be warmer than that."

He laid some woven clothing on the bed and stepped out of the hut.

Now alone, she got up and peered through the crack in the door. She shivered against the cool draft and rubbed her arm, only to find her dress in tattered shreds. The boy walked away from the hut and she turned to the clothes he had left. Her joints, stiff from being damp, and cold, made her slow to change. Just as she tied the top of the woven tunic, so it covered her scars there was a light knock at the door.

She stopped and stared at the door, not sure how to answer.

"You okay?"

The door squealed a little as it opened and she sat on the bed, pulling the fur blanket around her.

"Can you speak?"

"Yes."

"What's your name?"

"Zelia."

"Zelia? Can't say I've heard that name before." He gave her a faint, but warm smile. "Where are you from?"

"I… I don't know."

Her stomach growled, and she clenched the blanket as she pulled it closer.

"Sounds like someone's hungry." Zelia blushed, unsure of how to answer him. He offered her a hand. "Well come on, it's about time for dinner, anyways. Besides, my father will want to speak with you."

For a second she saw Rogath instead of Dotchavitch and shrunk back as what Rog had said charged to the surface.

"I don't bite, not hard, anyways."

She stood on her own, and Dotchavitch wiped his hand down his blue tunic.

"So, I have to warn you, my friends are rather… strange. Oh, and one of the twins can't talk and the other is a little… slow, so think nothing about it if they never say anything to you."

Why can't they talk? Have they had their tongue cut out? No, not if they're his age. Besides, what could they have done for that sort of punishment? Unless… Her teeth clenched and pushed back the images of torturing people.

"You cold?"

"Just remembering…"

Dotchavitch paused in the doorway, staring at her for a moment before stepping out into the waning light.

They met two pairs of scraggly teens before they even cleared the shadow of the building. The twins shoved one another as they bickered back and forth. She couldn't make out what the one was yelling, but the girl stomped and waved her hands in his face, her face flushed with rage.

"So, this is where you've been hiding the last few days." the youngest and scrawniest of the misfit group said.

"Guys meet Zelia. I found her on a shore a few islands over," Dotchavitch said. "Zelia meet Fifthry, Johnol, and the twins Senth and Sligh." He pointed them out.

She gave a slight nod of her head and shifted her feet under their gaze.

"What were you doing there?" Fifthry, the girl with fiery red hair, asked.

Should I lie? Would they believe me if I told the truth or think me insane? Would I have believed me? No. "I don't remember."

"She was unconscious when I found her. I think she may be a survivor of that attack we found the wreckage of the other day."

As she watched them, dragons approached. Their voices reverberated through her mind, almost like Rog, only their voices were so loud it almost hurt her to hear them.

"I don't know about this one. Stardust, where did you get this one exactly?" a high-pitched voice bounced through her head.

"We picked her out of some ice, she was half frozen."

Zelia glanced around at the dragons that had gathered and took note of which dragon she thought went to which rider. Listening to them, she could tell their colors matched their personalities, the bright red dragon seemed to be hot headed and authoritative, with a hint of misplaced sass towards the dark blue dragon who was the strongest of them. While the light blue dragon stood back from the conversation. His disinterested expression reminded her of the cool water of the tide, heeding itself only to the will of the moon as it crosses the sky.

The red dragon with spikes tipped in yellow flared her nose and pulled her scent in. *"She smells funny, like fire and…"* She sniffed the air again. *"And some other magic. Anyone know where Raven is? She would know."*

"Nope, haven't seen her in a few days."

"Hm, then let's find out."

Zelia watched as Dotchavitch's eyes widened, but he was too late to react when a wave of heat came over her from behind. Dotchavitch and his friends screamed and ran to stop the dragon. She only managed to put up a small wall of ice before the flames engulfed her and she collapsed to her knees, shielding herself from the fire.

"NO! Gulepia! Bad dragon!" Fifthry screamed over the others as the dragon's breath bathed Zelia in fire.

Zelia struggled with the need to latch onto the flames surrounding her, her core still chilled with ice. She gasped as her heart shuddered and rubbed against the shrapnel in her chest in a way it hadn't yet done. Her concentration faltered, and the ice wall shattered. Shards of ice rained across her back, propelled by the dragon's breath, some going deeper than others. As she fell forward, the flames subsided.

She struggled to cough as she sucked in ashes, then her breaths became slow and shallow. The world seemed to slow, then something rolled her to her back.

"Zelia? You… you're going to be okay."

She could tell Dotchavitch was trying to convince himself more than her. Her head lolled as he shook her and she wondered how long it had been since she'd last blinked.

"Shh. I can't hear her heart."

Johnol came into view for a moment, then she could feel something press against her chest.

"She's cold?" He snapped in front of her eyes, but she couldn't even force herself to react. "Dotch, I… I think she's gone."

"But how? She's not even burnt."

She glimpsed blood as Dotch slid his hand out from beneath her.

Dotch's jaw quivered for a moment before he wiped the hair from her face and gently closed her eyes.

"I shouldn't have let the dragons get so close to her, not so soon after the dragon trappers."

"We having a burial?" Johnol asked.

"It was my dragon that did it, I'll help you build it," Fifthry's voice shook and the charred grass crunched.

"I'll take her inside until it's ready."

"At least we know her name and can give her a proper send off."

Inside, Zelia struggled to tell them she was still there, but she was trapped. She could feel the warmth of furs as Dotch laid her on a bed.

Dotchavitch! Please, I'm still here. She begged, even knowing no one could hear her.

The cool breeze from outside ended as the door closed and they left her alone, trapped in her own mind. She tried to focus on what she could feel around her, to keep thoughts of her past from creeping in, but she was helpless to keep them away.

Just as she thought she had lost, the door squealed as it opened and the cool draft returned.

"Poor girl, just as things were looking up," the voice was the same as the one just before she woke. "Well come on, it's not right to keep her here."

"No, I'll carry her," Dotch said.

"Alright, I'll get the door."

A hand ran under her back, and this time it didn't hurt. Dotch lifted her from the bed and she shivered as he carried her outside.

"Did you see that?"

"See what?"

"She shivered."

"She's dead, she can't shiver." There was a sigh, and something brushed against her knees. "Son, I know you feel responsible for her, but it's too late, she's gone. Come on, it's time to let her go and the others are waiting. At least she will get a proper send off, which is more than can be said for the rest of her people."

"Dotch…" she tried to force words to her lips, but they wouldn't quite come.

As a light spray of sea water misted her face, she managed to move, nuzzling against Dotchavitch. She heard a splash, then he set her on something hard that moved up and down with the lapping of water against wood. As Dotchavitch moved away, his hand brushed hers and she grabbed it.

"Please don't leave me," she breathed the words and opened her eyes.

She could just make out Dotch's figure against the fire and starlight that shone behind him. He shook his head as he jumped back.

"No, you… you're dead," he nearly screamed.

She shook her head as she sat up. Her whole body tingled as if it were a muscle that had fallen asleep. There were a few gasps and whispers from the dark figures that lined the shore.

"What are you?" Dotch's father questioned as he placed himself between her and Dotch.

"I don't know how to answer that." She turned away, her shame of what she is rising to the surface. "I wish I did."

"How are you alive?"

"I don't die, not really, anyway. I just get trapped." She shivered, rubbing her arms as she scanned the open water, her gaze stopping on the flames. "I understand if you no longer want me here, but…"

"Come on." Dotch stepped around his father and offered her a hand. "I guess I should introduce you. This is my father, Chief Gondavitch."

"Thank you."

She gave a slight nod to Gondavitch and took Dotch's hand. As she stepped over the edge of the wooden boat, her legs buckled and Dotch caught her.

"You alright?"

"I will be, it just takes a while."

"This has happened before?" he asked as they moved closer to the open stone fire ring, the crowd parting as people stared.

"Not this exactly, but yes." She found it hard to look him in the eye as she asked, "May… may I explain later?"

He gave a slight sigh as he helped her perch herself by the fire.

"I'll talk to father. Johnol, get her something to eat and make sure everyone leaves her alone."

She turned away from the staring crowd and closed her eyes, trying to let the warmth of the fire creep in.

"Here you go."

Johnol handed her a wooden bowl of fishy smelling soup. For a second she thought to turn it down, but her hands shook, a reminder she needed to eat. She took a quick swallow and tried to ignore the fishy taste as she turned back to the flames.

"So, what are you,?" Johnol asked.

"I don't know anymore. I used to think I did, but…" her words trailed off and she opened her eyes, "things change."

She watched the flames in front of her, how they flickered around with the shifts in the wind. Then something gliding across the sky caught her eye.

Johnol raised his head, then let out a sharp whistle, calling the villagers to silence.

"She's back."

Dotch pulled Johnol back as a dragon landed behind her.

"What about Zelia!" Johnol protested.

"Get our dragons."

"So, the rumors and stories are true. The girl with the dragon tongue and control of fire and ice has finally come to our shores," the dragon's voice reverberated through her head. ***"I have heard rumors of your existence for years now. But feared I would not live to see the day you should turn up here to learn."***

She turned around, sitting with her legs beneath her and her back to the fire. The dragon before her was a midnight black, and she felt drawn to her for a reason she couldn't explain.

The dragon gave a great bow of her head. ***"Since word of your creation came to our shores, I vowed that you would be my rider. Being that, I, too, control fire and ice, I believe we are meant for each other. Though I wonder how you look so young. By my count, you should be nearing five hundred years old."***

Zelia struggled to reply, unsure of how to respond, so she said the only thing she could. "It's true that I am near five hundred. What is your name?"

The black dragon puffed out her chest with pride as she replied, ***"My name is Raven, and what should I call you?"***

"A fitting name. I'm Zelia."

As soon as she said her name, she questioned herself. *But why? I'm no longer that person.*

"You're talking to her?" Gondavitch demanded, looking aghast.

For a moment all she could do was nod as memories swirled around her thoughts, pieces of her life with Eadon, Koin, and Alrindel.

"Zelia? What troubles you?" the tone in Raven's voice was almost motherly.

"Something I used to have."

Raven lowered her head into Zelia's reach and she found herself entranced by how her scales felt beneath her fingers. Each scale was as smooth as the flat of an elvish blade with the curve of a flower petal. Raven was as black as the deepest and darkest of caves and her grey eyes seemed to pierce into your very soul. The other dragons had eyes that reflected light, but her eyes showed no reaction to the light of the fire. She couldn't help but feel drawn to the dragon who all but disappeared in the dark of night.

"What do you mean something you used to have?"

Zelia jumped as Dotch now stood right beside her.

"Kin," she shook her head, remembering the differences in language, "a family."

For the first time in years, she reflected on that night.

"They made this happen."

She lifted her hand, calling the flame to jump to her. As soon as it touched her, she put the flame out with a clenched fist. Her hand now covered in cracks and bleeding.

"You see, I'm not like you Raven. I don't belong anywhere."

"But you are. Come, I want to show you something."

Raven settled down beside her so she could climb on, and Zelia turned to Dotchavitch.

"Go on, but I'll be waiting for you."

She stared at him with a question in her eyes.

"All of our dragons chose us. It's what separates us from the trappers. Go on."

Once they had taken off, she glanced back at the villagers, they all stood staring up at her.

With a heavy sigh, she looked across the island and absorbed the view as it lit up in the dim light of the half moon. With eyesight that even surpassed that of Elves and Lumid, she could see it clear as day. The island was large enough a normal person could gaze in all directions from the highest hill and not see the ocean surrounding it. Framing the northern corner of the island was a sheer rock formation, a stream trickling down to a small pond surrounded by trees. The trees gave way to open pastures dotted with sheep and the occasional wild rabbit.

The village was on the southernmost point and had an assortment of homes. Some were dug into the dirt to avoid the wind off of the water, while others stood tall made of a mixture of timber and stone. She couldn't help but feel out of place as she had spent all of her life living among the trees and then held captive in a cave.

She laid back on Raven and looked up at the stars as they flew off into the night sky. The higher she got into the sky the farther she could see. The constellation Hyperia belonged to came into her line of sight. She couldn't help but long to return there, but she knew she never could, not after what she had done.

"We're here." Raven eased to a stop on the next island in the chain.

Zelia slid off at the edge of a beautiful waterfall. The moon reflected off the rippling pool of water and eased her nerves. Then Raven disappeared behind the waterfall.

A cave, why is it always a cave? She hesitated as she stared at the water. Raven peeked out from behind the water. ***"You'll be safe here, I promise."***

Raven held her wing over her as she passed beneath the rushing water. Once inside, the dragon lit up the dark cavern by lighting a fire from deep inside her fire lung. As she did, the true beauty of the cave came to life. Light reflected in all directions off the stalactites dripping down from the ceiling.

"I crack and bleed just like you. That's why the trappers left me here to die, now it is a reminder of how sometimes the darkest nights can lead us to the most beautiful things. Listen."

The wind blowing through the cave sang as it twirled around the rock formations above their heads. The hum of the wind reminded Zelia of a song she once heard Eleanor sing. Zelia hummed along with the haunting melody. It wasn't long before her humming turned into singing aloud with the melody of the wind. No real words to the ears of humans, but rather the ancient music of the Elves with its angelic melodies. It was the first time she had sung in over three hundred years as fear of punishment had kept her from singing even after being freed from the wizards. She found some peace in singing.

20

When Zelia stirred from her slumber, she didn't even open her eyes. She just lay there listening to Raven's heartbeat. Raven stretched beneath her.

"I should get you back."

"Raven, do you think they'll accept me for what I am?"

"They've accepted the dragons."

"But—"

"Zelia, you'll be fine. Now come on."

It was still well before sunrise when they returned to Dragon Island. As they passed overhead, she could see Dotchavitch sitting at the fire pit's edge, watching for her. Part of her knew he had stayed up, waiting for her to return, but she wasn't ready to face him.

"Raven, can we land on the other side of the village?"

"Of course."

She drifted down and landed with an easy grace. There was a lone tree, and she sat down at its base, listening to its soft hum.

"Zelia, there's something that's been bugging me." Dotchavitch's tenor voice broke her thoughts from the tree.

She turned towards him, seeing that he had dark circles under his eyes.

"You didn't sleep, did you?"

He smothered a yawn as if to confirm it and Zelia took pity on him.

"What would you like to know?" she asked him.

"There are so many things… yesterday you made it sound as if you had a family, but you're obviously not human."

"That…" her voice grew tight. "My past is a difficult subject." She fiddled with the end of her tunic. "I have had a family, but not in the normal

130

sense. Elves raised me, and I was taken in by Yargo after," she paused. "In between, I lived in captivity for a long time. I wish I would have died, so many could have been spared, including people I care about."

The faces of those she had killed rose in her memory and she could feel the tears rising to the surface. Her ribs tightened around the metal plate as she fought to hold the emotions back. Raven settled beside her, her cool scales brushing Zelia's arm and pulling her from the emotional edge.

When she looked back at Dotchavitch, he glanced away, his brow furrowed with guilt and regret.

"So, I'm about to head out. Would you and Raven like to tag along?"

She nodded, then she noticed Dotchavitch's sword.

"Are we going somewhere dangerous?"

"Who knows, maybe? Why?"

"Can… may I have a bow and arrows?"

"What about your powers?"

She lifted her hand, the cracks were smaller, but still visible. It took him a second, but he nodded.

"I'll be right back."

He disappeared into the village and when he returned, he was carrying a bow and quiver, along with a set of fur lined leathers which he held out to Zelia.

"Thank you."

He gave her a soft smile and nodded towards the dragons.

"Come on, let's get going."

Dotchavitch seemed lost in thought as they rode, so she let the silence sit. They were out past the main island chain when she glanced back to see that the other riders were flying after them and Dotch followed her gaze.

"Weird, they rarely follow me when I take off this early," he shouted.

"They don't trust me."

"No, but don't worry about that. Come on, we can make a pass around the island up ahead before they catch up." He leaned forward, urging Stardust to pick up the pace.

Zelia admired the island as they circled it, it was even larger than Dragon Island. Caverns, ranging from the size of tiny pockets to the size of huge ships, pierced the cliffs along the shore. A point stuck out into the ocean where a single lonely tree hung out over the rocky cliff. It seemed as if it pointed at Dragon Island.

A hill rose in the shadow of a small volcano and that is where they waited for the others to catch up. The moment her feet touched dry land; she sensed much that was going on beneath the earth. She could feel the ground move and shift several meters below the surface as if it were alive. The earth buzzed with uneasy power as the others landed beside her.

"It's unusually warm here today. We should leave." Fifthry fidgeted and scanned the island.

"Why? Because it's warm for Autumn? Let's go explore, maybe we'll find a new dragon," Dotch said.

"No. We should leave," Fifthry insisted.

Zelia left them to argue and walked off, but an uneasy feeling grew in her as she went down the hill.

"Are there any men on the island?" Zelia asked.

"Is she talking to us? She can hear us?" The trees creaked and cracked with excitement.

"Well, go on, answer her!" some of them encouraged.

"Wait, what was her question again?"

"Men…"

"Oh! Yes, there are men from a ship walking among our trunks," several of the trees replied.

"Wait, hold on, one at a time please," Zelia stopped them. "I can hear you, but I can't make sense of it if you're all talking at once."

The trees quieted and then the one beside her answered in solemn creaks, "Their boat lies hidden in the caves deep below our roots."

"Do you know what they're doing here?"

"We're not positive… but they seem to be searching for something. Something that drives them to carry metal nets and weapons." Zelia turned to return to the others, and the trees called after her, "Beware… we shelter many creatures amongst our branches. Everything from snakes and spiders to aggressive dragons… they won't hesitate to protect themselves."

"Are you alright?" Dotchavitch called and his voice made Zelia look round. Everyone was staring at her from the top of the hill.

"Why?" she asked as she climbed the hill.

"You've been staring at the trees down there for a while."

"Oh, well, there are other humans on the island. Most are in the caves and some are traveling through the trees."

"How do you—"

"Trees, I hear them talk… it's related to everything else."

"Trees talk?" Dotchavitch sounded disbelieving, and there were giggles from the others.

"So do dragons and all the animals."

The giggles became laughter and Dotchavitch turned to glare at the other dragon riders for a moment then looked back to Zelia.

"Alright, shall we go say hello to the visitors then?"

"I don't believe these people have good intentions. They hunt for something other than food."

"Sounds like dragon trappers... even more reason to go. Don't worry, we'll be careful. No one traps dragons on our watch." Dotchavitch waved her towards the dragons.

She shook her head without budging.

"You won't be able to spot them through the canopy. If you wish to find the ones' traveling through the trees, we'll have to go on foot."

"We don't leave our dragons," Johnol protested.

"You're right, you guys go find the ship in the caves and I'll go with Zelia to find the men in the trees."

Fifthry slid from Gulepia. "If you're going; I'm going. Johnol, you're in charge since Seabloom is our only sea dragon."

Seabloom's wings quivered with delight as she puffed out her pearly white belly. Julio, Senth's green spotted red dragon, rolled his eyes at Seabloom's little show. For a moment, Zelia marveled over the amount of expression the dragons could show as they huffed little whirls of smoke from their nostrils.

The twins groaned as they took off on their dragons.

"Why do we never get to be the leaders?" Sligh's volume more than made up for his twin's lack of voice.

Fifthry shook her head at Sligh and followed Dotchavitch and Zelia into the trees leaving their dragons on the hill.

"We'll keep an eye out from above," Raven said.

For a while, the trees guided Zelia, but then they stopped shifting their upper branches to show her where to walk and one spoke. "Look here, they're just ahead."

She peered through the gaps in the leaves and saw five figures. They were still out of earshot, so she jumped down to a lower tree branch.

"How do you do that? You walk in the branches easier than we walk among their roots," Fifthry said.

"Shh, they're not all that far off, just over the next hill. There are five of them." Zelia turned and disappeared back into the canopy without a sound.

Fifthry might as well scream 'I'm over here!' with how loud she talks.

Then Dotchavitch tripped over a tree root.

And how much racket they make.

It didn't take long for the five men traveling through the trees to hear their approach.

Zelia crouched in the canopy of the trees and drew her bow, ready to shoot as the men surrounded Dotchavitch and Fifthry. They were a rugged looking crew and carried all sizes of metal nets and weapons. Many of them had scars as if they had been burned and scratched by dragons.

Dotchavitch drew his sword as one man spoke.

"What are you and such a beautiful young lady doing way out here, boy?"

"I was just about to ask you the same thing. Except the beautiful young lady part. None of you are beautiful or a lady…"

"It's been so long since we've been in the presence of a true woman."

One of them moved towards Fifthry with an outstretched hand. He was about to touch her face when Fifthry's sword shot to his throat.

"Touch me and die, you nasty little piece of scum," she snarled.

The one who spoke first interrupted, "Now, now, no need to be hasty, little ones. You're outnumbered, and certainly out-armed."

Dotchavitch gave a defiant smirk.

"We're not alone. Even now we're being watched."

The men held their weapons a little tighter. "Then why don't your friends show themselves? Or are you bluffing?"

"Why would I show myself?" Zelia spoke with the wind, letting it carry her voice through the trees.

The man laughed. "You travel with a little girl?" He turned to where he thought the voice came from. "Come here little girl! We won't hurt you!"

She moved to another tree as she scanned the area, making sure no one else was nearby and replied, "Why would I do such a thing? Tell me, why are you here? What is it you hunt?"

The men glanced at one another, uneasy at her words no matter how young the voice sounded.

"Why don't you come down here? And we'll tell you."

Zelia jumped down right behind the biggest man with her bow drawn, three more arrows in her hand ready to be notched. "Now, why are you here?"

The man gave a deep laugh. "So heavily armed for such a little thing and doesn't even know how to draw a bow properly. Why don't you go run home to your mommy and daddy? The forest is no place to play."

She shifted her aim and shot one of his comrade's axes through the handle. The ax shook as it stuck to the tree behind it, the handle splintered around the arrow.

In the blink of an eye, she had a second arrow from her hand trained on the man.

"I do not play. Now tell me what you are doing here or the next one is going through one of your companions."

She smiled coldly to unnerve them, her years of torturing and killing people crept back into her mind. She knew all too well how to force a person's hand. *Please don't let it come to that ever again.*

"Where did you learn to use a bow like that?"

"Would you shut up before you get us all killed, Brian?" the man Fifthry held a sword to asked.

Brian waved him off with a careless flick of his wrist. "So?" he asked her.

She forced a smile as she looked down her arrow at him. "From the Elves of Elyluma. They have the finest archers the realms have ever seen."

Brian crinkled his nose. "Elves? The Ely what now?"

"Do you not know who you are talking to?" Dotchavitch put in. "Trained by Elves, voice of dragons and trees, child of the gods."

I never said anything about gods.

She stood unwavering even though Dotchavitch's unwelcome endorsement caught her off guard.

"You believe all that about this girl? She can't be more than fourteen winters old!"

"I have seen more winters than all of you combined. Now, I will not ask you again." The man laughed, and she cut him off. "Fine, if you won't talk. Start walking. Take us to your captain."

The man shrugged and put his sword away. "We were going to take you there, anyway."

He turned his back on Zelia and walked off deeper into the trees, away from the dragons. Dotchavitch and Fifthry followed behind the men as Zelia removed her arrow from the tree.

She threw the damaged ax aside and whispered to the trees, "Guide the dragons to us."

She walked on the branches just above the men. This way she could keep a close eye on their every move and have plenty of time to react should the need arise.

One of the men watched Zelia for a while before deciding on small talk to learn more about her. "You climb well for a girl."

She ignored him completely.

A few minutes later they came to a stream, and the trees parted for a short span.

The men slipped and splashed as they trudged through the knee-deep stream. Clouds of mud and sand puffed up and clouded the water with their every step.

When they reached the opposite bank one of them called out, "You'll have to get out of that tree to cross."

Zelia ignored the man and looked at a tree across the water.

"Would you lend me a branch?"

The tree sprang to life. It twisted and turned until a single branch stuck out in front of her. Startled, the first man to cross stumbled back and fell into the water, taking the others with him. She made the short leap to the branch, and it returned to its original position.

"Thank you." She patted the tree's trunk and looked down.

Even Dotchavitch and Fifthry looked shocked as the men muttered, "H-h-how? Trees don't move!"

Suddenly the trees creaked and cracked with so much alarm that even the men could hear them. She scanned the trees until she saw why. An unfamiliar dragon came barreling through the trees straight for Dotch and Fifthry.

The men struggled to their feet, splashing around in the stream, and trying to manage their iron nets. As the dragon neared, they threw the nets at the dragon with practiced ease. But this dragon wasn't so easily caught. It darted and wove around their attempts to ensnare it.

Once the men ran out of nets, the brown and red dragon turned to attack them. Zelia leapt in front of the group of men, Dotch, and Fifthry just as the dragon began breathing fire.

Zelia raised a hand in front of her, the fire stopped and shot out in all directions as if it were hitting an invisible wall of stone. Some leaves scorched, and the trees pulled back from the flames.

Zelia faltered, and the flames licked Fifthry's sleeve.

"Hey!" Fifthry jumped back, dusting off the hot embers.

Zelia's vision blurred with the effort to hold back the flames.

She locked eyes with the dragon as it stared at her in shock, his voice ringing through her head. ***"How—"*** He drew back as he asked, ***"What are you?"***

His head tilted as Zelia urged him on with a wave of her hand. "Go while you can."

The dragon weaved through the trees before turning to look back at her. With that last glance over his shoulder, he disappeared.

"Leave the metal nets. You won't be using them anymore," Zelia said without moving from where she stood.

"You heard her, get going," Fifthry shooed the men to walk and moved off behind them.

As soon as the men were out of sight, Zelia fell to her knees and just sat in the charred leaves. The heat rising off the blackened ground was almost comforting.

"Are you alright?" Dotch asked once the men were out of earshot.

She nodded. "You should go with Fifthry, I'll catch up in a few."

"Alright. Don't be too long."

She could hear a pause in his step just before he passed the nearest tree, and she closed her eyes. With a sigh, she rocked to her feet and started after the others.

21

The forest came to an abrupt end, and the ground fell away in a steep cliff to the ocean. Without a word, the men worked their way backwards over the edge of the sheer cliff and began picking their way down, one foot at a time.

The last one paused before he disappeared from sight. "Don't just stand there, there's only two ways down and this is the way to our ship."

Three long shadows passed over the men and they plastered themselves against the cliff. With only a glance at the dragons, Fifthry and Dotchavitch jumped from the cliff.

"Come on, Zelia, jump. I'll catch you," Raven said.

Dotchavitch and Fifthry's dragons circled up with their riders. Zelia slipped her arrow into her quiver, ran towards the cliff, and jumped. Raven swooped down and slid beneath her.

"Told you I'd catch you." Raven spread her wings and rejoined the others.

"Nice jump!" Dotchavitch called over the beating wings.

They glanced down, the five men who hung from the cliff had a mix of surprise and fear in their eyes.

The dragons circled, rising and lowering with the thermals coming off the island. Dotchavitch and Fifthry devised a plan while Zelia and Raven flew up well above the island in search of a glimpse of the other riders.

"Do you see them, because I'm not seeing them."

"No, they must be in the tunnels below the island."

She shook her head when she returned to Dotchavitch and Fifthry.

"I could go check the tunnels."

"No, I have a feeling we're flying into a trap and our friends might have already found it," Dotchavitch said.

"That's what I'm afraid of. Ever since that man said he'd planned to take us to their ship…" her voice trailed off. "What do they do with the dragons?"

"Usually kill them. Sometimes they force them to work, who knows what they'd do if the others found them."

She stared down at Raven's black scales and her mind shot her back to the past. A knife replaced her bow and a bound boy drenched in blood screamed before her. *No, they can't be like that.* She shook her head. *And if they are, I won't let them. Even if I have to break my promise.*

She glanced across to Dotchavitch and Fifthry. *How do I reply to the dragons in their tongue?* She mulled over accessing their tongue but had made no progress by the time the men reached their rowboat. They picked up their oars and set to work rowing towards the huge open mouth of a nearby cavern.

The dragons hung back as they followed the men. It grew dark in the cave until it was nearly pitch black. Torches and lamps lit the cave ahead. The lights bobbed up and down with the steady waves lapping into the cave from the open ocean behind them. The sound of moving water and beating wings filled the air.

The men on the rowboat grew anxious, fidgeting and looked back at them more often.

Zelia glimpsed the ship around a bend of the cave. Its sail was furled so it could enter the cave. It was a tight fit, and she guessed that once high tide came, the incoming sea would crush the ship against the cavern's ceiling.

Though they traveled quietly, the cave amplified all sound, creating echoes. It wouldn't be long before the men aboard the ship would hear the steady beating of dragon wings. If they couldn't already.

When the rowboat reached the bow of the ship one of the men yelled out, "DRAGON RIDERS!"

The ship became a maelstrom of activity as Dotch, Fifthry, and Zelia jumped off their dragons onto the ship. Zelia faltered as she hit the deck, and Dotch caught her.

"Zelia?"

"I'll be fine." She pushed his hand away, pulled a handful of arrows, and drew one.

"Go! We'll call for you if we need you!" she yelled at the dragons over the echoes of beating wings and yelling men.

"Are you sure?" Raven questioned.

"Yes, go!" Zelia climbed atop the railing of the ship with Dotchavitch and Fifthry in front of her.

The men from the rowboat scrambled over the railing. They were surrounded by a mismatched crew of men who all appeared to have seen long days at sea, with their long scraggly beards and salt crusted hair. The only exception was a set of young boys standing at the back of the group without weapons.

"Why this is a first!" the man spoke with a sharp tongue that cut through the air like a knife through paper. "Dragon riders who send their dragons away as they fight!"

An older man with a long, jagged scar across his face stepped through the crowd. It was obvious he was the captain as the crew parted for him. Her skin crawled as the captain's right foot scraped across the wooden deck with each step. The man came to a stop before them, a sense of death emanated from him and hit her like a stone wall. She bit the inside of her lip.

"They must know what we do here, yet they still land. What are ye names, my innocent little friends?"

Dotchavitch stood unmoving as the man edged closer until Zelia spoke. "Take one step closer and your men will be without their captain."

"Strong words for one so young. Why don't ye put your toys away and come here?"

There was a distinct undertone in his voice, and the release of a bowstring echoed through the cave.

"No!" Zelia dropped her bow, letting the arrow fly where it may as she shoved Dotch to the side, raising a thin wall of ice in front of him and Fifthry. The ice shattered as an arrow struck and Dotch threw himself over her and Fifthry.

"What do we have here?" the captain's voice boomed in the cave and Zelia tried to focus on him as she struggled to breathe; her use of fire and ice trying to break her apart.

"Let me go!" Fifthry screamed.

Something jerked Zelia up by her arm and flung her amongst the feet of men.

"Put her with the dragons, she's worth more than her weight in gold."

⟶

"Zelia? Zelia, wake up. Come on, Raven will have my scales if you die now."

Seabloom's voice reverberating through her head pulled her back to the present.

"Seabloom? Where... where are we?"

"Trapped, in a cage."

"What?" She rolled to her feet. "No."

In a panic, she banged on the door, only to yelp as a spike of pain ran through her arm, all the way through to her shoulders.

"Zelia? Zelia, get us out of here," Dotch's voice came from just outside the sealed metal cage.

"I... I can't," she spoke through panicked gasps. The dark, a cage. Trapped again. Fear raked through her, the past surging forward to haunt her and pain threatening to push her over the edge.

"Zelia, just take a deep breath, we're counting on you."

She forced a couple shaky breaths. "Dotch, I can't... I just can't go back."

"I know you can't, but right now I need you to freeze that lock as fast as you can so I can break it. Johnol, you and Seabloom get Zelia out of here."

"But she can help," Fifthry protested.

"I think this will hurt her, you saw how she collapsed. Have Seabloom go under as soon as you get off the boat, then send our dragons back in. The trappers have gone too far this time."

"Break it? Doesn't he think we've tried?"

"Hush Evergreen, it's not like we have another option."

"They could get the key."

"Zelia, we have a plan, but we need the dragons," Dotch said.

"Just don't leave me, please."

Her hand shook as she pressed it against the metal still warm from the breath of a dragon. The air cooled as the metal froze. There was a sudden bang, and she gasped as the vibration ran through her cracking arm. *"Raven..."* her own thought vibrated like the voices of the dragons and she sank against the cage wall.

One, two more bangs and the door opened with a screech. The wild dragons shot past, barely missing her as she sat in a heap by the door.

"She is the girl of dragon blood, help them as they have helped you," Raven commanded, a snarl in her tone.

"Uh, Dotch," Johnol paused, and she forced her eyes open.

"I... I'll be fine," her voice caught, "it just burns."

Her vision was blurry, but she could still make out Dotch and Johnol's faces as they lifted her onto Seabloom.

"Get her out of here, I don't think she could take much more. Go on, we won't be far behind."

"Just be careful," Johnol said.

There was a warmth behind her as Johnol climbed on and held her from sliding off. Seabloom snaked through the ship and splashed over the side, just keeping them above water as she went.

"Zelia."

There was a rush of wind as Raven doubled back and left the other dragons to deal with the trappers.

"She's like you, isn't she?" Seabloom asked.

"Yes. Would you carry her to land, the big hill?"

"Of course. You go back and help the others."

"Thank you, Seabloom."

➤

There was a bit of light still left in the sky as they landed back on the hill they had first stopped on.

"The others?" Zelia asked.

"They're right behind us. Is there anything I can do?"

"Not unless you know how to get Yalif."

"Yalif? The god of healing?"

"He's not a god, but yes. I'm just going to lie down."

"Here."

Johnol helped her down from Seabloom and laid her down. The cool grass felt good against her cracked and blistered arm. She only ever blistered when she went from fire to ice, never ice to fire.

22

"Why do we always have to get the firewood? Why can't we get the food?" Sligh and Senth complained.

"Do you not remember what happened the last time you got the food?" Fifthry questioned.

Sligh and Senth's faces showed their disgust and they stamped off down the hill. Fifthry headed down the hill in search of food.

"Who are they?" Johnol asked.

"They were being forced to work… still deciding what to do with them. So, how is she doing?" Dotch asked.

"I don't know, she hasn't said a word since she lay down."

"Are you alright?" Raven asked.

"I will be, just need rest."

Her thoughts were slow as Raven settled down beside her, chilling her scales from the inside out to sooth Zelia's skin. The relief from the burns caused her to prop herself up against Raven, so she watched the others, the will to sleep not yet with her.

"Looks like Raven is taking care of her for now, maybe we should learn what we can?" Johnol gestured towards the boys they had plucked from the crew and Dotch shrugged before descending the few paces down the hill.

⟶

"We were only on that ship for a week, maybe two weeks." The boy ran his thin fingers through his sun-bleached hair. "I really don't know. I kind of lost track of the days," his voice was scratchy with adolescence. "We're from an island quite a ways north of here. We're all that's left of our people.

143

The dragon hunters raided our village for food and supplies. They killed most of our people before dragging us on board to work."

"That wasn't until after they had their way with the women of our village." The younger boy, maybe fifteen years old and tanned from being in the sun, stared at the grass at his feet. "My brother died trying to protect our mother. I tried to help him, but…" his voice cracked, and he buried his face in his hands, "I... I froze."

"There was nothing any of us could've done." The older boy rested a hand on his companion's shoulder.

"What of the men of your village?"

"The dragon hunters claimed they sank their ships. Leaving none alive. But not before they found out where our village was."

Dotchavitch nodded and spoke quietly, "A similar story can be told of our village. When I was just an infant, a group of men did the same to our village. Our only saving grace was that one of our ships was at port when they attacked. With a great deal of effort and loss, we drove back the intruders, but not before Fifthry's mother was taken…" his voice trailed off as Fifthry started up the hill.

All was quiet around Zelia for a time allowing her to nod off to sleep.

➤

The dark crept in around her and she shivered.

"Get up!"

"What is it this time, oh great wizard Asenten?"

She rubbed her eyes with the heel of her palm before prying her eyes open to the welcome sight of light. The glow of Asenten's staff bounced off the damp cave walls in every direction. She knew it was just a dream, but the webs of the past held her all the same. For a moment, she wondered why Rog was blocking her, but her dream pulled her from those thoughts.

"I said get up! I have something for you." Asenten pulled a gag from a man's mouth.

"Let me go! Who the hell do you think you are?" the bound man spat.

"He's a wizard of the guild, a man beyond power. And I'm afraid he will never let you go. Not now that you've seen me," she said sadly, giving the man enough dignity to look him in the eye, to have someone remember him. She always did, she remembered all their faces and their screams.

"So, what shall it be my dear lad? Tell me the truth and I might let her make it quick," Asenten said.

"Her? You're threatening me with this child?"

"Please just tell him what he wants, it's easier for us both that way." Asenten slammed her to the wall with his staff and she didn't give even a whimper, she just waited silently for her breath to return.

"Did I ask you to speak?"

She shook her head and lowered her gaze.

"Good, now get your ice stone." She fell to the ground and snatched the little blue and white speckled stone from the cave floor. Asenten pulled the man to his feet. "Go on, you know what to do."

Ice crept around the man's feet and froze him in place.

"Release me! You... you monster!"

He struggled, but the ice didn't budge. She reached up and took his hand, it was warm to the touch and she wished all she had to do was hold it, let it thaw the ice she used to protect her heart. Then again, the ice around her heart saved some little pieces of her soul. The man shuddered, and his fingertips froze.

Her dream lurched forward, *she had thawed the man, burned him, and frozen him again. Now her palm rested upon his chest as she held back tears.*

"Tell him, and I'll make it fast. I'll make sure your soul passes over, no one should have to linger here."

"You're right, no one should be forced to linger here, even you," he spoke through chattering teeth. "I was wrong, you're not a monster. He is and don't let him convince you otherwise."

"That's enough!" Asenten shoved her down. "Finish it!"

The man gave her a nod with a mix of pity, sympathy, and forgiveness in his eyes.

➤

"Zelia? Wake up," a voice whispered through from the present, but she didn't acknowledge it.

Someone shook her. "Zelia, you need to wake up."

Her eyes flashed open, and she shot up from her half lying position, where she had rolled away from Raven. Pain pulsed through her, and she clasped the tunic across her chest. Blood rushed from her head and she

145

edged towards unconsciousness, her vision going black around the edges. Firm hands grasped her shoulders and kept her upright.

"Are you alright? You weren't breathing."

She shook her head against her spinning world. Johnol's expression twisted.

"How often does that happen?" he asked.

"It's only happened once, but I've not been alone much since then."

She rubbed at her arm, then remembered the burns.

"Thank you for waking me up."

Zelia rocked to her feet and walked away. She wasn't ready to share the reality of her past. She could feel Johnol's gaze boring into her back, as he explained what happened to Dotchavitch.

She plopped down on the side of the hill and watched as Johnol stood brushing himself off. Dotchavitch rested his hand on Johnol's shoulder and she zoned out, unable to focus on any one thing.

She was so out of it she didn't notice Johnol's approach until he was only a few meters away.

"Mind if I join you?" She just shook her head, and he sat down beside her. "Here, I brought you some rabbit."

They ate in silence as they watched the long shadows of their friends flicker from the light of the fire.

"Why didn't you just tell us? I mean, about your heart?"

"I wasn't sure and can't let myself seem weak, or have others care about me."

"What?" His head snapped towards her. "Why?"

"It only makes it harder to leave. Besides, people who care are more likely to get hurt trying to protect me... Sometimes I wish I could just disappear to a place where there's no one I could hurt."

"Zelia, we wouldn't be here if it weren't for you."

"You're right. You wouldn't have found those men if it weren't for me. Your lives wouldn't have been in danger if I hadn't come here."

"Then we wouldn't have found those two boys down there." He pointed towards the light of the campfire below them. "I, for one, am glad to have met you and nothing will change that."

"You already show that you would do something foolish for me." She turned away and used her hair to hide her face. "I don't want anyone putting themselves in danger for me."

Johnol moved to where he could look her in the eye. "That's not your choice to make."

"It should be." She turned away from him with her arms crossed, the urge to slouch gnawed at her as the steel plate in her chest held her straight. "I'm the one who'll be haunted by your decisions for millennia, or however long I'm cursed to stay here."

"I have a feeling you know good and well just how big of a difference one act can make to change the course of the future. You need to learn to accept what others choose to do for you."

She couldn't believe she was hearing this from such a young human, but a tinge of sadness still rose from deep within her and she muttered under her breath, "And if I can't?"

"You have to, or you'll always be fighting with yourself over what others do. Now, we should go join the others and get some rest." He stood and offered her a hand. She reluctantly took it, and he hauled her to her feet.

She followed him down the hill. The eyes of the two young boys they had picked up earlier that day followed her.

"Can either of you explain why those two," Dotch pointed to two green dragons that sat by themselves, "scooped you out of the water and followed us?"

"I… well, I don't know."

Zelia could tell Dotch wasn't trying to accuse the boys, but she wasn't sure that they understood that he was just trying to decide if they were a threat or not. She hadn't noticed the two new dragons before, but she was sure Raven had already approved them.

"Maybe it's because we were the ones who fed the dragons. Those two are the only ones who didn't try to eat us."

"How long were they on the ship?" Dotch asked.

"They and one of the other dragons were there when they took us."

"Well, since Raven and Stardust haven't chased them off yet, they should be safe enough. Are you both alright with riding them on the way back to our island?"

"We can go with you?"

"If they'll let you ride. We're too far out for us to double up for the ride home, but I don't plan on leaving you."

"We have to ride them? Like you do?"

"If you want to get off this island. That said, riding is much more fun than dangling from their claws."

The boys shared a nervous glance with one another before nodding. With that settled, the others went straight into debating who would take first watch.

"I'll take first watch," Zelia said.

Dotchavitch stared at her, surprised by her offer. "No, you need to rest."

"I won't be able to sleep for a while either way. You should all rest while you can."

They all stared at her, questions showing on all their faces. *Do I appear that tired?*

"My heart is still offbeat."

"What?" Dotch asked.

"I… I told you that Yargo took me in as one of his children, but I didn't explain why." She fiddled with a blade of grass, not sure how to continue. "Actually, I don't know why he took me in like that. He came to save me at Rogath's request and there was an explosion. I used ice to block the blast from hitting Yargo and his men, but…" she trailed off, not wanting to relive those moments of agony. "I have pieces of metal and rock in my chest. They affect my heart. So, I can't go back to sleep until it's at least closer to what it should be." They still stared at her and she rolled her eyes, trying to brush off the topic of her heart. "Or would you all rather sit here debating all night and no one get any rest?"

"I'll stay up with her," Johnol offered. "You guys go get some rest."

"I'll take second watch," Dotchavitch said as he stood. "Come on guys."

They all spread out to sleep. The two new boys slept off to the side, farther away from the dragons. While the others slept against and under the wings of their dragons.

Zelia and Johnol sat side by side, looking down at the trees with the volcano at their backs.

She laid back and looked up at the sky as a chorus of snores filled the air.

"Not going to sleep on me now are ya?"

"No, just wishing the clouds would dissipate so I can see the stars."

"I take it you like to look at the stars."

"Yes, though what I see is different from what you see."

"How's that?"

"I see many more stars than you and I can see the planets that circle them when the air is clear."

"Uh, so… you're like Lumid, the ever-watching guard of the passage?"

"Kind of. You know, I trust him more than Yargo."

"What? Why? Yargo is the highest of all the gods."

"Yargo is a seeker of knowledge first and foremost and I'm a mystery to him. At least Lumid just wants to protect me and is curious about my sight."

"So, you were serious back there, you have met them."

"Yes, and then I hurt them. I tried not to, but I couldn't stop it."

Johnol fell silent, and she forced herself to search for specks of stars through the clouds to keep her mind from wandering. Some time and many clouds passed before Johnol shook himself awake.

"You keep watch. I'm going to go wake Dotchavitch. You can come join me once he gets up here."

He watched her until she nodded before starting down the hill. A few minutes later Dotch plopped down beside her.

"So… I didn't want to ask in front of the others, but how did you end up here? I mean, why are you not still with Yargo?"

She sat up and stared at the flames, part of her wanting to reach out and let them burn her.

"I lived with them as family. They saved me, and I nearly killed them. No one around me is safe, not as long as they can control any part of me."

"Who?"

"The Wizard Guild. They created me, to kill everyone I care about. I'd kill myself again, but I already know I'd just come back. I always come back."

"I might know of someone who could help you. If they don't run us off their island first."

"No one can help me, not even those you consider gods."

"Maybe, but we should at least ask for their advice. Fairies are magical creatures after all."

"Wait, there are Fairies out here?"

"Well, not here, but not all that far from home either. You go get some rest. We'll talk more tomorrow."

"I… Dotch, thank you."

"You're welcome, now go on."

23

Her mind replayed the same scenes from before, only this time there was no one to wake her.

"I'm sorry," she whispered.

The ice jumped through the man and ended his pain in an instant, his face frozen in that pitiful stare.

Asenten slammed the butt of his staff into her side.

She gasped for air and froze when she realized where she was. Stars twinkled in the sky above her as she slipped from under Johnol's arm.

So many lives. She could almost hear their screams and she rubbed her side, where she had just been struck in her dream. *No, so many deaths.* She heaved a sigh and with a short climb up the hill, found the twins taking their turn keeping watch. When she tossed another piece of wood on the fire and sat, the twins fell over each other as they backed away from the crackle of the log burning in the hot coals.

"You two should go get some more rest. We still have a while before the sun comes up."

"But it's our turn—" Sligh protested until Senth's elbow connected with his chest.

"I can't sleep, anyway. And if I'm awake, you two might as well get some rest."

With shrugs and tired grins, the twins lumbered off down the hill where they fell atop each other as they lay down. Their snores began as quickly as they had fallen.

The flames and glowing embers took to the air, and she recalled the screams of the Darkans as they burned all around.

150

The longer she sat, the closer the flames drew to her. Her subconscious called to the fire she had hurt so many with. She edged closer and held out her hand, letting the searing scorching flames lap at her fingers.

She sighed as her mind continued to torture her with images of men, women, and children dying by her hand. Their screams and pleas pierced her ears, sending chills down her spine. Yet she sat, still unmoving, while the heat of the flames welcomed her with a twisted sense of warmth, pain, and comfort… Though her mind still wandered through some of the worst parts of her past.

With no warning, a hand gripped her arm and yanked her away from the flames.

"You have a death wish or somethin'?" the wiry boy voiced.

She jerked her arm out of the boy's grip, and he staggered back.

"H… how aren't you burnt?"

"I am, just not on the surface."

The boy edged away from her, before sitting in the grass. "So… How did you sleep?"

"Not all that well."

"Your heart?" he asked, seeming to be genuinely concerned.

"No." She heaved a sigh. "Dark memories from days long since passed."

"Nice to know I'm not the only one who's haunted by the past." His eyes flashed wide when he realized what he had just said. "Not that I'd ever wish for something bad to happen to anyone."

She gave him an understanding, though pained smile. "You know, I never got your name."

"Oh, I'm Kafthry, and he's Keller. I overheard the others last night. They only just met you?"

"I've only been in this part of the world for a few days now but I'm afraid it won't be long before I'll have to leave. I don't want to hurt anyone else."

They sat in silence as the sun broke the horizon. With the beautiful golden sunrise before her, she pulled herself from her dark thoughts to enjoy the view.

"You sure are fond of looking at the sky."

"You learn to appreciate it even more, when you've spent most of your life trapped in the dark."

"Sorry, but just how old are you? You act so much older than you appear."

"I'm not sure exactly. I couldn't track the days or the years when I was in the cave. Though I do know I'm somewhere around five hundred years old. Eleanor could tell me if I ever see her again. But age is just a number to me, since I don't age like any being here."

"You're how old?" Kafthry stared at her as if she was crazy.

"I didn't stutter, and neither of us is insane. Well, for my part, I suppose that's debatable." *I am connected to Rog after all.* She saddened at the thought. She hadn't felt Rogath's presence since he had blamed her and while she longed for his companionship, she dreaded facing him again.

Kafthry let her words sink in as the others stirred.

She stood and turned towards the trees. "You stay here and keep watch as the others wake. I'm going for a walk."

She made it only a few paces before Raven asked, ***"Where are you running off to now?"***

"For a walk."

"Want to go for a ride instead? We can make a lap around the island."

"Sure." She climbed onto Raven's back and they took off. *"Raven, do you think the Fairies can help me?"*

"Maybe, but they still follow the old ways. So, do you want to go fast or slow?"

"Slow, that way it gives everyone time to wake up. The Fairies, do they still speak their ancient language here?"

"Ancient language? I've only ever known them to have one main language, so I suppose so. Why?"

"Because I know it, or at least, I used to."

"Alright."

They looked out over the treetops towards the others.

"Looks like the boys made friends with Elm and Evergreen."

"Sounds like you did too," Zelia teased.

"I always make sure the other dragons brought home are safe."

"Why is it Dotch said you don't like people, even though you've been protecting them?"

"Because I'm old and they're young. Dotch wanted to be my rider, but he was meant for Stardust, not me."

"What will you do when I leave? You know I cannot stay, right?"

"Why do you feel you need to leave?"

"I..."

"You're not bound to the mainland; you can stay here."

Zelia ran her hand across Raven's smooth scales. *"I..."*

"You still feel you are bound there, just as I am bound here. I understand."

Raven swooped down and skimmed the water, then spiraled up to meet the others coming off the island.

"How about you give the boys the names of their dragons, before they come up with some strange name like Gulepia?"

"I happen to like my name," Gulepia almost growled. *"Besides, what type of names are Elm and Evergreen?"*

"The names our mother gave us when we hatched from the very same egg," Evergreen replied.

"You should tell them that! It's rare you know."

"Keller, Kafthry, would you like to know the names of your dragons?"

Both Keller and Kafthry nodded in reply.

"Kafthry, you're riding Evergreen. Keller, you're riding Elm. They say they're brothers, twins to be exact, hatched from the same egg. That's rare for any egg-bearing creature, let alone a dragon."

Kafthry and Keller exchanged a grin.

"What are you two smiling about?" Dotch teased.

"It's just ironic. We've always felt like brothers. You see, Keller was an orphan long before our earliest memories. His father died at sea when his mother was pregnant, and she died not all that long after he was born. The entire village took him in, but he spent most of his life with my family. If we hadn't been a few months apart, there might have been a rumor that we were twins, as we looked a lot alike when we were younger."

Kafthry's story of Keller's past reminded Zelia of her time as a small child, and she lost herself to her memories.

➤

"Starjaina!" Zelia called from her post on the vine fence.

The pure white horse lifted her head and galloped across the pasture.

"Want to race?" Alrindel asked as he rode up to join them.

"Are you not supposed to be at practice?"

"One quick race will not hurt. Come on, even Starjaina wants to."

The horse shook her head and eased alongside the fence. "Come on, let us show him what we can do."

"Let's give him at least a fighting chance, shall we?" Zelia teased as she climbed on and grabbed a clump of her horse's mane.

"Ready, set, go!"

They thundered across the pasture, Starjaina always keeping just a little ahead. Starjaina pranced as she came to a stop and Alrindel slid off his horse to rub its head.

"Either you are getting faster or Starjaina is getting slower." Alrindel told his horse, who shook his head in response. "No? You think she let us keep up?"

Zelia's smile beamed as Alrindel looked up at her, neither of them noticing the approach of another horse.

"What do you think you are doing? You are going to give Eadon a heart attack," Koin scooped her off Eadon's horse. "Now where is Alrindel? He is missing practice."

"Here I am." He ran up and jumped on Starjaina. "I was looking for Zelia."

"Sure, you were. Come on. And you, young lady, are supposed to be practicing your writing, if memory serves."

"But Eadon got called away."

"You can still practice, can you not?" Koin asked.

"Yes." Zelia lowered her head.

➤

"What are you so deep in thought about?" Johnol asked, startling her after she had been in her own mind for a while.

"My early childhood."

"What do you mean? I thought you said you were created by magic?"

"I was, but I had to start from the beginning just as any other creature. From what I understand, when they decided that they should not age me with magic, the Elven Queen Eleanor took me in as the other wizards traveled far too much to bother with such a young child. In turn, Eleanor handed me off to her trusted guard and friend Eadon. Even if he didn't want me in the beginning, he took me in as his own. I was the first outsider to learn among the elf children. Eadon has always had a soft spot for orphans. My elvish brother Alrindel isn't his son by blood either, his parents died towards the beginnings of the old wars." She let out a soft sigh. "I learned a lot alongside Alrindel, everything from language to how to fight."

"Okay… now I'm confused. You said life hasn't always been kind, yet it sounds like you had an awesome childhood."

"It was, until that day, until my first death. I only spent one hundred and forty of my five hundred years with the Elves. And my time with the

Elves only made the next few centuries all that much harder. They taught me that all life was worth cherishing and then Asenten forced me to tear men, women, and children apart piece by piece for the enjoyment of my captors."

"But you just said the Elves taught you to fight, how could they cherish all life if they train to kill."

"There's a difference between killing for selfish reasons and killing to defend yourself and the innocent. The line may not be clear cut, but it is there, and I have crossed it many times." Her gaze fell, and she slipped back into her self-hatred, the very thing Zivu had ordered her to leave behind.

"So… tell me, what are they like? The Elves I mean?"

She shook herself from her thoughts. "Elves? They're lovers. Lovers of beauty and knowledge, of all that is kind and beautiful in all the realms. Most of all they love music, the stars, their children, and their one and only soulmate. Even in death their souls are bound to one another."

"They sound beautiful, what do they look like?"

"Why is it that everyone wants to know what Elves look like, but they never want to know what, say, a Dwarf looks like? Is it because the women look so much like the men? They may not be beautiful to the eye, but their souls are as deep as their halls." A slight smile played across her lips and she glanced at her friends. "But yes, I shall tell you. They all have long flowing hair as fine as silk and eyes that pierce into the depths of your very soul with nothing more than a glance. Their skin glows in the light of the stars, to the point that they need no fire to see by on moonless nights. It's for that reason, they can often be found dancing under the stars."

"They... they sound beautiful," Kafthry breathed, both he and Keller were awestruck by her description.

"They are, even in heart and soul. Or at least most of them are."

"Why didn't you return? You speak as though you love it there," Johnol said.

"I... I do love it there." A feeling of love and longing of the purest sort washed over her but she shook it off. "But I can't let them put themselves in danger for me."

"You know, you can't run forever. Maybe you should go back. Not that we're trying to get rid of you," Dotchavitch raked his hair back, "it just sounds like you miss them. Like you belong there far more than here."

"You're right, they are my kin. I'm just not ready to face the wizards. I may never be ready."

"Maybe not on your own, but I have a feeling you won't be alone."

"Now who's being the wise one?" She forced a smirk.

The chain of islands came into view on the horizon, she could just make out a ship docked in the harbor.

"Dotchavitch, were the men of your village due to return today?" she asked.

Dotchavitch shook his head. "Not unless fishing was unusually successful. Why?"

"There's a ship docked in the harbor, similar to the one we saw yesterday."

"Stardust and I can fly faster than the others. Maybe we should fly ahead and check things out?" Raven asked and Stardust eagerly agreed.

Zelia relayed the message.

"We should stick together," Fifthry protested.

Dotchavitch squinted at the dark masses of the islands on the horizon. "Zelia and I will go make a pass by the island and circle back for you guys."

He glanced at Zelia with a grin. "Keep up if you can. Come on Stardust."

Stardust sped up and Raven took off after him.

"Oh, that little… you have yet to see fast. Zelia, you'd better hold on."

Zelia tightened her grip on the ridge along Raven's neck.

"Ready whenever you are."

Raven gave one hard flap of her wings and shot past Stardust and Dotchavitch. Dotchavitch's mouth gaped with shock. *It's a good thing there are not any bugs through here, he'd be catching a few.*

A moment later, Dotchavitch's jaw set and he leaned forward with a tightened grip. "Come on Stardust, let's show them what we've got."

Stardust sighed and picked up pace. He knew good and well he couldn't beat Raven with her wide wingspan, but he gave it his best effort.

They both sped along, leaving the sound of their beating wings far behind them. Dotchavitch and Zelia couldn't have spoken to each other even if they had wanted to.

They slowed their pace when they neared the island, and they were close enough for Dotchavitch to make out the ship in the harbor. To their dismay, Dotchavitch didn't recognize it.

She focused and could see men with bound villagers. "They are binding the villagers' hands. And I don't see your father."

Dotchavitch grit his teeth and slammed his fists on Stardust's back. "Those bastards! You go tell the others since Raven is faster. I'll go see what I can do."

She paused for a moment, but his look of determination and hatred for those men made her decide it was best not to argue.

Raven folded her wings and spun to face the others. This time she held nothing back as she flew back to the others. Raven didn't even slow down as she neared them, she just spun around until she faced the island once again.

"Come on! The village is in trouble!"

All the dragons sped up and Raven shot off towards the island.

When they neared, Zelia found some men surrounding Dotchavitch. They outnumbered him and he slashed at them in a desperate attempt to keep them back. *You fool, you're going to get yourself killed.* She sat back and made it rain arrows when Raven neared, waiting for the pause between wing beats to shoot. Each arrow met its mark and dropped men left and right. Half the men scrambled back in surprise and she even got two with one shot.

She slung her bow across her back. *"Drop me off here, if none of the villagers are on that ship, burn it."*

"What are you doing?"

"Saving Dotchavitch, don't worry about me."

Raven sprayed fire and slowed, allowing Zelia to slide off. She plucked a sword from among a man's ashes, the metal hot against her palm as she met the sword of another man.

She was a few huts down from Dotchavitch but could see the men had regained some of their composure and returned to fighting him.

The men around her shook off their daze and sprung towards her. Before she could meet any of them, Kafthry swooped down on Evergreen and plucked her from the crowd of angry men.

"Why did you do that?" she asked as she swung herself behind him.

Kafthry pointed ahead.

Raven and Stardust faced off with two dragons larger than even Raven. One was a rather round white ice dragon that sat half in, half out of the water. The other was a long and narrow red dragon.

The others darted here and there around the two dragons. Zelia stood on Evergreen's back.

"Raven, over here!"

Raven circled over and Zelia dropped down to her. They passed over the burning village and she willed the fires to quell.

"Zelia." Raven turned towards the shore.

A tall, broad shouldered man stood next to the burning ship. In front of him, he held Gondavitch with the blade of his sword to his throat. Fifthry dropped Dotch off on the shore and headed off to help the others deal with the ice and fire dragons corralled in the harbor.

"Let my father go," Dotch demanded, his anger showing as his sword jabbed the air with each word.

"You're in no position to be making demands, boy."

The men who had been ransacking the village now moved towards the harbor.

"Raven, Stardust." She nodded towards the men.

They bathed the approaching men in fire and ice to hold them back, though they were careful not to cause more damage to the village.

Zelia stepped to Dotchavitch's side. She watched the man's gestures, his rage, and even his arrogance.

The man sneered. "Icelore! Show them just what you can do!" The gigantic white dragon left his companion to deal with the other dragons and puffed out his chest with a deep breath.

"You don't have to do this. Let me help you, you can both be free."

"We can never be free, no one can kill him, we've tried." He lowered his head and blew straight at them.

She shoved Dotchavitch aside as the dragon's icy breath encased her in a spiky block of ice. Caught in an internal fight between fire and ice, she shuddered and strained. *Please don't let me shatter this time,* she thought as she felt the ice envelope her, to become a part of her. She had only ever done it once while in the cave and never so soon after using fire. A muffled scream filtered through the ice. *Dotch?* She forced her hand to close and the ice around her outstretched hand cracked. She willed the ice to break as she forced her arms apart and her icy tomb shattered.

Even Dotchavitch turned from holding his fallen father. "Z... Zelia?"

She stared down at Gondavitch, his insides showing where the dragon trapper had gutted him. Cracks ran down her face and grew with her every move, her ice form fighting with her inner flame. She chewed her frozen lip against the pain and turned her attention to Gondavitch's killer.

Rage at his actions coursed through her, yet she still didn't want to kill him. "I have fought becoming the very monster some of my creators wished me to be, and you have sought to become that monster. Maybe it's not what we have done, but what we choose to do. Tell me. What will you choose?" Ice formed under her feet as she walked towards the man.

In a last-ditch effort, the man made a move towards Dotch. Before he could get near him, she raised her hand and icy spikes shot out of the ground in front of him.

The pops and cracks of snapping ice sounded when she shook her head.

"No. Greedy and heartless beings like you don't deserve to live in this realm. The deepest depths of Fregnar's realm would suit you much better," some small part of her hoped to intimidate him into fleeing with his men.

The man raised his sword with a shaky hand towards her. "No! I won't go to the underworld!"

She cocked her head at his remark. "I can tell you; you won't be going to the hall of fallen warriors."

"How would you know!" His face twisted in anger.

"Because, Yargo has a hand in deciding who's allowed in Hyperia's hall of fallen warriors and I have more faith in him than that. Don't worry. Your death will be swift, which is more than I can say for most of your victims."

She could see the fear in his face, but he charged her anyway, determined to change the fate Zelia had laid before him. He made it only a step before jagged points of ice grew out of the ground and skewered him in place.

"You... you killed him!" The two huge dragons stared in amazement.

"You're free now. Go where you please." They stared out at the open ocean. *"Go, no one will stop you."*

Without a second glance or a word of thanks, they darted away.

"Get back here! You're not leaving without us!" The other invaders ran out into the water after the dragons.

She staggered towards Dotchavitch and her color returned to normal, streams of blood replacing the cracks.

Her legs gave out and Dotchavitch caught her.

"Are you okay?"

"You sure like to ask that."

She shivered and slipped into unconsciousness.

24

"Hey there, are you okay?" Kafthry was first to her side when she stirred.

"Better than I figured I'd be."

She sat up stiffly, her entire body aching with each movement. *Don't look so serious, I'm not dead.* She cracked a smile, hoping to ease Kafthry and Johnol's worry.

"So, how long was I out this time?"

"It's been a few days."

"Hm, best time yet." She pulled the wool blanket around her and sat back against the wall.

Both boys raised an eyebrow.

"It usually takes me much longer to recover from going full frost after so much as looking at fire. That's if it doesn't kill me. So, what did you do with the men who swam back to shore?"

"They're tied up in the hog pens. You know, we should go tell Dotch that you're awake." Johnol paused, "Oh, and the men are due to return today. Gondavitch had sent a dragon with a letter telling them to return when he saw a dragon trapper's ship on the horizon."

"I see. Well, come on then. I can give Dotch the news myself." She slung her bow and quiver across her back as she walked.

Dotchavitch stood with his arms crossed as he looked out at a ship sailing towards the island. The others hung back as she stood next to him for a moment.

"How are you holding up?"

Dotchavitch jumped at the sound of her voice. He stopped and composed himself a little as Johnol and Kafthry laughed at his reaction.

"I will be better once I break the news to the men." He motioned towards the ship coming in.

"I can do it for you. It's the least I can do."

"Thank you, but they need to hear it from me. Besides, they don't know you."

"If you change your mind, let me know."

"How about we go get something to eat? I'm sure you're starving," Kafthry said.

Not really. She shrugged and headed towards the dining hall anyway, leaving Dotch alone with his thoughts.

On their way out after eating, Raven met them. ***"Come on, the men are about to tie off."*** Zelia glanced back at Johnol and Kafthry, and Raven rolled her eyes. ***"Fine they can get on too. Just hurry up."***

"Come on, Raven will give us a lift. The men are about to tie off."

Johnol and Kafthry didn't even hesitate as they climbed on for the short hop to the shore.

They all slid from Raven as she landed on the beach just as the ship eased to a stop at the dock. The men busied themselves with tying it off, several of them eyeing the crowd. They obviously sensed that something was off. Kafthry stopped beside Keller at the edge of the crowd while she followed Johnol through the throng of people. There were a couple people left in front of them when Dotchavitch raised his hand, calling the crowd to silence.

"I'm afraid I have grave news for you." Dotchavitch blinked to stop the tears forming in his eyes. "Our Chief, my father, is… is dead."

There were some gasps from the sea-weary crew as the ship's captain demanded, "How, how did this happen?" He stared down at Dotch as though he had killed his father.

You're not alone in this Dotch. She pushed her way by the last few people to stand at his side.

"Yesterday, a captain of the dragon trappers showed up with a large crew and his two favorite dragons to take over the island," Zelia said.

Dotchavitch's voice cracked as he added. "By the time we got here, they had already tied up most of the villagers. I tried to save my father, but I was too late. I, too, would be dead and many more if it weren't for Zelia."

"And how do you know she didn't cause this?" The men pointed at her.

Dotchavitch stepped in front of her. "If you'd like to question my word, then that's your right. But I for one don't question where Zelia's loyalties stand. The fact of the matter is that no one would be here for you to come back to if it weren't for her."

Zelia glanced around at the crowd that had gathered. She saw the grief and heard the support in their voices, but the men didn't share their belief in her.

"If this will cause problems among your people, I'll take my leave. Just point me toward the Fairies."

One of the men jerked his head back, frowning. "Fairies? What in the gods are you talking about?"

Dotch grinned for the first time since his father's passing.

"Much has happened in your absence. Come on, we'll fill you in over dinner."

The men grumbled, but they couldn't argue with a proper meal, so the entire village went to the dining hall. Once they had eaten and their tempers had simmered, they informed the men of everything that had happened while they were gone. Though the stories weren't all sad there was a heavy sadness in the air for they had lost several good men and women.

Then one man turned and stared at Zelia. "If all that is true, show us something."

"I..." She chewed her lip.

"You don't have to," Dotchavitch said.

"No, I can show them something." She threw a horn of water across the table. Instead of splashing as water, it floated down as flakes of snow. She waved her hand up and down like the rolling waves of the sea and the snow jumped to life as if it blew across an open plain.

She made the snowflakes appear as wolves running over a snowy mountain. Then a slender figure with pointed ears appeared, only to be run through by what appeared to be a Darkan.

"No," she whispered and shoved back from the table.

She ran out to the water's edge and fell to her knees in the sand.

"I didn't do that. The image, it just came to me, like the visions used to. Lumid, I know you're watching me, what does it mean?" Zelia looked up to the sky, looking for an answer.

Hyperia's star twinkled in the starlit sky.

"I know you can't answer me. I need to talk to the Fairies, but not till we put Gondavitch to rest."

Later that night the village sent small boats out into the water carrying their dead and some belongings for them to carry with them into the afterlife. Dotchavitch was about to release a flaming arrow when a memory of pyres flickered in her thoughts.

"Dotch, may I? Please, you'll see why."

She took the bow and arrows from him. One by one, she set the boats ablaze as the villagers sang a song in remembrance of the people lost.

Their songs peaked and sparkling white orbs lifted into the night sky, just as Leena's soul had. Everyone gasped and Zelia slipped away from the crowd, having done her best to honor those who'd fallen to evil men.

"You've done that before?" Raven asked.

"A long time ago, for kin."

Zelia wrapped her arms around herself and leaned against Raven as she stared at the souls.

Once the souls of their loved ones had long passed out of sight, people trickled back to their homes with a newfound feeling of peace. Eventually, only the dragon riders and their dragons stood on the shore in silence and they soon came to her.

"That's not the first time you've seen that happen, is it?" Dotch asked.

She shook her head.

"Well, come on, we should get some rest before I take you to the Fairies."

"Wait, why are we taking her to the Fairies?" Johnol asked.

"She needs to learn something before she can return to the mainland."

"How do you plan to return? You have no boat and dragons can't fly that far without rest."

"We might be able to help her with that, if she's willing to stay for the winter." Dotch grinned at Zelia, and she sighed. "So, just going to sleep out here?" Dotch asked.

"Maybe."

Dotch shook his head. "Come on, let's get some sleep."

The others all got up and left her staring at the stars.

25

They had passed many islands when they came to one with high cliffs, waterfalls, and a thick forest. The trees were so dense across the island that they circled many times before settling on a tiny clearing overlooking a cliff that dropped off into the sea.

The forest before them reminded her of the forest that surrounded the Drakeon Empire, which nestled to the north of the Mountain of the Old Ones. She'd only been in the Elves' woods for a short time, but much like the trees before her, they emanated power.

The others moved into the forest with swords drawn, as they always did.

"Maybe this is why the Fairies don't like you." She gestured to their weapons with a wave of her hand. "We are intruding on their lands after all."

The others sheathed their swords, and she listened to the trees. Their chatter pounded in her ears, and she worked to understand their words.

"They speak only of us. The Fairies will find us soon enough. The dragons should stay here, though; they'll only get tangled in the undergrowth and we wouldn't want any of them lighting the trees ablaze."

"But we want to come!"

"Speak for yourself."

"Oh, shut up, you'll do as she says. Go ahead, Zelia. I'll make sure they behave," Raven said.

"Thank you."

She turned and slipped into the thick underbrush. She moved without a sound or a trace. Once they were a good way into the trees, they began to hear noises.

"What's that sound?" Senth asked, referencing what sounded like the jingling of bells.

"It's the Fairies."

"What are they saying?"

"Give me a few. I don't remember the language as well as I thought I did." She thought back to the time before her first death. "It's the language Alrindel and I were using when…"

"It's okay, you don't need to explain," Dotchavitch assured.

A sparkling light shot across the path ahead, and she couldn't help but smile.

"But, can you tell us what they're saying?" The others were all eagerly gathered around her.

She shook her head and followed the crisscrossing specks of light winding down the path. Soon she could hear a small waterfall. The air of the forest had a new crispness, and she grew more cautious of her footing. She was careful not to step on any of the little creatures that moved across the forest's floor.

The insects grew dense, and she slowed to a stop.

"Would you please ask the Fairies to come here? I don't wish to step on any of their little friends," Zelia asked the trees.

The trees creaked in reply, their quickened tone showing their surprise at a human talking to them. They even chattered about the respect she showed towards the creatures that lived amongst them.

A few moments later several very inquisitive Fairies surrounded them. Their figures were hard to make out through their sparkling light.

Once they slowed, she could see every little detail about them. They wore clothing made of leaves and flower petals and had thin wings that varied from dragonfly wings to wings like a butterfly. Other than their wings and their bright glow they looked very much like their distant cousins, the Elves.

At first, she spoke their language slowly, as she searched for the correct words. It had been a long time since she had last spoken the language.

"Do any of you understand the language of the humans?"

"Oh my gosh! She... she knows our tongue! Quick, go get someone of the royal family." One Fairy with the wings of a luna moth said.

Two of them shot off towards the sound of water. It took her a few to process their words as they spoke in quick spurts, like the jingle of bells.

Soon, a little Fairy Prince and Princess appeared.

She bowed her head as the Prince asked in a language the others understood.

"Where did you learn our language? Of all my fathers before me, we've never met a human who could speak our language."

"I learned your language as a small child on the mainland when I lived in Elyluma. A wise elf taught me many languages, many long forgotten by man and Dwarf alike. I didn't quite believe my ears when I heard the whispers of the Fairies in the trees. The language your people speak is one that has been long forgotten by the Fairies of the mainland."

The little Prince fluttered his painted lady butterfly wings as he stood a bit taller.

"You lived among Elves? But Elves hate humans!"

"That may be true of some Elves, but most of the Elves on the mainland have fought many wars alongside the humans. They have their disputes, but they get along fine with humans who are not as greedy as most."

"You speak as if you aren't one of them. But if I should believe my eyes, you are human."

"You are neither right nor wrong in either of those judgments. I was created to look as though I am human, though I am not."

He fluttered his wings as he processed that, then he flew off. "Come, I believe our parents should like to meet you, dragon riders."

The little monarch butterfly-winged Fairy Princess took flight alongside her brother.

"Come, the insects have cleared a path for you this way. Just watch out for the mushrooms."

They followed the Fairies to the edge of a pool of water dotted with lily pads. A small waterfall glowed blue and green to one side of the pool and a stream trickled out the other end. There was a downed tree along the edge of the water, and it was there the Fairies had them sit while they went off to find their parents.

In the absence of the Prince and Princess, ten little leaf people, wingless Fairies, watched over them.

She understood the need for the guards quite well, while the others were nervous with the little leaf people watching their every move. The longer they sat, the more leaf people she noticed. They watched them from the trees, and some rode small birds.

Time passed, and she whistled a little tune with the birds. One drew close and perched on her finger. The sparkling color drained from her rider's face. Zelia stroked the little bird's breast.

"You're a beautiful bird, but it's time you go back to listening to your rider."

With a tweet, she fluttered back into the sky.

Finally, the Prince and Princess returned followed by their parents, all clad in clothes made of leaves and flower petals. They were almost a mirror image of the royal Elves she once knew.

"Why do you bring humans to our home?" the King asked in their quiet and pretty language.

"He thought you might find it interesting that I speak your language. Though I only appear to be human. And I was taught your language by your distant relatives, the Elves," she replied in their language before the Prince could.

The Fairy King pulled back and made two quick passes around her.

"Well, you look human enough though you do not speak or compose yourself as one. Do your companions understand our language?"

"I'm afraid not. They know only their own language, where I have been taught all the languages known to the higher-born Elves."

With that information, the Fairy King changed languages though his voice was still tiny. "I've never known Elves to teach humans their knowledge. No matter how Elfish the human may act."

She smiled. She had never thought of how much Eadon and Alrindel had influenced her in the time she'd spent with them.

"What, you did not know how alike you are to the Elves?"

"I didn't realize how much Eadon and his son had imprinted on me. They took me in as one of their own when I was an infant, thanks to Queen Eleanor."

The Fairy Queen flew forward.

"Speaking of formalities and such. I do not believe any of us have exchanged names. I am the Fairy Queen Fairon. This is my husband King Forgon. And our children Prince Flon and Princess Flaina whom I believe you have already met. What are your names?"

"I am Zelia." She continued naming the others in the order they sat beside her.

The Fairies bowed.

"Glad to make your acquaintances. Now why are you on our fair island?"

"I thought you might be able to help Zelia," Dotchavitch said.

"It's complicated. I'm not human, wizards created me to kill the gods. I just don't want to hurt anyone else, but they can control me. We... I was hoping you might know of something that can help."

"If what you say is true, I do not know of anything that can give you what you wish for. But I can give you a piece of advice, you cannot run from the Wizards of the Guild. I assume they are who you are talking about, in which case only their deaths will free you."

"Surely not all of them have turned, dear," Queen Fairon said.

"They would all have to help willingly to create life, unless some were deceived."

"Do you think an elf with telepathy could be deceived?" Zelia asked.

"Anyone can be deceived, even royal Elves."

"Could one change someone's memories?"

"For a short time, but the memories would return, eventually."

"Thank you King Forgon."

"For what?"

"I know where I'm going."

Zelia looked up at the sky. The sun was setting, and they had traveled a long way that day.

"You guys should go ahead back," she said to her companions.

She turned to the Fairies. "If you do not mind, I would like to learn more about your people and your guards before I leave. I won't be able to return."

Fairon and Forgon exchanged a glance.

"I won't leave you alone here," Dotchavitch protested.

"I won't be alone. Besides, I've spent a great deal of time on my own; I'm capable of taking care of myself."

"Here, I'll stay with her if it makes you feel better," Kafthry offered.

"Me too," Keller interjected.

Dotchavitch rolled his eyes. "Fine."

With that decided they turned back to the Queen and King for their approval. The little leaf men showed their disapproval of the idea with crossed arms.

"We can sleep with our dragons in the clearing on the edge of the woods if that would make you more comfortable with our presence. Also, there is no need to feed us. I assure you I only seek to learn more about your people. Although the Elves hold vast knowledge, their knowledge is limited when it comes to Fairies and leaf men since so few stayed on the mainland. I wish to return with at least something to teach Eadon."

26

The royal Fairies debated and eventually accepted Zelia's offer, then said good day to the other dragon riders.

After they had left, the Queen and King excused themselves, leaving Prince Flon and Princess Flaina to answer her questions.

Zelia asked many questions, most of which pertained to their magic and culture. To make things easier for the Fairies and to make the leaf men more comfortable, she spoke in their language.

She learned that there are distinct groups of Fairies, though they all treat each other as equals.

"So, you're divided up with different classifications like the Elves?"

"Depends, can you give me an example?"

"Royals, healers, bowmen, and swayers are the major groups."

"Hm, not exactly. We're divided up by tree, water, flower, mushroom, moss, bird, bug, and a great deal of other things. But we all work together to keep the island alive and happy."

"So, you are all swayers of sorts, beings who can influence the growth of other things with song?"

"You could say that."

"So, what about the leaf men?" She glanced to the little men watching her, and their demeanor lightened at the mention of them. "I have heard even less of them."

"Well, you could compare their abilities to that of the elvish bowmen."

After she had asked as many questions as she could think of, Flon and Flaina had questions for her.

She answered their questions as best she could though some things they mentioned she had very little knowledge of.

The leaf men had warmed up to her. A younger leaf man who had a larger, pointy nose asked, "Tell me this, you have so many powers, yet you carry many weapons, why?"

"You can't always rely on your powers as they're not always the best tool for the job. Besides, it's rather hard to blend in as a human if you go around using magic all the time."

"How well can you use all the weapons you carry?"

"I'm best with the bow and do well enough with the sword."

"I should like to see your skills with the bow and sword, if for nothing else than to learn."

"There are a few things I could show you, but I don't have a skillful enough opponent here to show you much."

The leaf men pointed to Kafthry and Keller. "What about these two?"

She laughed and was glad the boys couldn't understand her.

"They're far better with an axe than a sword."

Keller sat forward. "What are you guys talking about?"

"They wish for me to demonstrate my sword skills on you."

He edged away from her. "Um, I'll pass on that invitation. I'm rather attached to my head and limbs."

"No worries, I rather like you being in one piece too. But there is one trick I could show them that won't endanger you." She drew her sword, and its surface glinted in the evening sun. "Draw your sword and hold it out in front of you as if you were sizing up your opponent."

"Why does it have to be me?" He groused and pulled his sword. "If I were your opponent, I would just give you my sw—"

She lunged and before he knew what happened, she held his sword alongside her own.

Kafthry elbowed Keller as he sat back down. "If only you could see the look on your face."

Keller glared at him.

"Oh, lighten up," Kafthry said.

She sheathed her sword and faced the leaf men.

"That's all I can show you with them."

"Where did you learn that trick? Your footing is a great deal like mine, but what you just did there is something I have never seen."

"It's a Dwarf trick. It's really simple, you just circle their blade with a quick motion to loosen their grip, then fling it out of their hand. If you're good, you can catch it."

The leaf men nodded.

Zelia paused to look at the sky peeking through gaps in the treetops. It was getting dark; they would have to return to their dragons soon.

27

"Kafthry, Keller, it's time we head back to the dragons before nightfall. In case we leave before we see you again, thank you for answering my questions and allowing us to stay."

Prince Flon flew in front of her and bowed.

"It was my pleasure. Though I wish you could stay another day."

She smiled as the wind blew through her hair, blowing towards their dragons and the mainland.

"I do too, but the winds are calling me back. If these two could keep up with Raven, we'd head back tonight as I travel by the stars quite well."

The Prince bowed again. "Well, it was a pleasure to meet you. Goodnight."

He moved from their path and gestured for her to continue.

The sun had just set over the horizon when they made it back to the dragons. Dotchavitch had left a small pack with a few things to eat in it, so they all ate and lay down to sleep. Keller wanted them to take turns taking watch, but she assured them the leaf men would not hurt them while they slept.

She could just make out a faint elvish chant emanating from somewhere in the forest as she fell asleep.

A huge army of Darkans moved south across the land towards a stronghold of the humans east of the Faithful Mountains. She didn't know the land that well, but she knew enough.

The scene changed, she looked down at The Hold, the Kingdom of the Mountains' fortress where they go in times of dire need. The sky was lit up with the light of the stars, and elvish bowmen marched to the gate.

Her dream moved closer.

"Alrindel?" she muttered.

He was at the head of the Elves alongside Koin. She couldn't hear what they were saying, but she could tell enough to know the Elves' help had been accepted.

Her dream lurched forward in time.

The Darkans had gotten inside The Hold's outer walls and were slaughtering everyone in their wake, even as they retreated to the inner wall. She watched helplessly as a Darkan ran a sword into Alrindel's back, the blade piercing the front of his chest plate.

Koin caught Alrindel as he staggered, choking on his own blood. And with a strangled breath, he collapsed.

She screamed out in her dreams and could almost feel the pain he felt. She felt the pain of losing him before he had been lost before she could see him one more time.

———▶

Drenched in sweat and shaking she shot up, suddenly wide awake.

"Zelia, are you okay?" Kafthry reached towards her.

She retreated from his touch and stood next to a tree on the edge of the island, the cold breeze coming off the ocean doing nothing to calm her nerves.

"Zelia, who's Alrindel and why were you just muttering his name in your sleep? Are you okay?"

She took a deep breath and sank down against the tree.

"Alrindel is kin, an elf. He took me in as his sister."

She shuddered and shivered in the cool night air.

"I have to get back to the mainland. I can't..." Her voice cracked as she buried her face in her hands.

"You can't what?"

"Let him and all those people die like that." She choked back her sobs and pulled herself together. "If you can't follow me, then stay here and I'll have one of the others come get you. I have to go."

Keller and Kafthry climbed onto their dragons and followed. Evergreen and Elm struggled to keep up with Raven as they shot across the ocean.

When the fires on Dragon Island came into view, Elm and Evergreen were panting hard.

"Can you two get them back from here?" Raven asked.

"Y... yes," they wheezed.

With their reply, Raven's pace quickened.

Dotchavitch and Johnol were walking up as she landed.

"Can I borrow a ship? I have to leave," she said.

They followed her for a few paces. "Why?"

"War is stirring on the mainland."

Keller and Kafthry climbed off their dragons and explained what they knew in a rush.

⟶

"Don't go doing anything rash. You should calm your nerves before setting out to sea," Dotchavitch said when he caught up.

She stuffed the clothes Dotch had given her in a pack.

"No, I should go now while the sea and the wind are ready to push me back. The fields were already in full crop, that means I only have until the end of summer to cross the sea, skirt around The Mountain of the Old Ones, and climb to the summit of the Faithful Mountains. Land travel will take over a week and that's if I don't stop to sleep or eat."

"You won't do anyone any good if you kill yourself trying to get there."

She slung the pack over her shoulder, and Dotch handed her the blanket off the bed.

"I know. I only said it, so you'll understand how much I have to hurry if I intend to save Alrindel's life." She stopped midstride, she owed Dotch a better explanation than this and she knew she needed his help to get back. "Alrindel was… is my brother. He took me under his wing when we were children. We did everything together. Competitions with him are part of why I'm so good with a bow. I would probably just be the wizards' puppet if it weren't for him and Eadon taking me into their family when I was an infant. I wouldn't be shown his death unless I can change it."

"And that's what I will do." She said it more for herself than she did for him. "So, you see, I have to go. Will you help me? Please?"

Dotch let out a long sigh. "Yes. You can take the smaller ship. It's a boat I found after the dragon trappers raided it last year and it hardly works for fishing, anyways. I don't think the men will string me up for giving it to you. And since they just got back, it'll be ready to go."

"I wish I had something to give you in return."

"You saved our village, it's the least we can do. But you won't be able to take Raven with you. It's too small."

"Raven already said she feels bound here. Hopefully, she'll understand."

Dotch nodded. "Then go say goodbye to her, I'll get things ready for you."

"Thank you Dotch, really."

➤——————→

Zelia found Raven staring out at the ocean, waiting for her. *"I'm sorry I'm leaving like this."*

"I could come with you."

"No, Dotch says the ship won't hold you. Besides, the humans on the mainland would hunt you down and kill you. It doesn't matter if you are friendly and I can't risk losing you like that. Besides, I need you to take care of them for me as I won't be returning."

Raven nodded, a veiled sense of disappointment and anger vibrating off of her before she flew off.

"Raven? I'm sorry."

Zelia watched Raven fly away, torn between her new friend and a family who she hadn't seen in centuries. An image of Alrindel gasping, his last breath leaving him as Koin held him, rose to the surface, and she turned from Raven. She had to save Alrindel, but maybe one day she could return and see if Raven was still here, if she would forgive her. She went to tell the other riders goodbye. The looks on their faces told her they would protest her leaving, but Dotch already had other villagers piling dried food and barrels of water in the boat's hold with practiced ease.

"Nothing you say can change my mind. I'm leaving and likely won't be coming back in your lifetime. So, take care of each other for me."

"Everything's ready," Dotch said as he came up to join them. "Are you sure you can handle the ship on your own?"

Zelia shrugged, Eadon had taught her a little about ships, but she never imagined she'd need the knowledge. "I'll manage."

"Keller and I talked about it. We're going with you," Kafthry said, Keller nodding his agreement.

Shaking her head, Zelia backed away from them. "No. Where I'm going you won't survive. Even if you could keep up with me once I get to dry land. I—"

"We're going and whatever happens to us will be on our own heads." Kafthry climbed into the boat.

"That's what I am afraid of," she muttered under her breath.

A few villagers came up with enough supplies for Kafthry and Keller to make the trip with her. Zelia shook as she watched Kafthry help the villagers. *They can't go. They'll die.* He glanced at her, and she knew then she couldn't sway the boys.

"Go tell Elm and Evergreen goodbye then! This is a one-way trip."

It tore her up to take more lives to face their end, but she knew she needed their help with the ship.

➤

By the time the boys returned, she had calmed herself. She couldn't let her emotions get in the way, not when so many lives depended on changing what was to come.

"Okay, we're ready to go," Keller announced when they returned.

She turned to the others who had gathered on the dock, knowing they were waiting on her farewell. "May the winds ever blow to carry you and your dragons across the open water."

Before their goodbyes could be dragged on any further, she nodded to the boys to drop the sails and let the winds of the coming storm push them as fast as the boat could stand. The dragons followed them out, but Raven beckoned them back with a hint of anger and sadness in her tone.

The island faded from view, and she sank against the rail of the ship.

Kafthry brought her a water skin and sat down beside her. "So, how long do you think it'll take us to get to the mainland?"

"Around a month. Then the hard part will begin."

Over the next couple of weeks, Zelia did her best to train Keller and Kafthry to defend themselves and to speak the common tongue. With all of it, they often fell asleep while they fished in the evenings. That's when Zelia practiced her control of ice, finding ways to use her shifting ice forms to propel the boat just a little faster.

One day the sky turned black with clouds and churned with rage. A storm brewed so large it often sent the ship flying through the air instead of floating on water.

She froze waves and moved the ship from one wave to the next with the expanding water, saving them from destruction at sea time and time again. The entire time Keller and Kafthry struggled to keep the sails and supplies tied down. By the time the storms cleared, she was drenched in sweat and saltwater, her legs shaking with the effort to hold her upright.

"Keller!" Kafthry pointed towards her.

For a moment, she wondered why, but then her knees buckled, and Keller caught her before she fell overboard where a section of railing had torn away.

"You okay?"

She fought to stay awake as her eyes tried to roll back in her head.

"I'll be fine, just need to rest."

"Then rest, we can handle things for a while."

"No, I…" she trailed off as sleep took her.

⟶

"Look who's finally awake."

Her vision was blurry as Kafthry placed some stale bread in her hand.

"You need to eat something."

"How long was I out for?"

"About a day, and the ship is in rough shape."

"How bad?"

"There's a hole in the hull too large for us to patch. We pulled everything we could onto the deck after you passed out. As it is, we won't make it."

She nodded and pressed her palm against the deck.

"Are you sure you can handle that right now?"

"I'll have to."

Her vision cleared from sleep as she gave him a faint smile and watched as a thick film of frost grew across the deck. The boat creaked as the bilge water under the deck froze.

"How long do you think that will hold?" Kafthry asked.

"Long enough."

She watched the sky as the sun set behind her to reveal the stars above. She identified constellations above and in front of her. They were only a few days from the mainland, which was good because she wasn't sure how long she could keep the hull sealed with the waters warming.

After a little while, her mind wandered to other matters. *What way are we going to take over the Faithful Mountains?* She knew they didn't have time to go around as most people did. *If it was just me, it wouldn't matter what pass I take. I could make handholds with ice if I had to. But, these two need the pass… a few peaks south of The Hold, but which one?*

She closed her eyes and recalled the maps she had seen and what she knew of the mountains. She counted from the southernmost peak, the pass they would have to take was between the fourth and fifth summit if her memory was correct. Even though the pass went across a low spot, it would take at least two days to cross.

28

The Mountains of The Old Ones came into view on the horizon as they neared The Trading Town's docks.

"So that's where you grew up?" Kafthry asked.

"Not exactly, but yes. We'll have to go that way after we find horses and gather some supplies. If we're lucky, the trappers will be in town and I can ask them about the pass."

⟶

She slung her pack over her shoulder as the ship eased to a stop alongside the dock.

"Don't go wandering too far. I'll catch up with you."

"Wait, you're leaving us?"

"No, I need to sell the ship and I'll cover ground faster on my own."

She glimpsed a familiar face wading through the crowd that had gathered to gawk at the strange ship as she jumped to the dock.

"Connan?"

"Zelia? But I thought you were dead. Wait, Asenten… you killed him?"

She started to look away, unsure of how to explain, but then she noticed how his demeanor and clothes had changed. He looked rundown, like a villager instead of a dwarven prince. Even the little pieces of gold that hung in his braided beard before were gone, replaced with little ties of leather.

"No, but can we talk about this somewhere else? Please."

Connan glanced around at the crowd, then waved her to follow him. He led her to a dark and dusty tavern and sat at a secluded table towards the back. He didn't say anything after they sat, he just stared.

179

"I didn't kill Asenten, but…" she trailed off, unsure how to explain. "When you came back, I ran because I couldn't leave, not because I didn't want to. Asenten and the others had trapped me there for years."

"What? Why?"

She shrugged. "They created me. Your friend James wasn't wrong when he questioned me being an elf. I lived with the Elves across the mountains when I was little. I don't understand why they did what they did, but Asenten had to die. He would have made me kill you and all of your people, because you had seen me."

"If that's the case, why did you run?"

"I didn't run. I was taken away to Hyperia. Asenten tried to kill me, or something, but his spell wasn't strong enough or maybe it was their healers."

"Asenten is what was keeping Darkans from taking over the mountain. And now we can't get rid of Kniteoff," Connan growled.

"Kniteoff, the dragon?"

"The one and only."

Zelia struggled with what Connan was saying. She had heard of Kniteoff, he was one of the last of his bloodline, of the dragons that lived thousands rather than hundreds of years. He seldom came near humans, let alone Dwarves.

"We used Kniteoff to try to stop the Darkans, but now we can't get rid of him. Thousands of my people were slaughtered because Asenten was killed."

"What? You're… you're saying it's my fault? I didn't know." Her mind raced to put the pieces together, but it felt like she didn't have all of the puzzle. *Wait, if he is alive…* "Did you tell the Elves about me?"

He nodded and leaned forward.

"Why were they shocked to hear your name? And why did they try to cover it up?"

"Like I said, Eadon raised me in Elyluma."

"Then… wait, you're the one the stories of the old wars hinted at. Of the girl who released the souls of the fallen King and his men as though she were his daughter."

"Connan, I'm sorry about the Darkans and your people, but Alrindel will die if I don't get across the Faithful Mountains soon."

"How did you know about the war on the other side, but not what happened here?"

"A dream, it's hard to explain. All of this is. But can you help me get horses and supplies? Please."

He studied her for what felt like ages before answering.

"I can't, but I know someone who can."

They walked out of the tavern and nearly ran into a man talking to Keller and Kafthry. Zelia couldn't help but admire the old man, the deep creases around his eyes showed his age, yet he was as fit, if not fitter than any young lad in the town.

"So, what are you boys doing with that boat of yours?"

"It's yours Jack," Connan said, "if you help my young friends here. They need three horses and supplies for a trip across the Faithful Mountains. No bedrolls or such, just the necessities."

She could see the concern in Jack's eyes.

"I wouldn't go traveling right now. The Darkans are stirring. People are saying war is in the air; even the trappers have been crossing back to this side of the mountains."

"Her kin are over there. You won't be able to keep her here so just help her get what she needs."

"All right, but only one problem with that. There are only two horses in town up for sale."

"What about that black stallion?"

"Eh, he may be from a king's herd, but he's too wild to ride."

"I'll take him," Zelia said.

"Then your death wish is in the pasture at the edge of the woods. I had planned to let him breed my mares, but if you can ride him, you can have him."

"Thanks Jack," she called after him as he waded through the crowd. "Thank you for the help Connan."

"Don't mention it. Oh, and you will help me fix this dragon problem if you survive the Darkans."

"In that case, until next time."

She gave him a short bow and headed off to the woods south of the town, leaving Keller and Kafthry to follow Jack for the time being.

She was just off the edge of town when she let out a slow and pretty whistle. The sound of it echoed off the trees and reminded her it was the same tune Alrindel used to call for his horse and a knot tied in her gut. She had forgotten where she had heard it, and it made the potential of losing him all the more real.

A warm grassy breath puffed in her face and eased the knot in her gut.

"You came." She had expected to have to search for him, not for him to come at the sound of a mere whistle. "Not so wild after all are you boy? So, what's your name?"

"Bête Noire, my grandmother told stories of someone like you. Someone who spoke to horses. Your whistle, do you know Alrindel?"

"He's kin. You know him?"

"I wanted him to be my rider, but the King sent me to the Dwarves."

"May… may I be your rider?"

She stroked his forelock as she stared into his eyes, hoping he would accept her.

"Hm, no tack."

"Alright."

He let out a light neigh before jumping the fence and turning alongside it so she could climb on.

"Oh, Kafthry and Keller, we need to get back to them before they do something stupid."

"Who or what are Kafthry and Keller?" Bête Noire asked.

"Friends from Dragon Island who have a knack for not knowing when to keep their traps shut."

"They can't be any worse than Dwarves."

"Perhaps, but at least Dwarves can defend themselves, Keller and Kafthry… not so much."

It didn't take them long to locate the boys as they stood in the middle of the market street in a heated argument with a tall, lanky man. The man's face turned red, and he drew his sword.

"Oh, it's on, you little runt!"

"I'm sorry to interrupt, but I would appreciate it if you left my friends alone, sir." She trotted up on Bête Noire.

"If you're such a big shot with a sword, get off that horse and show me," the man demanded in a rage that was apparently incited by Kafthry and perhaps a bit of alcohol by the looks of things.

"I won't fight you."

Zelia slid from Bête Noire and shot Kafthry a disapproving glance as the man charged. She ducked the sweep of his sword and drew a dagger from the small of her back.

She deflected his blade and moved to the side.

"A dagger?" the man demanded, the leather hilt of his sword popping as he twisted his hands on the hilt, tightening his grip until his knuckles shone white. "You must take me as a joke. Come on, pull your sword you little brat!"

"No. You're going to hurt someone," she said, glancing at the crowd around them hoping he would get the hint.

"Why you littl—"

"This is a new low, even for you, trapper." An elf stepped through the crowd that had gathered.

"Someone has to teach these little brats to respect their elders," the man grumbled as he put his sword away.

"If only you knew," she breathed under her breath and switched languages. "Thank you for the assistance. I do not believe we have met before. I am Zelia." She gave a slight bow to the elf.

"Where did you learn that language?" The elf reeled in surprise.

"Eadon of Elyluma taught me."

She could feel the stares of the crowd as they tried to understand their conversation over the sound of the cursing man.

The elf stared at her with wide eyes, and his light brown eyebrows rose. "But you're not an elf."

"Not going to give me your name?" She asked with a grin, unable to contain her amusement at his reaction. *I'm surprised you haven't heard of me; the Elves don't keep things from each other.*

His shoulders drew back as he bowed his head. "Oh, sorry, you may call me Eragon. I am a royal guard for the Drakeon Empire."

"Is King Erolith in the area then?"

"No. I am on my way to The Hold to see if the rumors of a war to come are true."

"Depending on what way you plan to go you will be there just in time to witness the battle take place. I would venture to guess the bowmen of Elyluma are to march out any day now to help the Kingdom of the Mountains defend The Hold from the Darkan armies marching south as we speak."

He tilted his head to one side, his eyes still fixed on her.

"How do you know this?"

"Eleanor," she said the name as if it explained everything. "I, too, am headed across the Faithful Mountains. Since we head the same direction, perhaps we can travel together? I assume someone else is with you. Darkan Territory is hard to pass even for an elf of the Drakeon Empire."

"You are a peculiar girl." Eragon skimmed the crowd for his companion. "Saria should be around here somewhere."

She switched languages as she turned to Jack.

"If you could hurry with those supplies and meet me on the southeast side of town that would be lovely."

Jack gave her a nod and slipped into the crowd.

Eragon changed languages to match her.

"I'll meet you there as well. As soon as I find Saria and finish gathering supplies."

She watched Eragon disappear into the crowd, then turned to Kafthry and Keller.

"You two can come with me before you get yourselves in trouble again."

She propelled herself off a half rotten stump in the middle of the walkway and onto Bête Noire's back. The crowd parted as she rode through with Keller and Kafthry close behind. Being new to the environment they tried to take as much in as possible, they walked with wide eyes as they scanned their surroundings. From time to time, Keller would stop and take a deep breath through his nose as there were so many new smells to absorb. Zelia wished she could see the town as they did, but she knew most of the people she'd killed had been from the Trading Town and if she stayed long enough, she would hear tales of people disappearing.

When they stopped at the edge of the town Keller looked Bête Noire over.

"So, this is what a horse looks like."

Bête Noire shook out his mane and nickered, "They've never seen a horse before, and you expect them to ride across the Faithful Mountains?"

She didn't switch languages so Keller and Kafthry could understand her.

"I'm sure they can do it. They managed to stay on dragons trying to keep up with Raven so I'm sure they can stay on a horse. Though we should teach them the basics."

She looked to the boys.

"Keller, Kafthry, pay attention because this is a crash course in riding. Horses are very different from dragons. The way you'll be riding, you'll have what we call a bit in the horse's mouth and you pull with one side and let out on the other to turn. If the horse refuses, you give a slight jerk on the side that you wish for them to turn towards."

Keller bunched his eyebrows. "Why don't you use one?"

She patted Bête Noire's elegant neck, a true trait of an Arabian.

"He hates tack. I use leg pressure and verbal cues. Leg cues are hard to learn as you'll be more concerned with staying in the saddle and most horses won't listen to your verbal cues. They're free spirited creatures and have minds just as you and I do, so they can be tricky. You got lucky with Evergreen and Elm; they accepted you right off the bat without any trials. The horses will try you. You have to be firm to begin with."

She went on explaining the basics for a while longer. Until Jack showed up with horses and supplies.

He handed each of the boys a lead rope and a heavy pack, then headed to Zelia with a pack for her.

"Take care of yourself now."

She slung the pack on her back as Eragon and Saria rode up on matching chestnut mares.

"The Elves are going with you?" Jack asked.

"Since we're all going the same direction, we might as well travel together. Thank you for your help, Jack. The ship is yours, just take care of yourself."

"Yeah, yeah, you too, little lady." He gave a dismissive wave as he headed back into the town.

Keller and Kafthry clambered onto the horses' backs. *At least you did one thing right, you two didn't get on backwards.*

Eragon snickered as he watched Keller and Kafthry.

"I take it your friends haven't ridden before."

"Not horses anyway."

Saria's long red hair shimmered as she turned.

"Then what have they ridden?"

"Dragons, though they'd only been doing that for a couple days." Eragon and Saria looked at her as if she'd lost her mind, so she continued, "They are from across the sea. I spent some time on Dragon Island. They didn't really fit in with the other riders so chose to come with me back to the mainland. No worries, we didn't bring any dragons with us. Now I have a question for the two of you. What has happened here? I always knew the Darkans would spread, but I never thought they would have the numbers to run the Dwarves from their homes."

"They not only spread from Darkan Territory, but from the Darkan Mountains in the north. Truthfully, we don't know all that much about what is happening across the mountains. Messenger birds haven't crossed them in over a month, from any of the kingdoms. King Erolith has grown concerned, which is part of the reason for our going," Saria said.

Keller and Kafthry finally joined them so they all turned towards the three giant peaks of the Mountains of The Old Ones.

"Then let me tell you what my dreams showed me. The Darkans marching south are at least one hundred thousand strong and I only got snippets of their forces. Everyone from the Kingdom of The Mountains will gather at The Hold. They won't be able to defend themselves against those numbers. Even with the help of Elyluma. That's unless I can take at least half of them out."

"Do what?" Both Saria and Eragon spun around to face her and spoke in unison.

"Have you heard the stories of the girl created by the guild of wizards?"

"I've heard rumors, but King Erolith never confirmed anything. Why is that relevant?" Saria replied.

"I am that girl. And I'll do everything in my power to save Alrindel, even if I'm not as powerful as they wanted me to be."

Images of Alrindel's death flashed before her eyes and she gritted her teeth to suppress those thoughts.

"Alrindel? As in Eadon's son?"

She nodded in reply.

Eragon continued, "Why do you care so much about him?"

"He's the closest thing I have to kin in this realm. I owe a lot to Alrindel and Eadon. Besides, the images of his death will haunt me until the end of time if I don't at least try to save him."

She glanced over her shoulder to Keller and Kafthry. "So, are you two ready to pick up the pace?"

They were both pale as they nodded.

With their okay, Bête Noire quickened his pace to a fast walk. His stride was so long the others had to trot to keep up with him. Keller and Kafthry gripped the horns of the saddles as they bounced around.

They rode until the sky was but a sea of stars, and made camp.

They were close enough that she could feel Kniteoff's presence as he hibernated deep inside the Mountains of The Old Ones. *So Connan was telling the truth.*

Keller and Kafthry gathered wood as Eragon and Saria tended the horses. And she wandered off to find something to eat.

It didn't take her long to find something. She picked big black berries from thorny bushes, using the broad leaves of a Maple tree to keep from staining her tunic as she carried them back to camp.

"How do you know those are safe to eat?" Saria questioned.

"I was raised by Eadon. Trust me, I know what plants are safe to eat."

Keller and Kafthry puckered their lips when they tossed a tart berry in their mouths.

"I hope everything doesn't taste like this here." Keller ran his tongue across his teeth.

"They aren't quite ripe, they get sweeter with time," Zelia said.

Eragon and Saria tried to hide their amusement to no avail as they snickered, and their glowing skin made their grins even more evident.

After they all had their fill, Eragon and Saria insisted they take watch that night.

29

When she woke, she climbed up and sat with Eragon as he kept watch from a tree.

"Did you know you stop breathing occasionally when you sleep?"

She nodded as she stared down at the others. "There are a great many things you don't know about me."

"Well, if you'd let me, I think I would like to learn more about you." He turned towards the others. "Should we wake them?"

"The sun will come up soon. So, I guess so."

"Wake up, little birdies. It's time to tack up the horses," Eragon spoke with a silvery voice and jumped out of the tree.

Kafthry sat up and rubbed his eyes. "What time is it?"

"I don't care, as long as you keep waking us up so nicely." Keller elbowed Kafthry. "Come on, Kafthry. Look at the bright side."

Eragon came up behind Zelia as she threw her rope around Bête Noire's neck. "Need a lift?"

She looked around briefly for something to use as a step up and when she saw nothing she sighed. "Yeah."

Eragon picked her up around the waist and set her on Bête Noire's back. "You know, many people tried riding him, but no one could get near him."

"He wanted Alrindel to be his rider. I copied his whistle so much when we were little that it just kind of stuck. He thought I was him when he heard it."

Keller and Kafthry lagged behind, and she offered them a smile.

"I bet the two of you wish you'd stayed behind on Dragon Island."

"Ha, ha, very funny, can we get going now?"

"Sure, let's see if you can keep up." She gave Bête Noire a nudge, and he stretched his legs to gallop ahead of everyone on the trail. "Easy, we have a long ride ahead of us."

"Just showing them what we can do!" He pushed a little harder but didn't even strain to thunder up the hill. "Slowpokes!" he called to the other horses from his pedestal atop the hill.

"Show off." The others scoffed between heavy breaths.

"You know you love me for it!" he lowered his head and munched on the grass while waiting for the others.

Keller and Kafthry held on for dear life as their horses galloped after the Elves. When they reached the top of the hill, they were as pale as ghosts.

"I think I prefer dragons," Keller spoke with a wobbly voice.

Zelia chuckled to herself. "I'm not sure about that. Bête Noire is a much smoother ride than Raven ever was."

Eragon's curiosity stirred. "Why did you go to sea in the first place?"

"I didn't plan to go there, I just kind of ended up near Dragon Island. They took me in, much like they did Keller and Kafthry."

Kafthry chimed in, "Then we went to an island of Fairies and leaf people!"

For a moment, Zelia couldn't help but shake her head, then she went along with the change of subject.

"They spoke an older language that was thought to be dead. They're very interesting little beings."

Eragon and Saria asked her many questions about the dragons, leaf people, and Fairies as they rode. It was about mid-day when a change in the winds cut their conversation short.

"There's a storm approaching," Eragon said.

Saria nodded. "Looks like a bad one. We should start looking for shelter soon."

"There's only one place left on this side of the mountain is the cave where they found Asenten." As soon as he said it, Eragon seemed to make the connection. "Are you alright with that?"

Zelia nodded her approval, but she was sure her expression showed how she dreaded returning there. They all followed behind Eragon in silence as none of them had a better suggestion.

A few drops of rain fell as the wind swept through the trees. The horses cantered with an uneasy pace as they weaved between the trees until they stopped in front of a cliff covered in vincs and roots.

She paused just outside the entrance and stared into the darkness behind the curtain of leaves. A flash of lightning struck nearby and shook her from her trance. She shuddered then entered.

Inside she saw remnants of her past life. But what bothered her most was the crater in the center of the room and the dried blood across the wall and floor. It was as if the cave was a sealed time capsule, a testament to the horrors she had faced.

Her lungs burned, and she felt as if a fist squeezed her heart as the memory of that night flashed before her eyes. She leaned against the cool cave wall as her chest constricted, her ribs pushing against the metal plate. She was about to double over in pain when Eragon's hand rested on her shoulder.

"You're not alone here."

Keller gasped when he saw the crater and dried blood. She had told him a little about this place, but she always glossed over what had happened here.

"Are you okay?" Keller asked, kneeling beside her.

She closed her eyes and forced herself to take a deep breath.

"I'm fine."

She put on a brave face for Keller and Kafthry. She might appear younger than they do, but they looked to her for guidance.

"A little help here?" Saria called.

With a light squeeze of her shoulder, Eragon hurried out. Keller and Kafthry set up their little camp, while Eragon and Saria led the horses in and untacked them.

Zelia sat closest to the entrance with her back against the wall and stared at the crater. That day kept replaying through her mind.

➤

"Zelia is coming with us, release her now," Yargo demanded as he stood between her and the wizard.

"Never," Asenten spat as he raised his staff and chanted, "Fe father en dais lath en thesinos."

"No!" she screamed and jumped from behind Yargo. Everything seemed to slow as Asenten's staff slammed on the ground and she threw a wall of ice in front of Yargo and his two warriors. A blast of fire, metal, and rock caught her and threw her through the air. She landed with a sickening crunch against the far wall.

Metal clanged, then silence hung as she lay crushed, her heart thudding against the cold stone beneath her.

"My lord Yargo..." Gaeru's voice bounced in the cave and in her ears.

A gentle hand turned her over and cradled her limp body close. Her eyes flashed open to see that Yargo held her.

"Plea... please, don't leave me," she begged, through ragged and choked breaths.

→

Her friends shifted to steal a glance at her, and their movement brought her back for a moment. Outside they could hear rain as the wind whipped by. Then the crashing sound of thunder shook them.

Everyone but Zelia jumped. She just sat there until the sound of thunder quit reverberating through the cave. Then she leaned her head back against the cave wall.

Eragon finished tying the horses up so they couldn't bolt during the storm and sat next to her. His usual Elfish demeanor was replaced with one of compassion and understanding. Even his Elven glow had dimmed to match her emotions.

"We're here for you if you need us."

She let out a deep breath and leaned against Eragon. She might have just met him, but she needed someone, anyone to lean on.

Eragon wrapped his arm around her and sat unmoving, becoming a steady warm presence for her to cling to.

It was a while before she closed her eyes and fell asleep. Neither one of them ate that night, and the others divided watch amongst themselves.

Sleep wasn't much better than being awake for her. As once again her mind dragged her through the past.

→

"Do it!" Asenten demanded.

"No, she's just a child. I've done everything you've asked, but I won't torture her, not like that."

"Fine, then you can watch."

He drove a blade through Zelia's shoulder and into the cave wall. Her eyes watered, but she didn't let out so much as a gasp as she stared into the flames that seemed to glow behind his eyes.

191

"No looking away or I'll bring another for you to watch."

He patted her check and turned back to the girl he had tied and gagged in the corner.

Once he had tied the struggling girl down, he removed her gag and she screamed, begging for her life. Asenten took no heed of her pleas and began to pick her apart, piece by piece.

"Enough," Zelia yelled over the girl's screams, she couldn't take it anymore.

"What are you going to do about it?" Asenten mused.

"This."

She clenched her fists and made ice shoot across the cave, ending the girl's life in an instant. She drove spikes of ice at Asenten, knowing full and well the spells would give her all his injuries, all his pain. But he moved at the last second, and they only hit his side and shoulder.

———▶

Her heart pounded in her ears as she shot upright, choking down a scream.

"Zelia?" Eragon asked.

No, I can't, not here. She ran past Saria and out into the storm. She didn't make it far before she collapsed against a charred stump. Lightning struck all around her, her hair bristled with electricity, but she sat unmoving in the pouring rain. Her ribs burned as they tried to move with her rapid breaths and raindrops froze mid splash all around her.

She was drenched yet covered in ice when Eragon pulled her into his arms without waiting for her approval. She crumbled in his arms, and, for the first time in centuries, she let herself cry. It wasn't just a cry of pain but rather of turmoil from centuries of pent-up emotions. The ice no longer spread; her emotions finally being released outside her powers.

The storm raging around them drowned out the sound of her sobbing. She buried her face in the crook of his neck with her arms pulled tight against her chest.

The rain lightened as one last tear ran down her face, and she sat back.

She wiped her eyes with the back of her rain-soaked hand.

"Thank you, Eragon."

Eragon hugged her once more.

"Anytime, Zelia." He sat back and continued, "Now, we should go dry off. As soon as I figure out what way the cave is."

She wiped her eyes one more time as she took his hand and led him through the trees.

Saria looked them over when they entered. "You guys look like drowned rats."

She forced a smile at Saria's joke.

"Here, I can fix that."

She waved her hand over Eragon and then herself. Eragon looked down at himself; he wasn't even damp, but there was now a small pile of snowflakes around their feet.

"Uh, thank you."

"It's the least I can do."

30

Eragon woke when she moved.

"Are you always up this early?"

"Yes. Here, come with me. I want to show you something that I noticed last night."

She waved for him to follow her as she passed through the vines.

A dense fog rose from the ground, wet from the previous night's rain. She slipped around the edge of the cave. Above the cave entrance stood a huge hedge tree, the roots draped around the opening as if they were loose tug ropes strung out to dry.

Zelia climbed up the tree and Eragon followed her until he came up beside her. They were well above all the surrounding trees and could see a long way off.

They sat there in the top of that tree, watching as the sun broke atop the peaks of the Faithful Mountains far in the distance. The fog lit up with a golden glow to match the sky. Specks of red and green treetops broke through the fog here and there.

She flashed Eragon a smile and slipped from the tree. She craned her head back to see that his glow had faded with his heart in his throat. Then, with a deep breath, he gathered his wits and followed suit. He was as graceful in the trees as any elf she had ever seen.

He smiled when he landed beside her.

"Are you sure you aren't an elf?"

She swept her hair behind her ear.

"I wish." She watched as wheels turned behind Eragon's eyes. *Just what are you thinking?*

"Come on. We need to get going," Saria called up and interrupted their thoughts.

Zelia turned from Eragon and jumped from above the cave onto Bête Noire's back.

Kafthry tossed Zelia her pack and climbed onto his horse. Both he and Keller had gotten better at getting on their horses, even if they waddled around anytime they were back on foot.

Once they were saddled up, they headed out.

"You know, you never said what your orders were if the war was already upon them when you got there."

"They did not give us orders for that," Saria replied. "They only sent us to be their eyes and ears."

"We won't just stand by and watch, especially if Alrindel is there," Eragon added.

"Now you talk as if you know Alrindel," Zelia said.

"We crossed paths a long time ago. He holds an unwavering hand against Darkans."

"That may in part be because of my first death. The one Asenten took advantage of to gain control of me. He and the wizards he was closest to demanded that I demonstrate my powers to them and to do so they sent me into a horde of Darkans. I had never used my powers before, I didn't even know I had them. That's also when I found out that using too much fire and ice together will kill me and anyone nearby. Well, I don't really die."

They came to the river as she glanced around at them.

Keller pointed to the river. "I thought you said it was a small river. How the heck are we going to get across that?"

Zelia slid from Bête Noire's back, judging the speed of the currents.

"The nearest bridges are not for several leagues in either direction and they're nothing more than felled trees as this river only shows on the maps of trappers. You are welcome to use one of them or you can follow me," Eragon said.

"Wait, I can freeze it."

She turned a ghostly white as she walked out to the center of the river. She hadn't really intended for her powers to turn her to ice. But she hadn't used fire in a while, so her body took to it a little too well.

Bête Noire crossed as Zelia turned back to the others.

"Come on, I can't hold moving water very long."

Their horses didn't want to cross the icy river, so she switched languages. "It's fine, cross the river."

The horses stared at her and blinked a few times before crossing over.

She used the ice to get back onto Bête Noire, then unfroze the river. It took her a while to return to her normal color as she didn't force it.

Saria looked over at Keller and Kafthry. "Why do you two look unsurprised?"

"Saw her turn to ice when she got caught in dragon ice and then killed a dragon Trapper Captain. Only that time she cracked as she had used fire just before, or at least I think that's how she explained it."

Eragon cocked his head as he turned to Zelia. "Cracked?"

"In ice form, I shatter if I've used fire recently. In full fire, which none of you have ever seen and hopefully never will, I explode if I have used ice recently. My environment decides how long it takes me to reform. Though I'm not sure how that'll work now that I have a steel plate holding my ribcage together."

"Why do you tell us so much about yourself when we tell you so little of ourselves?" Saria asked.

"I have many reasons for doing it. But I'm hoping you'll be less likely to jump needlessly to your deaths for me. Besides, the last time I tried to hide what I was, a dragon tested their theory about me with their fire breath. It didn't go so well, they tried to give me a burial at sea."

She switched topics. "It won't be long until The Pack of the Ridge challenges us. Don't pull any weapons when they show up."

"How do you know they are nearby?" Saria asked.

"The trees, they like to chatter about wolves."

It was getting dark and Keller and Kafthry were having a hard time seeing. So, Saria moved back beside them.

"They're here," Zelia whispered.

Seconds later wolves howled all around them, and a chill ran down her spine. She smiled as she switched languages and announced herself. "Dain, it's me, Zelia. I come with friends, try not to scare them too much, please."

Huge white and silver wolves stepped out into the moonlight.

Then an even larger black wolf stepped out of the shadows. "Zelia! It's been a long time. We were on the other side of the mountain until we heard the trees stirring up a commotion about your return. We had to come see it for ourselves. Just where are you going?" He flicked his tail as he sniffed the air.

"To the Hold, and before you say it, I know war is impending. That's the reason I must go."

Dain scratched his ear with an eye closed.

"Come on, there's an abandoned trappers' cabin nearby, we'll keep watch. You guys don't look like you've slept well in a while."

As he got up and turned, flicking his tail, she thanked him.

Bête Noire continued after the black wolf while she waved the others to follow.

Eragon rode up next to her. "So, what did he say?"

"Dain says they'll watch over us as we travel through their territory. We can all rest easy for the next few nights."

"Why would they do that?"

"Not long before Asenten's death I saved Dain from some Ogres; he was just a pup back then."

Dain came to a stop. "Here you are. Sleep well, Zelia."

Before she could reply, he disappeared into the trees. She slid from Bête Noire. "Go eat while you can boy, see you in the morning."

She stepped into the dusty cabin and Saria lit a candle from her pack so they could all see to pick their spots to sleep.

31

Zelia woke to Dain's cold wet nose nudging her.

"Come on, wake up."

"What is it Dain?"

"You stopped breathing and your heart doesn't sound right."

She nodded towards the door and crept out of the little cabin. Dain followed her to an open area where the sun was rising in the distance.

"Zelia, what's going on with you? Is that why you look so exhausted?"

She gave a slight nod and sat in the damp grass. "A lot of things have happened."

"Why were you in that cave? Where did you go?"

"Asenten was holding me captive. Someone came to free me, and he attacked them. I put myself between them and got hurt, so they took me back with them."

"I went looking for you again, my mother didn't believe me when I told her about you. When I returned, all I found was blood. The trees said someone from somewhere else took you, but now you're back and fighting the Darkans?"

"They're going to kill someone I cared about. No, someone I still care about. I can't undo what I have done, but maybe I can change what will happen. I have to at least try."

"And I have to believe you can do anything you set your mind to, you saved me."

It had been so long since she had petted Dain that he flinched when she reached up to stroke his head. Then he leaned into her hand, and she scratched him just behind his ear.

"I guess I should go wake the others. Thank you, Dain."

Dain shook out his coat. "Don't mention it."

The sky had just lightened enough to see by when Zelia whistled softly alongside the birds. The others inside stirred as she picked up her bag. With the others packing, she set to work tacking the horses. Eragon and Saria came out to join her as she slipped from a tree onto Bête Noire.

"How long have you been up?" Eragon asked.

"Not long. Come on. We have some ground to cover."

She stopped under a pear tree and tossed a few in her pack before taking a bite of one, the tart juice dripping down her chin. A couple minutes later they set out towards the Faithful Mountains.

The next few days they slept under the stars and were light-hearted as the wolves howled all around them and the Faithfull Mountains grew before them. Eragon and Saria even taught Keller and Kafthry a few songs as they traveled.

The day came for Zelia to say goodbye to Dain. He sat amongst his pack as one by one the wolves disappeared back into the trees. After they had all gone, he stood and lowered his head to her.

"Take care of yourself, Zelia."

His pack howled a call of goodbye as he, too, disappeared into the trees.

⟶

She took the first watch that night. When time rolled around for her to wake her relief, she didn't budge.

Eragon woke up on his own as he was next to take watch. He found her high in a tree looking down at the horses. She didn't say anything when he approached the tree, so he climbed up after her.

As he reached the branch she was sitting on, she scooted out away from the trunk so he could sit against it.

Eragon looked down at the horses.

"You should go get some rest."

Zelia sighed as she leaned against him, her head resting against his shoulder.

"It's been getting worse, hasn't it?"

She let out a shaky breath as she didn't know what to say.

"You don't have to talk about your heart if you don't want to, but if there's anything I can do…"

"I used to stay with Rogath, listening to his heart as we slept. It seemed to help."

"Why didn't you say something before?"

"I can't seem weak to others."

He ran his fingers through her dark brown curls. "You're anything but weak. You are possibly the strongest person I know. Now get some rest."

Before he could say anything more, she dozed off right there in that tree as she leaned against him.

Eragon sighed. "Sleep well, Zelia."

⟶

She woke a little before sunrise.

Eragon smiled and joked, "Sleep in trees often?"

"Not as often as I would like."

She had turned to face the east that night when she took first watch. They sat watching the sunrise across the mountains.

The others were stretching and rubbing the sleep from their eyes. When Keller spotted them in the tree he called out, "I thought it was my turn to take the morning watch." He raised his hands. "Not that I'm complaining or anything."

Eragon slipped out of the tree. "Zelia kept watch later than she was supposed to, so I saw no reason to wake you to watch for such a short time."

Zelia climbed out of the tree behind him. She appreciated that he didn't mention why she had kept watch past her turn.

Keller shrugged. "Then you two get to rest the whole night through and we'll take watch tonight."

Zelia held a pear in her teeth as she slung her pack over her shoulder.

Kafthry squinted at her. "Do you ever unpack anything?"

She pulled the pear from her mouth, leaving little indents where she hadn't yet taken a bite. "I only unpack what I need when I need it."

She went off to the horses and fed the last few bites of her pear to Bête Noire as she leaned against his head, her eyes closed.

After a moment of peaceful bliss, she moved over to a tree with some low branches and used it to climb onto the stallion. She set out to scout their path a bit while the others packed up.

It was midday when they crossed into an area frequented by ogres. They decided to continue on into the night to get to an open area where it would be safer to stop.

As night fell, Eragon led the way since he had been through the area before. Saria led Keller and Kafthry as they jumped at every sound coming from the trees. They had never seen an ogre and weren't wanting to change that.

They were just a few minutes off from their stopping point when Bête Noire froze in his tracks and Zelia listened to the trees, they were too quiet for her comfort.

She nodded to Eragon before circling back to the others. Keller and Kafthry were useless in the dark as the light of the moon didn't even pierce the dense canopy. Zelia was tempted to use her control of ice to locate the ogres, but their only weakness was fire and they wouldn't be able to start one by hand fast enough for it to help. She kept her flames ready, and they continued towards the clearing in the trees.

Eragon notched an arrow.

"Don't waste your arrows," Saria warned.

With an arrow nocked, he asked, "Then what do you suggest?"

"Leave them to me," Zelia said.

When they reached a clearing, Zelia pointed to some logs scattered around the site. "Let me know when you're ready for me to light it."

"Stop right there," a voice boomed, the growl to its speech giving it away as an ogre.

"Show yourselves!" Zelia said.

An ogre bellowed from the trees, "Impatient little one, this one is!"

The tallest ogre she had ever seen moved branches out of his way as he stepped into the open.

"Such a loud noise for such a *little* person!"

Another one walked out of the trees. "Not even big enough to use as a toothpick is that one?"

Zelia pulled her sword and spun it at her side as another one laughed from the trees.

"Not a very bright one, now is she? They should know swords and arrows don't hurt us!"

She spun the sword around again and rolled her shoulders back to loosen them from the long day's ride.

"I know."

The ogre laughed as he reached for her. "You're not worth eating but I will make an exception."

Just as the ogre was about to grab her, she jumped and ran up his arm. Her sword lit ablaze as she drove it into the top of his head, the fire burning a path through the ogre's skull. She clung to the hilt as he staggered back bellowing in pain, swatting at his flaming head.

Before he could crumble to ashes, she jumped to the next ogre.

Her sword sank up to the hilt and held as the blue flames spread across the monstrous creature.

She dropped to the ground as ashes fluttered down.

"Anyone else?"

Several smaller ogres ran out of the trees with screams of anger. She sank the blade of her sword halfway into the earth. Flames snaked across the ground like cracks on a frozen pond until all the ogres crumbled to ash.

She pulled her sword from the ground and stood.

"You have a little ash, well, everywhere," Eragon said, his amusement thinly veiled.

She glanced down at herself. "Yeah. You said there was a stream up ahead, right?"

"Yes, and we shouldn't stay here after all that racket. Everything in the area will have to come check out the commotion." He scanned the area for a moment, then turned back to her. "Would you like a hand up?"

With a sigh, Zelia nodded and let Eragon lift her onto Bête Noire's back. This time she and Saria rode in back as that's where danger was likeliest to come from. Eragon led them through the trees until they came to a small stream, the water gurgling as it carved its way through the forest.

They all topped off their water reserves and let the horses get their fill while Zelia slipped downstream to clean up. The water was near freezing, even this far from the mountains, so she made a flame hover around her hands as she splashed water over herself before sticking her hair in the water. She wished she could control it like Rogath, she'd have been clean and dry by now. She paused, letting out a long breath. *I'm sorry Rog. I wish you could forgive me.* When there was no response, she dried herself best she could without singeing her clothes and headed back.

When she returned, Eragon was waiting to help her get back on her horse.

She yawned and Eragon teased, "Not going to fall asleep on us while riding, now are you?"

She blinked a few times. "I'll try not to," she said, unable to think of the last time she had restful sleep.

"Awe, poor Zelia is tired. You could ride with one of us. You know, so you don't fall off if you doze," Keller teased.

Saria shot him a hateful look. "She's just a child! She may be older than any of your kind could ever hope to live. But she is a child none the less. You would do well to remember that." She turned her nose up and turned her back to him.

"He's just joking," Kafthry jumped to Keller's defense.

Saria's horse moved in front of them. "Don't you see she is trying to be strong for everyone around her? Any elf her age hasn't even seen bloodshed, yet she carries the weight of the world on her shoulders. She may be five hundred years old, but that isn't even fifteen years old for a human. You two need to get your acts together!"

Keller's veins visibly throbbed as he argued. "You wait just a minute!"

"Enough!" Zelia yelled before anyone could say another word.

When she did her heart skipped a couple beats, and she gasped. Her eyes fluttered as her vision went fuzzy. She tried to focus in one place, but all she could make out were the outlines of those around her. Then her knees buckled beneath her.

Eragon caught her, kneeling to bring her head closer to level with her heart. "Zelia. Zelia. Are you okay?"

He searched her eyes for a response.

The others all dismounted and circled around as she closed her eyes and took a deep breath.

"I… I'm sorry Zelia. I didn't mean to..." Keller's voice trailed off, unsure of what to say.

She took another deep breath and blinked a few times before speaking.

"It's not your fault." She took another breath. "My heart's been giving fits ever since that night on Fairy Island. It's just catching up with me."

Something moved in the trees across the stream and she sat up, regretting the movement the moment she made it.

"We can't stay here. But I can't stand up or ride on my own right now. Not until my heart catches up...," she paused to take a breath, "with the rest of me."

Eragon stood up with her in his arms.

"Here, will one of you hand her to me once I get on. I know of someone who may be able to help."

Something rustled even closer in the trees as they climbed onto their horses.

They rode a few hours north, and the sky lightened with the morning's sun as they reached a clearing in the trees. A little log cabin and barn sat high on a hill looking up at the mountains.

32

"I thought we said we never wanted to see your face again Eragon," a gruff, dwarven accented voice greeted them.

"I know." Eragon said and Zelia could feel him glance at her as she sat shaking in his arms, slipping in and out of sleep. "But she needs help."

Someone sighed. "Bring her inside," a female said in Elven. "Nordock, put your ax away. Eragon wouldn't be here without good reason."

Wood creaked as Eragon slid from his horse, cradling her against him. Then the air was warmer and smelled of tea and honey.

"You can put her there. Do you know what happened to her?"

Eragon removed Zelia's weapons, piling them against what sounded like a wooden wall and laid her on the bed. She wanted to help, to not be helpless, but her chest ached, and her eyes were heavy with exhaustion.

"She has shrapnel in and around her heart and lungs. From what I understand it's been there for over a year. She stops breathing in her sleep."

"How long has she been in this state?"

"A few hours. She sat up and spoke for a few before we headed here. Sealia, I just… I don't know what to do for her."

Zelia could feel the warmth as someone else approached her side.

"I'll do what I can for her, but from what you say she shouldn't be alive."

Something pressed against her chest, silky strands of hair tickling her neck. Zelia's heart skipped beats, and she struggled to suck in enough air. Then a hand rested on her forehead.

"Try to wake her. I'll make some herbal tea to help her steady her heart rate and warm her up. That's the best I can offer."

Sealia turned away, but Eragon shifted, stopping her.

"Thank you. Really, I mean it."

"I do it for her. Not you."

There was a pause as floorboards creaked and Eragon turned back to her, moving a piece of hair out of her face. "Zelia, wake up now. We still need you here. Zelia, wake up."

"I'm awake," she whispered and rolled to her side, clutching the front of her tunic for a moment before she sat up. The moment she sat straight it felt as though a metal band wrapped around her skull and she wavered.

Eragon grabbed her before she could fall back again and whispered, "I've got you. We need to steady your heart."

She leaned against Eragon's chest as he hugged her. She fought to keep from falling asleep as she tried to steady her short shallow breaths into longer, deeper breaths.

Sealia came around a corner, a cup of tea in hand.

"Good, you got her to wake up." She sat on the edge of the bed. "Do you think you can drink? It should help."

Zelia turned, still leaning against Eragon, and took the cup in trembling hands. She stared at the cup in her shaking hands for a moment, willing them to steady before taking a sip.

Her voice cracked when she spoke. "Tha… thank you."

She closed her eyes to hide her aggravation with her body.

"Do you know where you are?"

She took another sip of the tea and spoke with a hoarse voice.

"Somewhere near the Faithful Mountains, and yes, I know why we're here."

Sealia stared at Eragon. "Why are you here?"

Eragon turned away from her gaze.

"King Erolith sent us to find out about the war brewing across the mountains. I found her taking on a trapper with a dagger in Trading Town's market. She thanked me in elvish and then we figured out we were headed in the same direction. She travels to The Hold, to save Alrindel."

Sealia sat back with surprise. "Alrindel?"

She looked down at Zelia with new interest. "You know Alrindel?"

Zelia nodded but didn't speak.

"How?"

Please, I can hardly talk. She tilted her head back to look at Eragon.

"Eadon took her in as an infant. Alrindel and Eadon are the closest things she has to kin here. She watched him die at The Hold in her dreams.

There's a lot more to her than you would ever guess."

Kafthry, Keller, and Saria came in followed by the Dwarf calling out, "Horses are taken care of. Except for that wild black one. So, how is she?"

Zelia shivered as she glanced at the Dwarf. He was young with stringy red hair. He stood with his shoulders back and his thumbs in his leather belt, he even blushed a bit as Sealia kissed his cheek.

"She'll be fine. She's just having problems with her heart."

He raised his eyebrows. "Heart you say?" He turned to Eragon, his expression grim. "What are you doing dragging a young lady around these parts with a bad heart?"

"I—," Eragon stopped when Zelia held up a hand.

She spoke in a quiet voice as she tried to keep it from cracking. "I would have made the trip with or without traveling companions."

Zelia shivered again and closed her eyes as she leaned against Eragon. She forced her breath to steady, and.

Eragon swept the hair out of her face and pressed a hand to her forehead. "Zelia, are you sure you're fine?"

She wrapped her arms across her chest.

"Just tired." She closed her eyes as she listened to his heart.

They all stood still for a moment before the Dwarf spoke again, "You all look beat. Come on. We'll find corners for you to sleep in."

"Go, I'll keep an eye on her," Eragon said.

Saria stayed behind for a moment. "Make sure you get some rest too."

Eragon forced a tired smile. "I will. Go, rest while you can."

Once they had left, Zelia pulled away from Eragon still holding her chest as she did.

"You need to get some rest. I'm going to go check on Bête Noire. I need to get up and move around, it usually helps." *Though I don't ever remember it being this bad.*

The Dwarf overheard Zelia as he entered the room, the floor creaking with each of his steps. "Go get some rest Eragon. I'll keep her out of trouble." He pointed a thumb over his shoulder. "There's a space for you back there."

She nodded when Eragon glanced at her, so he got up and went to lie down.

Once Eragon was out of the room, she moved to the edge of the bed.

"You know, I never got your name," she said.

She stood leaning against the wall as the Dwarf replied with a deep bow, centimeters from touching his nose to the floor.

"Nordock at your service."

She moved towards the door with a hand against the rough wood wall to steady herself. "Well, would you like to meet that wild black horse you mentioned earlier?"

Nordock raised a bushy eyebrow as he came towards her. "That's your horse?"

She rested her hand on his shoulder as they stepped through the doorway.

"Yes and no, he has a free spirit. No one can truly own him." She looked out at the pure black horse, his coat gleaming in the morning light. "Bête Noire, come here."

Bête Noire raced across the pasture and stopped with his head pressed against her chest. "You scared me Zelia. I think you scared all of us."

She spoke in his language as she ran her fingers through the coarse hairs of his mane. "Sorry boy, I didn't mean to."

He raised his head and brushed his velvety muzzle across her cheek. "I know, but why didn't you tell anyone you were having problems with your heart? Well, more problems than usual."

"You all had enough to worry about. And it's not like there's anything that can be done about it."

Nordock broke in. "Um, I take it you can speak to animals?"

"Animals, the trees, dragons." She took another deep breath. "I also know all the languages the Elves learn as children, among others."

"That's a lot to know for someone so young." Nordock patted his belly as he rocked on his toes. "Makes me look bad."

She faced him with a tired smile.

"I age as the Elves do, if not slower. So, I've had plenty of time to learn and I had a good teacher."

Nordock scratched his beard with his thick stumpy fingers. "Just how old are you then?"

She heaved a sigh and sat in the grass. "Somewhere around five hundred."

She ran her hand over the wet grass. Warm droplets of water wet her fingers as her hand ran across the grass tips. It gave her a feeling of the peace and simplicity of nature that relaxed her. Her heart began to beat with a rhythm it had not kept in quite some time and her breathing steadied with one last shuddering deep breath.

Nordock sat beside her in the damp grass. "So, what's this about your heart?"

When she finished telling him about the explosion, she let out a long yawn into the back of her hand.

Nordock stood and offered her a hand. "You look as though someone's run you through the mud and put you up wet a few too many times. You should go get some rest."

"Can't argue with that."

She entered a room with shuttered windows where her little mismatched band of traveling companions was spread out on the floor. Most of them were fast asleep, except Eragon who sat up when he noticed her.

"Come here. Are you okay now?"

"Better than I have been in a few months."

Eragon flashed a sleepy smile and yawned.

"Good let's get some sleep." He pulled her over as he lay back with one hand under his head and the other arm draped across her.

They slept well into the night, the longest any of them had slept in a long time.

They woke to Sealia standing in the doorway, the sweet scent of some sort of stew drifting in through the open door. "So, who's hungry?"

Keller and Kafthry sprang to their feet; they were always ready to eat. Zelia, Eragon, and Saria were slower to stir. They came out to a makeshift table large enough for all of them to sit around.

Saria elbowed Eragon. "Guess we know how to get the boys up and going from now on."

Eragon laughed. "Yeah, just imply there's food."

"It has to smell delicious too," Keller said as he accepted a bowl from Sealia.

Zelia chose the seat where she could watch the horses out the open door. She sat in silence as everyone dished out breakfast, or rather dinner as it was late in the evening, the sky already filled with stars.

After everyone had their portion, Nordock turned to Zelia. "Are you okay?"

She drew a deep breath and pulled herself from her daze. "Yeah, just thinking."

Eragon cocked his head, his expression solemn. "About the Hold?"

She picked up the spoon and half-heartedly messed with the food in her bowl.

"I still haven't figured out how to save them. Sometimes he dies—" She shook her head. They didn't need the details. "He always dies, no matter how I change my decisions."

Saria put a hand on Zelia's shoulder. "We'll figure it out. But for now, we should eat."

She forced a smile, though she knew her eyes still told of her worries. "Then let's eat."

Keller and Kafthry joked and told stories while they ate. Their stories told of their time since meeting Zelia, so she tuned them out. But from time to time, everyone would glance over at her in disbelief before returning to their meals.

As soon as she finished eating, she went outside and drifted towards the forest's edge. She rested a hand on a tree's trunk, and it offered her a happy hum as wolves howled in the distance.

A stick snapped behind her and she sighed. "Coming to check on me, now are you?"

Nordock hooked his thumbs in his belt as he came up beside her. "Yeah, Eragon wanted to come, but I told him I would."

She ran her fingers through the deep ridges in the tree's bark and turned towards him. "I'm afraid you followed me down here for nothing."

"Well, I'm guessing you came out here to get away from Keller and Kafthry's stories. They talk as if their life began when they met you. No stories about themselves."

"That's because they are all that is left of their village. It's painful for them to talk about their past. They told Dotchavitch, another dragon rider, but I wouldn't ask them to tell their story again. Those boys are more broken inside than they let on. They'd given up hope before the dragon riders saved them."

Nordock wrapped his arm around her shoulders and pulled her to him as they walked.

"You have a big heart for someone so young and broken herself."

She started to correct him, but he stopped her.

"I know you're older than me. But it's like expecting an elf child to run off to war! I take it that's what you plan to do, isn't it?"

"Yes, and the only thing that would hold me back is death."

His arm dropped from her shoulder as he stepped back to face her.

Suddenly she felt as though she was being watched, but instead of alarm, she felt warmth and knew it was Lumid who was watching them. She couldn't help but look up to the stars with a smile.

Nordock followed her gaze before staring at her. "What are you smiling about?"

"Lumid is listening and watching."

"Who?"

"Someone who many consider a god. He can see across the galaxies and hear the grass growing in the field with the help of The Bridge."

Nordock nodded with a tightened lip.

"Okay, I'll take your word for it. Well, you should go sleep more so you can head out in the morning."

"If Keller and Kafthry weren't so useless in the dark, we could leave now."

Nordock shook his head. "These parts aren't safe to travel at night."

As though daylight is better. "Well, good night."

➤

Sleep came, and she found herself arguing with Alrindel as they stood on the outer wall of the Hold.

"I want you to go stay with the King, be part of the last line," Alrindel said.

"No. I came here to fight beside you, not him."

"Until two years ago, I thought you were dead and then Eleanor forbade us from looking for you."

"Would you two stop? This is not the time or place for this," Koin said. "Look around you. You are making them more nervous."

"Shields!" the call seemed to echo down the wall as people repeated it for others to hear.

Koin pushed the two of them closer to a higher portion of the wall as a volley of arrows rained down on them.

"Koin!" Alrindel yelled, scrambling to catch Koin as he fell, only to get hit himself. Together the two people she cared about most collapsed, Alrindel doing his best to support Koin on the way down.

"No, no, no… it wasn't supposed to happen this way." She frantically ripped strips of her tunic off, stuffing it around the arrow protruding from Alrindel's chest.

"Koin first," Alrindel said, his breath already gurgling.

She glanced at Koin, but blood already drenched his front and he lay eyes open, unblinking. She shook her head. "He's already gone. Alrindel?"

"I… love you," he choked the words out between strangled gasps.

"Zelia, wake up. It's just a dream."

Something shook her, and she shot to her feet flames in her hand. The shock and fear in Eragon's eyes pierced the veil of her dream and she stumbled back. *No.* She smothered the flame and darted from the room. *What have I done?*

"Where's the fire?" Nordock asked as she ran from the house.

"Zelia!" Eragon called after her.

She ran into the trees and fell to her knees. The shock and horror on Eragon's face replayed in her head. *I... I could have hurt him. I could have killed him.* She rocked with her arms clutched around her chest.

Leaves rustled as Eragon came up behind her and she scrambled away.

"St... stay away from me." She hid her fear with a veil of hair as she turned away with her side against a tree. "I don't want to hurt you."

He grabbed her and she tried to shove away as he hugged her, but he held her tight. "Shh, I know."

She couldn't fight it any longer and crumpled in his arms, tears streaming down her face.

When her sobs quieted, Eragon spoke in a soothing tone. "Zelia, do you know what you saw in your dreams?"

"I saw Koin and Alrindel and..." She shook her head and pulled closer to him.

"You saw Alrindel. What was he doing?"

Her heart raced and her breaths caught in her throat. "He... we argued and Koin died, then he was choking on his own blood. I thought that path had changed, bu— " Her words cut short as her breath quickened, leaving her gasping.

"Shh. You needn't say more." He held her tight and the beat of his heart slowed as he soothed her.

After some time, her heartbeat fell in line with his and she pulled away with a deep breath. "I don't care what the fates show me. I will save him, both of them. Even if I have to take the Darkans to Fregnar myself."

She wiped her eyes and pushed past the others.

By the time the others followed her up the hill, she had already grabbed her belongings. She cinched her sword belt around her waist as she walked past them back out the door and called out for Bête Noire.

Before she even got onto the stallion, the others had packed and saddled their horses.

She put on a brave face and turned to Nordock and Sealia.

"Thank you for everything."

With that, they all rode off towards the pass.

33

They were riding through the trees at a steady pace when the panicked screeches of a bird sounded from the trail ahead. Zelia didn't wait for the others, she just urged Bête Noire on. When she caught a glimpse of the creature, she was taken aback. It had the head, wings, and front legs of an eagle, but the body, back legs, and tail of a lion.

"What's that?" Keller gasped.

"A griffin, but what is it doing here?" Saria whispered.

A man stooped over the giant beast, one foot propped on the griffin's wing. "I wonder what you'll bring at market."

Zelia drew her bow and cleared her throat to capture the man's attention.

The griffin struggled against his bonds and let out a cry for help as the trapper dug his heel into his wing. The griffin's mouth gaped open as he tried to let out a screech of pain, his wing bowing under the man's weight, but no noise left his throat.

"What business do you have in these parts by yourself young lady?" the trapper asked.

Eragon and Saria rode out of the trees with bows drawn. "She's not alone."

"Would you kindly remove your foot from my friend?" Zelia's gaze drilled down her arrow at the man.

"Friend? Your friend?" A tree creaked behind the trapper as he continued, "Now I think I've heard it all. A girl who calls a beast her friend! The boys are gonna love this!"

The tree twisted around and knocked him on his butt. "I've had quite enough of you!" The tree creaked as she ranted on, "You little disrespectful, inconsiderate, destructive, oh you little!"

Zelia choked down a laugh.

"I believe you've angered the trees. I would have to say it would be foolish to step on their roots any further, being this deep in the forest and all. And I wouldn't dare think for a moment that this is the only tree that can move. They all can be vengeful if provoked."

The trapper scrambled away from her and the tree that had knocked him down. "You little witch!"

She slid from Bête Noire's back.

"If that's what you wish to call me, so be it. I may be able to hear them speak, but I don't control them. They have free wills of their own and do as they please."

Eragon and Saria brought their horses around to block the trapper from getting to her while she knelt and soothed the griffin. "Shh, it'll be okay. You're safe now."

The griffin let out a soft screech as she cut the ropes binding it.

"Thank you, thank you, thank you! I am forever in your debt. If there is anything you should need, I would be more than happy to assist you." The griffin curled his head clear to his breast with his bow.

The image of Alrindel's death flashed before her eyes and she took a step back.

"There... there is something, if you're willing. In a couple weeks' time, I'll need help fighting the Darkans at The Hold. I need someone to fly me out into their ranks so I can kill as many as possible. You needn't fight, I wouldn't ask that of you. I just need you to fly me out into their ranks."

The griffin flicked his lion's tail. "You will have my help and I may bring some friends along." The griffin shook and spread his wings. "Well, I must be off." He leapt a few times and took off into the air. "See you at The Hold!"

She climbed onto Bête Noire, and Keller pointed to the trapper.

"So, what should we do with him?"

"Leave him to the fates. The trees will warn the creatures of his traps. That'll be his punishment."

Keller shrugged as he rode after her.

They rode in silence for some time before Saria asked, "So just what are you planning?"

Zelia dug her fingers into the rope around Bête Noire's neck. "Something crazy, but none of my other plans panned out in my dreams. I should be able to take out half of the army in one swoop." *If they don't shoot me down before I can do it.*

"Just how do you plan to do that?"

"You'll see, unless I come up with a better plan."

"It'll be getting dark soon, we should find someplace to stop," Kafthry suggested with a yawn.

"There should be an opening a little way ahead where we can stop," Eragon said.

When they stopped, Zelia didn't even bother to eat. She just curled up and was fast asleep by the time Eragon pulled her close.

→

She opened her eyes to the point of a sword in her face. The man holding it sneered. "Ah, aren't the two of you the cutest thing ever. Draw your sword. We can finish our little argument here."

The other two trappers held knives to Keller and Saria's throats. Keller didn't keep watch very well.

"Zeli..." She held up her hand to stop Eragon.

"It's okay. His swordsmanship is shoddy at best. Besides, he's followed us this far, he won't stop. May I borrow yours?" His sword was better than the one she had from Dragon Island.

Eragon slid the hilt into her hand.

"Oh, you're gonna get it little runt."

The angrier the man, the worse he fights. Let's see how far I can push him. She spun the sword around at her side and rolled her shoulders back with a crack.

"Fine, it'll be nice not to hold back. We could make this interesting and all three of you could fight me at once. At least that way it'd be closer to an even fight."

The man almost growled as his face turned red and he hacked at the air as he charged. She stepped to the side and gave the enraged man a wide berth.

"I guess not. Pity, I was hoping for a challenge," she lied.

"You little brat, someone's got to teach you a lesson!" Enraged he bellowed and charged her.

She blocked his haphazard blow and spun her sword around with a twist of her wrist.

His sword fell to the ground with his twitching hand still attached.

He collapsed to his knees and gripped at his stub. His eyes grew wide and his face paled as he watched his blood spray into the fire. Time seemed to slow to an agonizing pace as he scrambled to stem the bleeding before he passed out.

Keller and Saria took the opening to overpower their captors as they looked on at the other trapper in shock. She should have helped them, but she battled with the urge to help the dying man as he bled out on a bed of red and green moss. Eadon had raised her better than this, but he also wouldn't condone this man's actions either. *He'll have lost too much now.* She sighed, she couldn't save him, but she didn't have to kill the others. She wiped a drop of blood from her cheek with the side of her hand and walked over to the trapper. A few drops of crimson blood still dripped from her sword.

"You just couldn't leave with your life intact, could you?"

She wiped the sword on his tunic and pulled a rope from his pack.

"Now your lives truly belong to the forest." She turned to the other two trappers as they stared at their fallen friend.

The sky lightened with the first rays of daylight by the time they finished hoisting the hogtied men into the tree. She stuck a knife in the trapper's bound hands.

"Be careful not to cut the wrong rope or you'll go for a little tumble and still be tied up."

She jumped down to Bête Noire's back, and they set out on their way with the trappers watching upside down as they disappeared into the trees.

Once they were out of sight, Kafthry beamed at Zelia.

"You were awesome back there!"

"That was just a show to get him angry. And while I could use a challenge, I don't enjoy fighting."

It was then they broke through the line of trees and the grey barren face of the mountains stretched before them.

Saria sighed as she looked up at the mountain's snow covered peak. "We'll all have our challenges soon enough."

They cut across the side of the mountain, close to the trees until they found the scarcely used path. It wound up the face of the mountain until it disappeared over a ridge.

They hadn't made it halfway up the barren portion of the mountain when night came and forced them to stop. The path followed the edge of a spring, so they all had their fill of water that night and refilled their water skins. They spread out and drifted off to sleep to the sound of trickling water as the stars blazed overhead.

34

It was about midday when an arrow whizzed by Eragon's hood-covered head. Zelia drew her bow as she turned to see where the arrow had come from.

A man veiled in a black cloak stood a short distance up the mountain slope. His dark eyes stared down the shaft of another arrow.

"What business do you have in the pass?" he spoke with a gruff voice that sounded forced as it carried across the barren pass.

"Depends on what business you have here." She aimed into the wind, ready to shoot him down.

His near perfect teeth gleamed as he grinned.

"So, the girl speaks for the group. That's something I haven't seen before. How about you answer my question first? I do have the high ground."

She released her arrow and drew another. "Do you now?"

A moment later, her arrow sliced through the man's bow string, the remnants whipping across his fingers as his wooden bow sprang straight. The man shook his hand as the severed bowstring swayed in the breeze.

"Lucky shot."

He pulled his hood back before stooping to pick up her arrow, rolling it between his fingers. The chiseled shape of his face and wavy black hair seemed familiar, yet altogether strange to her. Even his rough beard nagged at something in her memory.

"Where did you learn to make arrows like this? Only the Elves of Elyluma use that knot."

"And how do you know that?" Zelia asked.

He half slid, half walked down the steep slope as pebbles and snow rolled beneath his feet. He held his straightened bow and Zelia's arrow in one hand, his other grazing the ground as he descended to the path.

"Koin's a friend, he taught me that knot."

She relaxed her bow. "It would seem we have something in common. Koin's also a friend of mine."

The stranger's eyes narrowed. "Wait, you must be Zelia."

"How do you—"

"They couldn't send a search party after they found the cave, so Eleanor and Eadon asked me to look for you."

"And who are you?"

He jumped across the mountain spring and bowed holding his useless bow and her arrow across his chest. "I'm The Bounty Hunter to most. But the Elves know me as Skylar of the Mountain Kingdom of Old. As for your earlier question, I'm in search of some trappers that should be west of here."

"We ran into them a few days back. They won't be causing any problems for a while."

He raised an eyebrow, so she continued. "I killed one of them and we left the other two hanging in a tree, hogtied. I made it so they can get free, but that won't be for a while."

"Taking all the fun out of it for me? Guess I won't be getting my bounty for the one trapper then."

"Forget your bounty. An army of Darkans moves south. They aim to attack The Hold. If you're truly of the Kingdom of The Mountains, then you'll want to come with us."

He ran a rough hand through his hair. "Truthfully, I'm the great grandson of the late King. Not the King who rules now. My full name is Skylar O'Fell."

"O'Fell?" An image of burning pyres flashed before her eyes and his familiarity made sense, he looked much like the late King. "But they killed all the O'Fell family after we left."

"That's just what they wanted everyone to think; my grandmother escaped into The Wild."

Zelia shook her head. "Okay, if the people don't matter to you, then maybe this will since you call Koin a friend. He, Alrindel, and many elvish bowmen march south to aid the Kingdom of the Mountains. Many of them will perish at the sword of Darkans." Her gaze fell from his. "If not all."

"You see as Eleanor does?"

"Sometimes." She offered him a hand. "Here, Bête Noire will allow you to ride, just this once."

Skylar hesitated, then climbed on behind her.

She waved her hand in front of her scrunched up nose as they started down the mountain. "I think you've been hunting trappers too long. You reek of rotten beaver castor oil."

"Just try not to breathe through your nose." He grinned ear to ear.

"So I can taste it instead? Thanks, but I'll pass." She shot him a glare over her shoulder.

"You'll get used to it… eventually."

➤

It took them all day to traverse the pass, but they came out on the other side just as the sun was setting.

Skylar fiddled with his knife and struck up a conversation to end the day's silence as they sat around their small fire. "So, where are you two from?" Skylar asked, gesturing to Keller and Kafthry.

"Zelia found us on the ship of a dragon Trapper. They'd put us to work on their ship after destroying our village." There was a solemn pause and then Keller perked up. "We were dragon riders with Zelia for a short time. When she decided to return to the mainland, we came with her."

Skylar turned to her. "Is this true?"

She nodded, but her gaze never left the flames. "They speak the truth, however far-fetched it may sound."

"Eadon spoke of you as if you were kin. Why's that?"

"Eadon took me in as an infant upon Eleanor's request. He raised and taught me as his own for a hundred and forty years. I remember many a night singing and dancing under the stars with Alrindel when he was but a young elf."

Skylar gave her a puzzled look. "But you're not an elf nor are you from the royal line, so how…"

"Appearances are not always telling. I'm only part human, just as you are, only less so. I age as an elf, if not slower. So, your great grandfather was Dane O'Fell, the King that united all men of the Forgotten Lands under one man? I should have liked to have met him. He was a just ruler."

"Yes. Eadon used to tell me stories of him," Skylar said.

Zelia yawned into the back of her hand and leaned against Eragon. She fought sleep for a while before she drifted off.

————▶

Zelia woke to see Skylar staring down the side of the mountain and she thought of his bow. She shuffled through her pack and went down to sit with him.

"I believe I owe you this."

Skylar took the bowstring with a grin. "Well, you're just ready for anything."

She lay back against the steep slope of the mountain and looked up at the morning's stars. "Not everything. Some things are beyond my control."

Skylar turned to look at her as she lay barely visible in the night's light. "Was it my imagination, or were you not saying everything yesterday? There was something about your tone when you mentioned Alrindel."

"I'd rather not talk about it. It haunts me enough without speaking of it."

Skylar got up, dusting himself off. "Well, if you're keeping watch, I'll go help the others pack up."

————▶

He went over to help Eragon saddle the horses, but she could still hear him.

"Need a hand?"

"What do you want, Skylar?"

"What's Zelia not telling me about Alrindel? I asked her, but she said she'd rather not talk about it. Something tells me you know."

"She sees his death in her dreams. The worst time was a few nights back. It's his death that drives her. She's determined to save him and the people of The Hold."

"That's a lot for someone so young to carry."

Eragon tightened the saddle's girth with a jerk. "That's not even the half of it. She tries to be so strong for everyone around her, yet she's so broken on the inside. I wish there was more I could do for her."

Skylar slung a saddle onto the next horse. "She's lucky to have someone like you looking out for her."

"Someone needs to."

————▶

Zelia walked up to them with her things packed. "I take it Eragon answered your question. Good, now, Bête Noire won't let you ride with me again. He rather dislikes human men. So, who will lend Skylar their horse and ride with me?"

"I will." Eragon gave Zelia a lift onto Bête Noire and hopped on behind her.

Skylar led them down the mountain since he knew the pass better than they did.

It wasn't much longer before they reached the tree line and Skylar pulled his horse to a stop. "We have two choices. We can continue along the edge of the trees for a while and get there faster or we can take the easier path through the woods."

She looked to Keller and Kafthry. "Are you two up for a more challenging ride?"

They slumped their shoulders. "Yeah, the faster path it is."

They turned and headed north along the edge of the trees that crept up the side of the mountain. It was a tedious task to walk along the forest's edge. The horses often slipped and lost their footing, but they always stayed on their feet.

One time Bête Noire would have fallen down a ravine if a tree growing on the edge hadn't been there to stop them.

Caught off guard by the sudden jarring motion she clung to Bête Noire's mane.

Skylar glanced over his shoulder. "Not much farther and we'll call it a night. Zelia, are you okay?"

She raised a shaky hand. "I'll be fine."

Skylar looked to Eragon for answers.

"She has shrapnel in and around her heart and lungs."

Skylar's gaze turned to her as a flash of pain crossed her face before she could squelch it.

"Do you need to take a break?"

She shook her head. "Wouldn't do any good, just keep moving."

She spit out blood as they came to a stop. Skylar's rough exterior seemed to melt away at the sight.

"You should rest."

"I'll take first watch. I can't sleep right now, anyway." She slid from Bête Noire's back.

"Why's that?"

"My lungs are still bleeding. Can't sleep until they stop or at least I shouldn't." She shrugged and sat beside him as he set to work starting a fire. "I thought Eadon raised you, shouldn't you know that?"

"How long have you been like this?"

"About two years. The day after the explosion I began training with Yargo's sons. Magic practice with Rog and swordsmanship with Terik.

That's until I moved wrong and just about collapsed." She flipped a smooth flat rock between her fingers. "It took a while to get used to the lack of range of motion. Metal plates don't bend all that well."

"So, that's why you are so good with a bow. You trained with gods."

"No, I learned that alongside Alrindel. I wasn't very graceful as a young child, so I worked hard to beat their best bowmen. You know, you never told me about yourself."

Skylar stirred the fire for a long while. "I was five when Darkans killed my father in The Wild. The wolfbloods took me in for a while until the Darkans came for me. I couldn't watch them kill all of them, so I ran. They chased me into the woods of Elyluma. Eadon was among the Elves who saved me."

"And he took you in?"

He nodded.

"Seems we have similar beginnings, give or take a few centuries."

"For someone who has seen and been on the receiving end of so much darkness, you're incredibly light-hearted."

"I'm not, but it's either that or break at this point."

With that, she got up and disappeared into a nearby tree for her watch.

35

Skylar sat staring into the darkness of the changing leaves when he woke. The chill of the morning staved off the usual chirp of crickets and left an eerie silence in its place.

"I see now why Eadon took me in. He was hoping to fill the void you left in his heart. Last I saw him he was… different. He was always happy as most Elves are, but last year when he heard you were alive, there was a new light in his eyes that I'd never seen before. I guess in a way you and I are family."

"I think I'd like to consider you kin, if you live through the coming battle."

"Don't you mean we?"

"No. I don't die, I just… get trapped. It's better me than… " *Don't think that way, you'll save them.* She shook her head. "The people of the Kingdom of the Mountains should take refuge at The Hold soon."

Skylar chucked the rock he held into the woods. "We won't be far behind them. A couple days at most if we break off into the forest here."

"Then the forest it is."

"I'll call you over when breakfast is ready." He headed towards the fire.

The next few days were uneventful. The eyes of a wolf peered at them through the underbrush from time to time, but none of them stepped from the shadows.

When they came to the edge of the trees, they looked out over open grassland towards The Hold. It was dark, but they pressed on until a guard of men stood before them.

"Halt! Where do you hail— " He cut short at the sight of Skylar. "You, you're *that* bounty hunter. Why are you here?"

"Addre Xen." Skylar gave a slight bow of his head. "We come to offer our help."

Addre laughed so hard he almost fell off his horse. "You? Help?" he managed to choke out, then his laugh cut short. "Bind them."

"Zelia?" Kafthry asked.

"Don't resist."

"You knew this would happen?" Eragon asked.

"No, Skylar wasn't here before, but fighting won't help."

Guards stood on the walkabouts with drawn bows. A man beckoned and the great metal gates creaked as they swung outward.

"Xen! Why are you bringing prisoners when Darkans chase us?" A grey-haired man stood part way down the stairs with thumbs hooked on his belt.

"Let me go." Zelia shook free of the man who held her. "I request counsel with King Gregory."

"Gregory? You speak as if you're a friend, yet I know I have not met you." He glanced over their horses and lingered on Bête Noire. "And you ride a horse from my herd."

"We have not met, but I knew the O'Fell family and seek to protect the very thing they died for."

"And what would that be?"

"Your people and I bring news from Queen Eleanor." A ring of flames flared around her wrists and her bonds crumbled to ash as she turned to her captors. "But I believe we have more important things to discuss. Release my friends and don't forget the bounty hunter."

They backed away as she headed for Bête Noire. She slipped the rope from his neck and whispered, "Please go, you'll be safer far away from here. I need you to be safe and I will see you again."

"Fine. I would say be careful, but I know you won't." He reared towards the men who had dragged them all there, then ran out the closing gates with a flick of his tail.

King Gregory stared at the closed gate for a moment, then waved them to follow.

"Come. We will speak in private."

Zelia turned to Keller and Kafthry. "You two stay here, learn the grounds and rest. War will be upon us all soon enough."

Wooden doors shut them in the stone room with a bang. A map of The Hold and the surrounding areas spread across a table in the center of the room. Two candles flickered atop the map.

King Gregory wavered as he leaned against the table. "You need not use titles. We all bleed the same here, even you." He glanced at her and then to the Elves. "Now, what news do you have for me?"

"The Darkan Army will be here before next light. They travel with creatures the like of which this world hasn't seen since your great grand-father's time. I know what must be done. But I think it best I wait until we greet the rest of our council."

A chill ran down her spine as the call of a familiar horn echoed down the hall.

A young boy burst into the room. "The Elves, the Elves are here!"

Gregory pushed his way out of the room and descended the stairs. She didn't need to see to know who he went to greet, but she couldn't help but shove her way to the top of the stairs. Even having seen them in her dreams, she paused at the sight of them. It had been so long since she had seen either of them. Koin glowed in the starlight as he stepped forward with Alrindel at his side. He must have become Koin's second, a rank held only by the most skilled fighters.

"We come on behalf of Queen Eleanor to offer our hand in battle."

Gregory looked down at them from the little platform beside the stairs. "Why? You have no stake in this."

Koin's silky white hair shimmered as he nodded, a grim look spread across his face.

"If you had taken the time to get to know us better, you would know Elyluma seldom stands by while darkness wipes out innocent lives."

Skylar descended the stairs, leading her part of the way, and put his hand on Koin's shoulder.

"We'll gladly take your bow, Koin." He nodded to Alrindel. "And yours, brother."

"Glad to see you here, Skylar. We figured you'd have crossed the moun-tains by—" Alrindel stopped and stared at her. "Zelia?"

At his recognition, she leapt down the last few steps and wrapped her arms around his neck.

"It's been a long time, brother."

He froze, and she squeezed him tighter before he returned her hug. "That it has."

"You all know each other?" Gregory's bewilderment showed in his voice. Alrindel pulled back from her hug.

"They are my kin. Zelia lived with my father and me for over a hundred years, though that was long ago."

"H… How long?" Gregory staggered back.

"I age as an elf though I appear to be human. There are many things that neither of you know about me. But we don't have time to discuss that or to catch up," she said, giving Alrindel a sorrowful glance.

"Wait, hold on a second. How do you know this piece of scum?" Xen pointed to Skylar.

"Skylar is no scum." She stared Xen down. "He is kin to elf and man alike. Skylar?" She asked for his approval, he nodded so she continued. "This is Skylar O'Fell of The Mountain Kingdom of Old, the last living descendant of the Hyperians on this world, the great grandson of King Dane O'Fell."

"All these years we thought all the O'Fell line had died and here you've worked for me!" Gregory said.

"Zelia's right, we have more important matters than Skylar and Zelia to discuss," Koin ushered Gregory up the stairs.

We still need a miracle. She searched the dark skies above the mountains, then started up the stairs with the others.

A blinding beam of white light shot down on the path behind them and lit the wall better than the sun itself. The light disappeared before any of them had a chance to turn.

There before them lay a wood chest with a slender gold cylinder sitting atop a single piece of parchment.

"Lumid, what is this?" she whispered.

"Father sends it, don't let the humans touch it," Rogath's voice seemed irritated as it drifted through her mind for the first time in what seemed like ages.

"Rogath, I'm—" she stopped as Rog slammed the connection shut. "Don't—" Before she could finish, a guard grasped the golden cylinder.

His hand turned black, and he fell to his knees.

"No…" She ran up and pulled the cylinder from his hand. She froze with the surge of energy.

When she blinked, the energy eased. She ran her free hand over the terrified man's blackened arm and, as he scrambled back, his hand returned to normal.

"It's best you didn't touch things sent for someone else."

She picked up the delicate piece of parchment. It was written in ancient symbols, the language of the Hyperians. Roughly translated it read:

A gift for you in your battle against the darkness. I know it was the wizards, if only I could get Rogath to see that. For now, it is up to you to save these people as the wizards left to help you are few. I had the staff altered to amplify your powers.

One more thing, inside this chest, I have placed enchanted armor fit for the finest of queens, wear it well. We are with you in spirit and know you will do well. Good luck my dear.

Yargo

She handed the letter to Eragon and opened the chest to see the fine leather armor.

"Thank you." She stared at the dark void between stars. "For everything."

"Do you know this language?" Eragon showed the letter to Alrindel.

She cinched the ties on her armor and spun around to face them, pleasantly surprised by the way the armor moved with her.

"Yargo just changed the tides of the coming battle." The cylinder in her hand grew into a staff, and strange markings covered its entire length. She had seen Rogath draw some of them in the air to cast spells, but she never understood them.

"What do you mean?" Alrindel asked.

"You'll see when the time comes." She returned the staff to its original size and placed it in its holster on her back. "For now, I wait for—"

"What's that!?!" A man pointed to the sky.

"Griffins?" Saria stared as three winged creatures circled.

"Lower your weapons! They're friends, not foes!" Some men didn't lower their bows and Zelia raised her voice even more. "If you shoot at my griffins, I'll shoot you before they ever hit the ground!"

The remaining men lowered their weapons after a nod from their King.

Zelia ran to the top of the inner wall and whistled to get their attention.

All three griffins landed in front of her, and she bowed her head. "Thank you for coming."

The griffins bowed their heads in return. "The pleasure is ours. Now be warned, the Darkans draw near. They will be here within the hour."

She turned to Gregory and translated what the griffins had just said. He nodded, then called out orders to arm every able-bodied man. Skylar went after him to help.

"We will each take a rider, just this once."

"The griffins offer to take a rider just this once." She turned to Eragon and Saria and ran her hand over the silky feathers of the griffin closest to her. "I'll ride him, but you two are welcome to the others."

She then turned to Koin and Alrindel. "They will need you two here. Now, let's go help Gregory and Skylar get the others ready, we'll need all the help we can get."

Once the others were busy, she pulled Skylar to the side.

"I need you to do something for me and I can't trust the others to do it. What I'm about to do will leave me defenseless for a while. The griffin will circle back to pick you up once he drops me off in the middle of the Darkans' ranks. Once the blast is over, I need someone to pick me up. Can you do this for me?"

There was a moment where he just searched her eyes, questioning what she was about to do. "You have my word," he said at last.

"Good, it's all set then." She paused before she walked off. "Don't breathe a word of this until I've departed. The other griffins won't take flight until you give the signal."

Skylar's hand rested on her shoulder as she turned away.

"What do you plan to do?"

"Use the staff." She slipped from his hand and disappeared into the gloomy crowd of men and boys preparing for war.

36

The steady beat of a great drum vibrated through the air, booming over the ruckus of the army flooding the plain before the outer wall. The taste of fear was almost palpable, only the Elves and King stood stoic in the face of the impossible odds.

"We could use the power of the Fenari," Alrindel suggested to Koin.

"What about the Fenari?" Zelia asked. She had heard of them, their magic and impenetrable skin making them nearly impossible to kill without special weapons, but she had never heard anything about being able to use their power.

Koin gave Alrindel a warning look before he answered, "No. Eleanor said we would doom everyone if we did. We cannot risk it."

She could tell by Koin's demeanor that he would hear nothing more of the topic, so she left them on the outer wall and went to where the griffins waited.

"Are you ready?" the griffin she had saved asked.

"Yes," she said, though she knew she would never truly be ready for war.

He nodded. "I shall follow your lead."

"Thank you. Skylar knows the plan," she turned to the other two griffins, "he will tell you when to go."

When the Darkans stopped with a loud bang of their drums that echoed off the stone, Zelia nodded to Skylar and took to the air.

She couldn't help but glance back as Alrindel yelled, "What's she doing?!"

Alrindel shook Skylar by his chain-mail shirt, fear and anger ran wild in his wide eyes. Skylar rested his hands on Alrindel's shoulders.

"Brother, if you don't trust me then trust her." Alrindel turned to the other two griffins but Skylar gripped his shoulders. "They have their orders. Zelia needs to do this if we're to have any hope of winning."

"Where do you want me to drop you?" the griffin asked, bringing her attention back to the task at hand.

"Back there, where the Darkans are thickest and remember, fly fast when I drop."

She glanced over the huge black mass of troops and hoped she'd picked the place she would have the most impact.

"Almost there," he said.

She grabbed the staff from the halter on her back and steeled herself for the drop.

"Now."

She leaned, letting herself slide from the griffin's back and for a moment she stared up at him, part of her wishing she had asked his name. Then she turned in midair and let the flame that burned with rage, fear, and anger ignite inside her. She let it fill her and then she poured it into the staff, the staff filling her with power in return. Fire erupted from her in a wave like she had never felt before.

The Darkans beneath her didn't even scream before succumbing to her flames, and she rolled as she landed in the clearing. The staff slammed on the ground as she came to a stop and she pushed everything she had into the fire that spread around her. When her body shook with the effort, the fire inside her threatening to eat itself alive, she released it. She wavered, leaning on the staff for support as she stared at the path of destruction she had blazed.

In the distance, past a field of smoldering weapons, Darkans ran in all directions, screaming as they clawed over one another to escape the scorching heat. She heard a screech and glanced up to see a griffin descending towards her with Skylar, the two others carried archers who picked off Darkans who dared run across the smoldering field to reach her.

Her knees buckled as she collapsed the staff, replacing it in its holster. She tried to stay sitting up, to wait for Skylar, but her world tilted, and she closed her eyes as the ground came up to meet her.

"You better be alright or Alrindel will kill me for not trying to stop you." Skylar hugged her limp body close to himself as the wind whipped by them, the flapping of wings faint in her ears.

———————————▶

"Will she be okay?" Alrindel's soft voice asked beside her.

"I'm fine. It just takes a lot to control such a large burst, even with the staff." She put her hand on Alrindel's and forced herself up, her world spinning for a moment before righting itself. "I have no intentions of leaving you so soon. I just got you back."

"Are you two going to just sit there or come help?" Koin called from the outer wall.

They exchanged glances, and Alrindel sighed. "You're not going to stay here, are you?"

She gave him a faint smile and started towards the outer wall. They descended one set of stairs, then turned to the next. Zelia slowed as they climbed, but she did her best to shake the exhaustion.

Alrindel and Skylar instructed man and elf alike to shoot for the joints before they turned their sights to the Darkans.

The three of them stood side by side with Koin as Gregory called out, "Get ready!"

The Elves drew their bows, holding the next three arrows in their drawing hand.

Then the order rang out, repeated down the length of the wall, "Fire!"

The Elves worked as one while the men fired at will.

"I see you haven't lost your touch with a bow," Alrindel spoke as he drew his bow.

"I see you've improved with age, and you're not half bad, Skylar."

"I manage." Skylar drew another arrow with a smirk.

For a moment it seemed as though they might have a shot at winning, then a swarm of huge beetles flew in from the north. The swarm was so thick they blocked out all the light from the stars and moon. They could only see the light from their fires.

Even the glow from the Elves faded in a night devoid of stars.

She could feel the darkness creep in all around her as she doubted if she had done enough, should she have waited for this? Should she have cleared the skies rather than the field? Her heart and soul bled for these people and Elves.

She shook herself from her dark thoughts as she looked to Alrindel. Even in the darkness he still glowed, his spirit still held strong even in the face of almost certain death.

Almost. She thought. Not once had Alrindel lived through the battle, nor had they won the battle in any of her dreams.

She glanced over to see a screaming man get knocked from the wall by a spiraling swarm of beetles.

The griffins dropped Eragon and Saria off, and they scrambled to Zelia's side.

"Did you know about the beetles?"

Just as the griffins took off into the swarm, the griffin Zelia and Skylar had ridden fell out of the sky. He took as many beetles and Darkans with him as he could, holding some in his claws and beak as he plummeted.

"You knew that would happen?" Saria asked.

She nodded and pulled her staff back out.

"Sacrifices had to be made. They knew they wouldn't come away from this alive." The other two griffins fell out of the sky, one after the other. "From here I don't know what happens. My dreams didn't go any farther than this, other than to show me that everyone had died."

"One thing's for certain." She watched Alrindel shove a wooden ladder from the wall. "We're on a different path than any of my dreams have shown."

"We need light," Alrindel said it as he struck the Darkan that clung to the wall.

Zelia searched inside herself for an ember to light the skies with as she stepped away from her friends, but the loud bang and screech of metal against stone stopped her dead in her tracks. In that still moment before the second bang of the battering ram, a red and yellow feather fluttered to her feet. She scooped it from the floor and a loud caw rang out as beetles fell from the sky.

She looked up to see three huge birds flying through the storm of beetles.

Men cheered as the sky lit ablaze with the passing of the three fiery-winged creatures. Giant flickering shadows moved across the ground as the birds glided through the swarm.

Giant beetles rained down in every direction and took many Darkans with them as they hit the ground.

The fiery birds made another pass through the beetles, then dove into the Darkans with one last screech that chilled her to the bone.

Thank you, may we meet someday. She kissed the feather, and it blazed in her hand. As the ashes blew from her fingers, she whispered to the wind. "May rebirth be swift for you and your sacrifice not be in vain."

"Brace the gate!" A voice yelled above the others and Zelia raced for the stairs, Skylar on her heels. They shot Darkans as he descended.

"Did you know they were coming?" Skylar asked.

"No, I've never even met a phoenix." She spun around and slid her sword beneath a Darkan's armor. "I only heard tales of them and have no idea who sent them."

Men screamed as the door cracked and splintered open. A stream of Darkans flooded the gap between walls.

"Retreat!" King Gregory called out.

What men remained at the gate or were not yet caught in the wave of Darkans looked to her as Skylar and Alrindel came to her side.

"Go! We'll hold them off. Skylar, Alrindel, keep them off me."

She pulled her staff, but this time the staff glowed blue as cracks grew up her fingertips and the air around her chilled. She shuddered as the ice smothered the last few embers of fire in her veins. Even with changing to her ice powers, the well of energy she pulled from was almost empty and she scrambled for a way to stop the Darkans, to buy them time to regroup. The cracked pedestal on Hyperia came to mind, and she slammed her staff on the stone, willing her powers to focus on the seams in the stone above the gate. There was a groan and a crack, then the wall crumbled, crashing down on the Darkans.

Alrindel caught her as she swayed. He scooped her up and ran through the inner gate with Skylar on his heels. The gate drew closed with arrows whizzing by in either direction.

"I'm glad you're on our side," Gregory said as she wilted against the wall.

"I just hope it's enough."

She shook and watched the cracks recede down her arms, leaving trails of blood where they had been. She grasped her side as a spike of pain emanated from her wound. *When did I get shot?*

Alrindel killed the last of the Darkans that had made it through the inner gate and froze when he saw her slumped against the wall. "Zelia." He knelt beside her.

"I'm fine. This happens every time I use that power," she lied and dragged herself to her feet, knowing if she told him the truth, he would lock her away from the fight. "I'll be back in a few, help the others." She headed deeper into the hold while the others fortified the inner gate.

She slipped around a corner into a room that had been full of weapons but was now empty. The wall felt cool against her clammy skin as she leaned against it. *It's not that bad, you can get it on your own.* She shoved two fingers through a gap in her armor and into her side. She wrapped her fingers around the splintered shaft of an arrow and gasped as she pulled it from her side.

Something moved in the corner of her vision as she dropped the bloody arrow shaft with a shaky hand and slid down the wall, her eyes closed.

"Do any of the others know?" Koin's concern bled through his every word.

She shook her head, and looked down at her hand covered in warm, crimson blood.

"It didn't hit anything important. Would you help me stop the bleeding?"

He started to rip a strip of cloth from his tunic, but Zelia shook her head.

"I need you to seal it."

She pulled a dagger from her belt and his eyes grew wide as she heated its tip.

"Are you sure?"

She nodded, and put the handle of the dagger in his hand.

"It's the fastest way. Trust me, I can handle it."

Koin pressed her shoulder against the wall, pinned her legs to the ground with his knee, and put the hot dagger against her skin.

She forced her body to let the dagger burn her and stifled a scream with clenched teeth. As soon as he pulled the knife away, she fell forward into his arms as her body shook with the first signs of shock.

Koin held her against him as if comforting a small child.

When the shaking turned to more of a shiver, she leaned back against the cold wall with closed eyes. The smell of burnt flesh permeated the air.

"Thank you, Koin." Her voice shook. "Please don't mention this to the others, at least not yet. They still need my help, but they wouldn't take it if they knew."

"Why are you doing all of this?"

"Alrindel is supposed to die, everyone is supposed to die here."

"How?"

"I've been having dreams. It's not the first time."

He offered her a hand to her feet.

"Just stay close," Koin said. "The arrow might have been laced with poison and I'm certain the arrowhead is still in you."

⟶

When they returned to the inner wall, they found Alrindel, Skylar, and Gregory arguing about what to do.

"That's enough! Arguing amongst ourselves will do us no good. We have lost far too many to hold," Koin took charge.

She came up beside him as the unforgettable sound of cracking wood came from the inner gate. "Koin is right, and I don't have the strength to pull off another blast like that. Even if I gave it everything."

233

She turned to Gregory. "Arm your women. Weapons lay idle in the chambers, don't let them go down without a fight. I'll ride out and take as many down with me as I can. You're all more than welcome to join me, but I would not ask it of you." She glanced to Alrindel. *Maybe I can't save you, but you wouldn't stay even if I begged.*

"Zelia, you know we stand with you, no matter what." Eragon rested a hand on her shoulder, and all the others nodded in agreement.

"Father! The gates are about to give way!" a man yelled up from the bottom of the stairs.

Gregory mumbled under his breath, then nodded.

"Fine, we'll arm the women and take as many Darkans with us as we can."

Kafthry ran up as Gregory walked off, he frantically searched everyone's face. "Has anyone seen Keller?"

No. I never should have allowed them to come. She glanced to the others and Skylar put his hand on Kafthry's shoulder.

"I'm sorry, but if Keller is out there, then he is gone."

Guilt washed over her and she turned away. *You can't snap, not now. You can't change what has happened, but maybe you can change what happens next.*

After a moment, she turned back to Kafthry.

"I want you to go with the women and children as the last line of defense. The younger boys we're sending with them need someone to lead them. Will you do this for me?"

Kafthry wiped a tear from his eye with a nod and took off after Gregory.

Skylar turned to her as she watched Kafthry disappear into The Hold's innermost chambers. "I'm sorry about your friend. But you were right to send Kafthry off with the women and children."

She put on a brave face and headed for the horses near the front gate.

"Let's make it worth all the sacrifices."

She winced as she climbed onto a horse. Part of her wanted to ask her name, but she knew she was only going out there to die and she didn't want another name to haunt her sleep.

Gregory soon rejoined them. "They know what to do, now let's give them a fighting chance."

He climbed on his horse and rallied his men.

"We no longer fight for a kingdom, land, or wealth. No, we don't even fight for our own lives any longer. Now we fight for the lives of our women and children! Will you stand and fight with me one last time?"

Men yelled all around the room as their battle horn blew with a long deep call that vibrated into their very cores.

The broken inner gates swung open, and they charged into the ranks of the enemy. They slashed and cut through Darkans left and right as they charged out.

Most of their horses made it past the haphazard climb across the outer wall, then succumbed to the enemies' spears and swords.

Eragon and Saria fought side by side some little ways ahead while Zelia, Skylar, and Alrindel stood with their backs to each other as they cut through Darkans. They were slowing, but none of them were willing to give up just yet.

She turned towards Eragon just in time to see a sword driven into his chest and she froze. *No!*

Saria slashed at the Darkans and caught Eragon as he let out his last breath. His eyes stood open as his face relaxed from the expression of pain and surprise to the blank stare of the dead.

Eragon. Zelia's sword chattered to the ground and her vision narrowed until all she could see was Saria holding their fallen friend.

A mix of emotion fell over her and she clenched her fists. In the end, anger and rage won. Darkans and beetles all around crumbled to ash, burning from the inside out just as rage burned through her. Blood streamed down her face, sticky and warm on her cheeks. She had never used her powers this way before and she knew it was tearing her apart, but she didn't care as a numb feeling fell over her.

"That's enough!" Skylar snatched her into a hug and shook her back to reality.

She took a couple ragged breaths and looked out at the eastern slope, where she could faintly see a wizard.

There was a flash and the crackle of electricity as her eyes hazed over with a red hue from the blood and she blacked out.

37

She was numb and couldn't move, but she knew she wasn't dead as air whispered in and out of her lungs. Voices bounced off stone walls, and she strained to listen.

"She's been running from who she is, from her past," Skylar said.

"How do you know?" the voice was strangely familiar, but she couldn't place it.

"Because I've been there. Well, go on, I'll watch over her for a while."

She listened as footsteps left the room and echoed down the barren hallway.

Once the echoes had faded, Skylar spoke again, "When are you going to wake up already?"

She pried her eyes open and her voice cracked as she tried to reply, but nothing else escaped her lips.

"Easy there, you've been out for a while. We were beginning to think you weren't going to make it."

She tried to speak again, but he shushed her.

"Shh, no need to speak."

When she regained feeling in her arms, she rested her hand on Skylar's and forced her voice to work.

"Alrindel?"

Skylar swept a single strand of hair from her face.

"He's no worse for wear than the rest of us. I can go get him if you like."

Hearing that Alrindel was alive staved off the last of the numbness, and a smile crept across her face.

"I'll be right back." He squeezed her clammy hand and left in search of Alrindel.

How am I alive? The armor... She sat up and pulled her cleaned armor from the bedside table. She ignored the sharp pain from her side where the arrow had struck her. It was minor in the scheme of things.

It seemed like it took an eternity to put the armor on, but with every piece she felt her strength return. *This is why I was able to fight so long, but what was that I did there at the last? I've never done that before, and I didn't use the staff. Wait, where am I?*

She cinched down the last tie for her armor and headed down the hallway. The sound of footsteps and voices guided her until she walked out onto a balcony. *The Kingdom of The Mountains? How long was I unconscious? What did they do with the bodies of all those lost?*

"She's alive," the crowd below murmured over and over again.

"See, told you she lives!" Skylar patted Alrindel on the shoulder.

Alrindel cringed with every pat until he turned and returned the favor with gritted teeth. "Thanks, brother."

Boys just have to antagonize. She glanced around at the mismatched group of friends before her. *Wait, where are Saria and Kafthry?* Her smile faded, but before she could ask about them, the crowd fell silent as Gregory walked out with a wizard close behind.

"Vainoff?"

She breathed the wizard's name as he gave her a sad glance.

"Zelia, he's not one of them," Koin whispered in her ear.

For a moment, she thought back to the few times she saw the wizards gathered in the mouth of the cave. Not once did she see him there. Still, her stomach twisted in his presence.

Gregory turned to address the people, "Today we no longer mourn those lost in battle. Instead, we celebrate those they left to carry on their memories! Though there are many to thank for success against the darkness, I believe we can all agree on one above the others. There's one among us who is a god among the living. One who is a flame shining ever bright on the darkest of nights, it is to her we owe the lives of our children, friends, and family! May we all bow to Zelia, god among men!"

He turned and got down on both knees as he bowed to her. Everyone in the crowd did the same, and she couldn't help but back away. Only those who knew her stayed standing.

"Get up. I'm not a god. Nor do I wish to be called your savior," her voice carried across the crowd as King Gregory met her gaze with wide eyes. "I'm a product of my creation, an abomination. Having power doesn't make you a god. It only makes you a tool."

Her footsteps against the stone walkway rang out as she disappeared into the castle. Behind her all was silent, and she didn't dare cry, not here. Zelia didn't stop until she reached a balcony a few meters off the ground at the other end of the castle.

She sat against a cold stone pillar and looked across the fields of grass to the sun setting over the snow tipped mountains.

She could feel Lumid's gaze upon her.

"How I sometimes wish I was back there with you. But even Rogath hates me now, he thinks of me as an abomination. Incapable of control."

"You are not an abomination." The low voice of Vainoff stated behind her, and she flinched. "Different, misunderstood, and a tortured soul, maybe, but you are no abomination. Now come, no being, god or no god, should speak to a King in front of his people such as you have."

She shot to her feet, her back to the un-railed edge of the balcony.

"You may have helped create me. But you have no right to tell me what to do. The others kept me locked up most of my life, but I know well what most think of me. Even now I see it in your eyes. I'm not what you intended me to be. The all mighty wizard fears his own creation."

A dark shadow fell over them, and Vainoff's face seemed to glow as if lit in the shadows of a cave.

"Enough! You do not know what I think!"

For a moment, Asenten's face replaced Vainoff's and she shrank back to the edge of the balcony. Her heart shot to her throat, racing as she found herself trapped back in the first years of her imprisonment.

Vainoff took a forceful step closer, and without a second thought, she jumped from the balcony. She stumbled when she hit the ground, but re-gained her footing and ran off towards a small patch of trees to the north.

In a split second, Vainoff realized what he had done and called after her. "Zelia! I didn't mea—" The thundering of her heart drowned out his words as she ran past Bête Noire, to a clump of trees.

She collapsed against a trunk, shaking, gasping for breath. Bête Noire nuzzled her as she sat curled up against a tree, but then she heard leaves crunch behind her and Bête Noire charged off.

"Zelia! A little help here!?!" Alrindel jumped between trees to avoid the thundering hooves of the black horse.

"That's enough Bête Noire, thank you," her voice cracked, and she lowered her head.

"Hey, boy, I won't hurt her," Alrindel assured. "I just want to check on her."

Leaves crunched as Bête Noire backed away and Alrindel eased forward.

She flinched at his touch, and there was a long pause before he pulled her to him.

"I don't care what you or anyone else says. You'll always be my little sister."

She shivered against his warmth, and he held her tight. His breath smelled of honey as he hummed, just as he had done when she was an infant.

A twig snapped, and Alrindel paused to see who it was.

"Zelia. I'm so sorry," Vainoff started. "I did not mean to scare you. You are so strong and good willed that I sometimes forget how broken and young you really are. Please forgive me."

Ca... can I forgive him? She sat for what seemed like an eternity, willing the answer to come to her. "I forgive you."

He breathed a sigh of relief before she had finished.

"Though I fear I shall never trust you."

She glanced at him and his age showed as he stared at the fallen leaves.

"I understand. If you are willing, I would like the chance to earn your trust back."

"Maybe someday."

She leaned her head against Alrindel's chest and pulled in the honeyed scent of his breath.

"Maybe someday is better than never, so I'll take it. Now, it'll be getting dark soon. You three should come inside and put that away, Skylar. You know very well you can't hit me with an arrow."

Once Vainoff had gone, she wiped her dry eyes and put on a smile. She stood and turned to Alrindel with a hand outstretched.

"Come on. We're supposed to celebrate the lives of those lost today."

"There's that smile I've missed so much," Alrindel said, though the tone in his voice told her he saw through the facade.

He took her hand, but hardly used it as he stood.

"So, where are Kafthry and Saria?" she asked as they walked back towards the castle.

"Yeah, about that." Skylar rubbed his neck and shoulder. "Saria had to return to the Drakeon Empire to report, and Kafthry volunteered to go with her. I think he's smitten with her."

She kicked a small stone as she walked.

"I'm glad he went. It'll be good for him to get a fresh start and I know Saria could use the company."

"I'm sure you'll cross paths with them again. Your fates are intertwined." Alrindel put a hand on her shoulder, and she leaned against it with a heavy sigh.

38

When they reached the edge of the crowd, a young girl stumbled and fell at Zelia's feet and all eyes turned to her. The music and dancing turned to a deafening silence. The tip of a quill could have been heard hitting the stone walkway. Candles flickered, and the breeze died down as she fought the urge to shrink away.

She could feel Alrindel's warmth at her back, and she drew a deep breath. *You can't let them fear you, or you fear them. They've been through enough already.* She talked herself up in her thoughts and offered the girl a hand. As she helped the girl to her feet, she did the only thing she could think of. She began to sing:

Oh, how the stars shine bright
On the starry night.
With the moon casting
Shadows on the ground.

Dance around we must
In the light of the night.
With the stars above our heads
And the hearts of those lost with us.

Celebrate their lives
As they look down at us.
For they dance
Among the stars.

241

In the halls of Yargo
And about the grounds of Niflheim.

No longer mourn their deaths
Celebrate their lives.
Set free your worries and woes.
For tonight, we dance under the stars.

The crowd was still silent when Alrindel took up the song with her. A couple lines in Skylar, Koin, and the other Elves joined in, followed by King Gregory. Soon everyone sang, some added extra verses here and there as their voices rang out into the crisp night air.

As the song repeated, she noticed something flutter near the front gate and she slipped away to investigate. In the middle of the alley stooped a huge bird that resembled a cross between a golden pheasant and a peacock.

The phoenix bowed his head and cawed, "My lady. I thought I should introduce myself while I wait on the others. They should be reborn in another day or two. Their ashes were spread out more than mine. I am Flits, the second in command of The Phoenixes."

She returned his bow. "Nice to meet you, Flits. Your help was much appreciated. Would you like to meet the people you helped save?"

"I don't know." Flits preened the feathers under his wing.

"Come, they'll be glad to meet one of the brave souls who saved their lives and they'll miss me if I'm gone for too long." She waved him to follow.

Flits hesitated, then flew after her as she sifted through the crowd.

She found King Gregory on the balcony and stopped to address him first. "There's someone whom I think you and everyone else should like to meet."

He stared at her for a moment, seeking her intentions. "Alright, let me get everyone's attention." As he stepped closer to the edge of the low balcony, he cleared his throat and the crowd quieted.

She moved to his side. "There's someone I would like all of you to meet. He's one of the creatures who gave their lives to save all of you."

She raised her hand towards the long black silhouette above their heads. "Meet Flits, the second in command of The Phoenixes!"

Flits landed beside her with grace, and his long tail trailed behind him. He puffed out his chest and bowed to King Gregory. "Your majesty."

She translated, and King Gregory bowed back to the fiery red and yellow bird. "We owe you and your friends many thanks for your help in The Battle for The Hold. If there's anything we can do for you or your friends, please do not hesitate to ask."

"Silly man! I only come to see you, Zelia. I need nothing from him!" Flits flapped his folded wings.

She couldn't help but laugh at Flits reaction.

"What's so funny?" King Gregory asked.

She shook her head and quieted her laugh. "Nothing, Flits appreciates your offer, but he doesn't need anything."

"Translate properly or don't do it at all." He eyed her jokingly, though she could tell he wanted her to repeat him.

"Fine, I'll translate it word for word. What he said is, 'Silly man. I only come to see you, Zelia. I need nothing from him.'" She held up her hands with a shrug. "Don't shoot the messenger."

"We only came to aid another phoenix. To save those she loves."

Her smile faded when she translated and looked down at her friends who had gathered around the bottom of the stairs. She ran her hand across Flits's silky feathers as she passed in front of him. "I'm done translating for the night."

Flits hooked his curved beak over her shoulder.

"I guess I'll be off then. Know that if you ever need us all you must do is ask the wind, for it is the carrier of the birds."

Flits let out a happy caw as he took off and disappeared from view.

She sat on the stairs a few steps from the ground so she could look her friends in the eye.

"So, what are we going to do now?"

Koin walked up with perfect timing.

"We will help the villagers on our way home. We hoped you would come with us."

His green eyes searched hers with a silent message. He knew she had to go with them. The arrowhead in her side had become infected, and she needed Eadon's healing skills, but he was kind and kept this to himself in front of the others.

She nodded and let out a long yawn. Seeing that, Skylar pulled her to her feet.

"Come on. I think it's time for you to get some rest. You still look like hell."

"Thanks. How's your shoulder?" She patted his shoulder, and he messed up her hair.

"You little squirt."

"Sibling-like already, I see." Once at the top of the stairs, Alrindel spun around them and walked backwards. He held up his hands up as if framing a painting. "With a little work, people might believe you two are related."

Zelia and Skylar exchanged a glance before all three of them burst out laughing. Her laugh cut short with a spike of pain from her side, but she hid it with a yawn.

"I guess not." Alrindel shrugged and spun to continue down the hall with them.

➤

The next morning, a loud sawing snore from across the room pulled them from sleep.

"Shh, let's get ready. No need to wake him."

Alrindel grabbed his stuff and ushered her out of the room.

Once they were clear of the sleeping chambers, Alrindel hummed as they went to fetch water for their trip home.

She sat on the edge of the well as he pulled up a pail of water.

"Alrindel, you know the Darkans didn't do this on their own, right?" she asked.

"What do you mean?"

"The Darkans. Their timing is all too convenient. The other wizards, they know I'm back, don't they?"

"Yes, but don't worry about that. We won't let them take you again," Alrindel assured.

"You can't stop them."

"Maybe not on our own, but we're not alone. More importantly, you're not alone." He picked up her hand and pulled her to her feet. "Come, let's watch the sunrise before we head home."

Home? She froze. *Yes, it is my home, so long as you and Skylar are there.*

"Zelia? Are you okay?"

"Yes, Alrindel. I was just thinking."

"Sometimes you think too much. Come, let's go watch the sunrise."

➤

Koin already sat on the balcony when they got there, and he patted the floor for them to sit with him. They watched the stars fade and the sun rise in the distance with Koin. Someone walked up behind them and Koin glanced back before settling against the pillar.

"You Elves sure spend a lot of time looking at the sky," Gregory said as he stood behind them.

"No matter how many times I see the sunrise or the stars in the night sky, their beauty never ceases to amaze me," Koin said.

Gregory grunted as he sat beside them.

"See that bright star there?" She pointed to a star straight above them, its light still blazing through the lightening sky.

Gregory nodded.

"That's Hyperia. I would suggest smiling and saying hello, Lumid's gaze is upon us."

"Who?" Gregory shifted his weight and stared at her.

"The all-seeing, all-hearing gatekeeper of the bridge between realms. A statue of him used to grace the halls of this castle..." she trailed off, not wanting to ruin the good will Koin had come here to build.

The stars disappeared as the sun broke over the tops of the tallest trees in the distance, sending streaks of pink across the sky and lining the edges of the clouds in white light.

"Well, we really must be going." Koin sprang to his feet.

Gregory got to his feet, the battle and his age catching up with him as he creaked into a standing position. Skylar appeared in the doorway as Gregory thanked them for everything they had done.

Gregory rambled on when Skylar walked up and hugged him.

"Oh, shut up you old coot. Next time if you need help just ask."

Koin turned back to face them. "Skylar is right. Our hand is always here if you need something. Do not be afraid to ask, consider our alliances here in the east stronger than ever."

"And friends can be found wherever you look, even in the most unlikely of places," Zelia said with a glance to Skylar.

Gregory shook his head. "The four of you have more wisdom in a drop of your sweat then than I possess in my entire body!"

Skylar patted him on the shoulder, guiding him from the balcony. "Believe me when I say it's not just the years that make them wise, but their outlook on life that does. Spend a few years with them and they'll rub off on you."

Gregory laughed. "Maybe my youngest boy should go with you if that's the case!"

Skylar walked down the hallway with him. "Tell him to practice with a bow and then maybe in a few years he can tag along with me for a while."

"We might just take you up on that offer some day."

Their voices faded as Alrindel and Koin jumped down from the low balcony. Bête Noire waited for her, so she lowered herself onto his back.

They were already at the front gate when Skylar caught up with them. A few dozen Elves followed him. Many wore bandages or walked with limps.

The Elves sang a cheerful song as they moved along.

After a while, Koin egged her on, "Come on, sing with us. I know you know the songs. You may fool them, but I know better. Share that beautiful voice of yours!"

The others clambered in agreement until she gave in. "Fine, I'll sing one song."

Birds tweet, their sound so sweet
As their wings flutter.
At morning's first light
Their songs can be heard
Ringing through the air
For all who might hear.

Nothing comes and
Nothing goes
Without their music
going to and fro.
Nothing sweeter can be heard
In all the wood among the land.

The Elves broke in:
That is except for Zelia's voice!
As it carries across the winds.
Loud and sweet to the ear,
Nothing but a soprano here!

He he, ha ha!
Though winter creeps in
Spring feels near
With Zelia's song!

Now they all sang together, even Skylar joined:

Birds tweet, their sound so sweet
As their wings flutter.
At morning's first light
Their songs can be heard
Ringing through the air
For all who might hear.

Nothing comes and
Nothing goes
Without their music.
Nothing sweeter can be heard
In all the wood among the land,
but Zelia that is!

On we go to home,
To the Elven kingdom
Of the east!

They all moved a little faster as they sang their cheery tune. Zelia shook her head every time they added her to their song. They continued to sing well into the evening and stopped when they came to the edge of the first village along their path.

39

Smoke rolled up from a smoldering thatched roof at the other end of the village. Random belongings were scattered across the dirt paths. The Elves set to work helping put out the few fires that still burned.

Koin stopped Zelia and one of the other Elves, but waited for the rest to disperse into the village before he spoke.

"You two are to rest and do not lie to me Lighnif, I see your limp getting worse. As for you young lady," he turned to face her, "we are not taking any chances with that infection. We should have left long ago, but we were afraid to move you any more than we did."

"Go ahead, I will keep an eye on her," Lighnif offered and ushered her towards a tree.

"What, so now we're babysitting me?"

"If we have to," Koin replied.

"Thanks, love you too Koin."

His expression softened, and he pinched the bridge of his nose. "Please, just go rest."

"Alright, we will. You should go make sure Alrindel and Skylar don't get in trouble."

With a heavy sigh, Koin headed off into the village and Zelia eased down against a tree.

Lighnif sat next to her with a sigh of relief. Blood seeped through the bandage wrapped around Lighnif's thigh, and when she touched it, she cringed.

"Here, let me." Zelia pulled a fresh bandage from her pack and sat up on her knees.

Lighnif leaned her head back against the tree with her eyes closed as Zelia untied the bloody bandage. It was a clean wound, but it had broken open with the long day's walk.

"So, tell me. How long have you had a crush on Alrindel?" Zelia asked.

Lighnif's cheeks flared with a cherry glow as her eyes flashed open. "Does he know?"

"No, even Elvish men are quite oblivious." She cinched the bandage down to stop the bleeding and Lighnif cringed. She tied the bandage off and sat back against the tree.

"Have a lot of practice at this I take it?"

"Yes, no one else would do it for me." She chewed the inside of her lip and watched the fallen leaves rustle in the breeze.

"Of all the times I saw Asenten over the years, not once did I ever think him capable of anything as evil as what he did to you. How do you move on after living through something so horrible?"

Her shoulders sagged with the weight of the topic and she leaned forward, her elbows on her knees.

"You just have to take it one day at a time. You can't let what you see every time you close your eyes dictate your every waking moment. Not a day goes by that I don't struggle with what I have done and seen. It's just something we all must learn to live with." A spike of pain emanated from her side, and she held it.

"How's your side? Koin told me about you getting shot, I had to reopen it because it got infected. Your bandage probably needs changing."

Lighnif rocked to her feet without putting any weight on her injured leg.

"Come, there's a hut around the corner that has a fire going so I can get a better look."

They knocked on the short hut's door.

"Come in," a voice called from inside.

A little old woman shuffled around the single-roomed hut, putting her house back in order. The comforting smell of a well-tended fire spread about the room.

The woman stopped and turned towards them, the firelight casting deep shadows across her wrinkled face.

"What can I do for the two of you?"

"I need someplace to change a bandage." Lighnif motioned towards Zelia.

The woman looked them over. One of her eyes sat lower than the other and seemed to have lost its sight long ago. "Happy to help the women who fought to save our lives. Need anything else?"

Lighnif paused in thought for a moment. "Clean water if you have any."

"Be right back." The women winked and slipped out the door.

"Come on, off with the armor." Lighnif loosened the ties and dragged Zelia's weapons and armor off of her.

Zelia removed her tunic and there was a slight gasp from the old woman as she stood with the door half open.

"Well, let's have a look at it." Lighnif untied the bandage and waved for the woman to bring the water.

Zelia winced as the bandage pulled from her side. She ran her hand through her hair and stopped part way through as she looked down. Black and blue veins ran out from around the inflamed hole in her abdomen. *I should have healed by now, but this…*

Lighnif rinsed the wound out. "Looks better than it did. Eadon will be able to do more for you once we get back, we lost the healers who came with us in the battle."

It must be the powers I used. I knew I'd be drained, but this is different. She shook the thought and forced a smile as Lighnif dried her side.

"You're doing well for a novice. Eadon will be proud of your work."

A smile flashed across Lighnif's face as she wrapped Zelia back up.

"You really think so?"

Behind her, the door creaked open and Alrindel slipped in.

"Oh, sorry. Didn't realize anyone was in here." Then he realized who's scarred back was in front of him. "Zelia?"

She slid her tunic back on and pulled her long brown curls out of the collar as she turned to face him.

"Yes?"

She could tell by the tone of his voice that he hadn't known. She watched anger and a flood of other emotions boil beneath his surface.

"It's not as bad as it looks."

Alrindel pulled her close with a hand at the back of her head.

"Even if it's not half as bad as it looks, it's too much. You should never have gone through everything you have. I... I..."

"There's nothing you could have done. Besides, what I went through made me who I am today."

She closed her eyes and laid her cheek against his shoulder.

"Everything okay?" Koin asked from the half-open doorway.

Lighnif nodded as Alrindel turned towards Koin.

"Did you know about Zelia's scars?"

Koin shook his head as he glanced at the dirt floor.

"Not until a few days ago when we noticed her side had gotten infected from the arrow she took during the battle."

Skylar stopped with his arm on the doorjamb above his head. "I knew it. There's not much privacy to be had on the side of a mountain."

Zelia shook her head at Skylar's remark.

"We should all eat and get some rest," Koin said. "We've got a lot of ground to cover in the morning."

Skylar rubbed his neck. "Let me guess, laygoose bread again?"

Alrindel grabbed Skylar's shoulder as he passed through the doorway. "Right as always is the bounty hunter."

Skylar brushed Alrindel's hand away. "Oh, shut up."

Zelia shook her head and scooped up the rest of her belongings. *Boys. But how can you not like the sweet taste of elvish bread?*

Koin passed out rations as they sat in the thick green grass under the open stars. He gave each of them half a piece of laygoose bread.

The laygoose bread crumbled as she bit a piece off. The smell of honey and cinnamon filled the air.

"So, what path do we want to take from here? We can go through the woods to the main gates or we can follow the well-worn paths to Riverdain and hitch a ride on a barge going upriver," Koin said once they had all taken a few bites.

Lighnif rubbed her leg just above her wound.

"We should go on to Riverdain. Some of us are still healing and the path there is easier," Alrindel said.

Skylar paused from cleaning his fingernails out with a knife.

"Sounds good to me, there's a bounty on a guy in Riverdain. Maybe I can pick him up along the way."

"Always thinking about work." Alrindel gave Skylar a light shove.

"What?" Skylar tossed up his hands with a grin. "There's a tavern there, and that attracts all kinds of characters. Besides, squirt here interrupted my tracking of some trappers back at the pass."

She rolled her eyes. "Yeah, characters like you. Besides, those trappers will be long gone from those woods by now. They upset the forest and won't be trapping much of anything for a while. If it makes you feel any better, I'll help you find the two that are still living come spring. If I had to guess they'll be in The Trading Town once they find they're unable to trap anything."

"What did they do to upset the forest?" Lighnif asked.

"One of them trapped a griffin and tried to break his wing just to be spiteful. I let him go, and he snuck up on us with some of his friends that night. One man with him was the same man who had challenged me in The Trading Town the day I returned to the mainland. He was rather upset that I drew a dagger instead of a sword to fight him. Eragon had stepped in to defend what he thought was a defenseless little girl." A smile flashed across her face as another thought jumped to mind. "Eragon was quite surprised to hear me speak Elvish."

"Back up a second, that griffin wouldn't happen to be one of them from The Hold would it?"

"The one that dropped me in the middle of the Darkan forces is the one I saved that day."

"So how did the one trapper end up dead?"

Her face fell, and she watched Bête Noire graze a little way down the hill.

"His companions held knives to my friends' throats to force my hand, so I cut off his hand and he bled to death. We left the other two trappers hogtied and hanging from a tree. I left them a knife so they could free themselves, though they would have a rough trip to the ground."

Skylar swept a piece of hair out of her face. "You showed them more kindness than anyone else would have."

"And that explains how you met Eragon and Saria. Have you ever not made friends someplace?" Alrindel joked.

She covered her mouth with the back of her hand and let out a long yawn.

"Couldn't have said it any better myself. It's time we all got some rest." Koin lay back on the thick grass with his fingers laced behind his head.

With another yawn, they all drifted off to sleep.

40

The next morning, they ate their laygoose bread as they walked. Zelia convinced Lighnif to ride Bête Noire for at least a while, on the premise that she needed to walk. She loved to walk with the Elves as they always moved with purpose in their step, never dragging their feet. Even injured, they walked at a pace faster than most as they sang their happy tunes to pass the time.

It was midday when they came to the next village. They helped here and there, and then set out again, this went on for the next few days as they traveled towards Riverdain.

Just as they prepared to set out once more, a young freckle-covered boy ran up to Zelia.

"Wait! I have something for you!"

The small child reached up, standing on his tippy toes, and put a small blue flower in her hair.

"Thank you for saving my mommy," the boy said.

The boy's mother stood in the doorway of their ruined home with a proud smile.

Zelia moved the boy's dirty blond bangs out of his eyes.

"Thank you. Now, you'll take good care of her for me, won't you?"

The little boy glanced back to his mother as he ran his foot over the charred remains of his village's crops.

"I don't think I can, I'm not strong like you are."

She rummaged through her pack and pulled out a wolf pup's tooth tied in twine and put it around the boy's neck. "Strength comes in all shapes and sizes. Even the smallest act of kindness can show great strength. Never question your worth or lose sight of all that is beautiful in this world."

She gave him a faint smile and walked off as he marveled at the wolf tooth in his hand. When he looked up and realized she had left, he ran back to his mother, proudly displaying his new prized possession.

The others stood watching the boy when she rejoined them. Alrindel glanced at the flower in her hair.

"So, what was that all about?"

"He thanked me for saving his mother."

"Someone has an admirer," Skylar teased. "So, what was that you gave him?"

"Just the tooth of a wolf pup, I found it while we were traveling with Dain's pack."

"Careful there, don't want to give anyone the wrong impression."

Skylar messed up her hair, and she knocked his hand away.

"Sorry, we can't all be as heartless as you," she teased. "So, where do you hope to find your bounty when we get to Riverdain? I would like to make our time there as short as possible."

"Figured I'd start where I always do, The Tavern."

Alrindel rolled his eyes. "That's just an excuse for you to drink."

Skylar shoved Alrindel. "That may be true, but that's also where I usually find my quarry."

Alrindel walked backwards in front of him for a few paces.

"Fine, a wager then? If he's not there, you haul my next kill from the hunt back."

"And if he is, then you come with me on my next bounty expedition," Skylar spoke with a honeyed tone.

"Deal." Alrindel spun back to Zelia's side with a new pep in his step.

The sun was setting as they came into Riverdain. She stared up at an iron barred window as they passed the only building that didn't seem to be falling apart with time. *'Town Hall, Court House, & Jail,'* she read the sign hanging above the door.

"The mayor is corrupt," Skylar whispered in her ear.

"Then why don't we do something?"

"Because that is not our decision to make," Koin answered. "I'll come get you when we have a ride upriver."

Alrindel nodded, and they turned down a little market street. It was already getting dark and the street was rather barren. Music drifted from a building at its end, where the glow of lanterns shone through the tiny windows.

People glanced at them as they entered, but quickly returned to their drinks and dancing. The bartender greeted Skylar as he leaned against the wooden bar at the back of the building.

"What'll it be today, Bounty Hunter? The usual?"

"Two meads and uh," Skylar faced Zelia, "what do you want?"

She hopped onto the stool next to him. "I don't need anything."

A man draped his arm across Skylar's shoulder, flicking his pudgy fingers. "Taking in strays now are ya?" He stepped forward and placed his grimy hand on her shoulder. "She'd make a nice toy with a little work."

Zelia grit her teeth as she looked down at his hand, then up at his disfigured face. One eye was half covered with a pudgy flap of skin while the other eye drooped.

"Remove your hand from me or I just may remove it from you."

The man grabbed a handful of her hair and pulled her head back. "Someone should teach you some manners, you little tramp!"

Skylar reached for his sword and Alrindel drew an arrow, but she didn't need the help. She kneed him in the crotch and the man doubled over. She grabbed her golden staff from its holster as she slid off the stool.

Between the pain from her side and seeing village after village of ransacked homes and burnt fields, this poor excuse of a man drew the last straw.

"I've had quite enough of men like you. Tell me, do you have a death wish or something? You'd think one would assume that someone carrying weapons would know how to use them."

She spun the staff around and gripped it with both hands as it connected with the man's head with a hollow CRACK.

His head bounced off a nearby table before he fell to the ground in a heap. Alrindel relaxed his bow, and Skylar moved his hand away from his sword.

"Anyone else wish to try me tonight? No? Good." She spun the staff, collapsing back to its traveling size and slipped it back into the holster on her back.

Skylar leaned back against the counter. "Nice hit."

She watched the man over her shoulder as he rubbed his head and staggered back to his seat. "Less bloody than using a sword, yet just as satisfying."

Alrindel shook his head. "You rubbed off on our innocent little sister."

"I for one think it's a good thing."

"Hey! I was careful not to kill him and I'm not exactly our dear Bounty Hunter's *little* sister."

"You're still smaller than me, short stuff."

She shook her head as Skylar and Alrindel took the first swig of their drinks, then a gruff voice sounded from the doorway. "Whose black horse is standing out here untied?"

She spun around to face the tall man draped in rough black fabric.

All the men about the tavern held their heads low and stared into their drinks, avoiding the man's gaze as he scanned the room.

He overlooked her until she spoke, "That'd be my horse."

The man smirked as he swept his hood back to reveal golden eyes that gleamed like a wolf's, but there was something more to them.

"That's a lot of horse for such a little lady."

"Trust me, she gets along just fine." Alrindel faced the stranger.

"This runt with you?" The broad-shouldered man looked Alrindel up and down.

"Only I get to call her that." Skylar turned.

The man's expression changed as soon as Skylar turned.

"Well, you don't say! It's Skylar the Bounty Hunter! I thought you'd jumped the Faithful Mountains for the winter."

Skylar's serious expression broke into a grin. "And I thought you'd headed off into The Wild for the winter. Guess we're both full of surprises."

They hugged each other with a pat on the back. Then sat down and Skylar ordered another mead for his friend.

Alrindel rubbed his thumb and middle finger together as he turned back to the bar. "Going to introduce us to your friend?"

The man grinned as he jabbed a thumb in their direction. "Yeah, who's the runt and the elf?"

"Nikolas, runt here is my sister, Zelia," he messed up her hair, "and he's my brother, Alrindel."

"Now, I had heard about your elf brother, but this is the first you've said anything about a girl."

"That's a rather long story."

Nikolas leaned on the bar. "How long of a story could it be? She can't be over sixteen winters old."

She and Alrindel smirked at his comment.

"Unless she's an elf." Nikolas raised a bushy unkempt eyebrow.

Zelia swept her hair behind her ear. "No, I'm not an elf, though I did spend many winters with them long ago." She spun a gold coin across the bar to the bartender. "As you well know, appearances are not always telling."

"Did you tell her?"

"No, but her knowing doesn't surprise me."

Alrindel sat forward. "Know what?"

"He's a wolfblood and something else," she replied in a hushed tone.

"Oh, them."

"So, maybe you can explain to me how the two of you met?" Zelia asked.

Nikolas scratched his short, rough beard. "As I would like to know more about you. Not often someone recognizes what I am, but what do you mean 'and something else'?"

She searched his eyes a little closer, noticing again the black streaks that ran through his golden irises. *Fregnar,* she thought the name of the god of death, but thought it best to wait until they were away from prying ears.

"You about done here? We have a ride home if we leave within the hour." Koin came up behind them.

Nikolas looked Koin over. "Another friend of yours Skylar?"

"More family than friend. I'll be back in a second." A man in the corner got up and started for the door, but Skylar grabbed him and slammed his head on the table. "You thought you could just run off? Well, usually I'd give you a fighting chance. But it would seem I have a deadline so off we go." He bound the man's hands without heed to his curses.

Zelia cringed as she slid from the stool. All the pain she'd been ignoring and pushing back flooded in at once.

Koin grabbed her and searched her eyes. "The infection spreading?"

Nikolas put the back of his hand to her forehead.

"She's burning up. What the hell kind of infection takes someone from looking fine to this?"

"We need to get her home." Alrindel scooped her up without waiting for her response.

"I'm fine. I'll be fine," she muttered and grabbed at her side. She pulled herself closer to Alrindel and bit her lip with her eyes clamped shut against the pain. She concentrated on steadying her breathing and heart rate.

She wasn't sure how he did it, but Nikolas convinced Koin to allow him to come with them upstream. The Elvish barge captains worked hard to push the overloaded barge upstream at a faster pace than usual.

"Get Eadon!" Skylar called out when they neared the docks the next morning.

By the time they tied off, Eadon had started down the short wooden dock. He glanced at Skylar and Alrindel, then down at her. Koin and Lighnif explained what had happened and what they had done as they followed Eadon to the main house.

"Zelia?" Eadon's tone was soft with an undertone of pain.

"Umhm."

"We have to get the armor off."

She nodded and pried her hand away from her side. They removed her armor and laid her on the bed. Alrindel and Skylar held her down.

"I'm sorry Zelia, but the arrowhead is still in you." Eadon looked as if he could have cried. "I have to remove it, or the infection will continue to spread."

She gave a slight nod and a moment later something cold and sharp cut into her side, sending both a spike of pain and a shiver up her spine.

She tried to hold back her scream by biting her lip as she had always done, but without adrenaline, there was nothing to keep her from feeling his every move.

A pained gasp escaped her lips. She could hold it in no longer and she let out a blood-curdling scream. She didn't understand it. Why did it hurt so much? She knew she'd been through far worse without so much pain. Eadon's warm hand slid into her side and fished around for the arrowhead.

Just as Eadon began to withdraw his hand, a tremor spread across her body. Her breaths shortened and her eyes rolled up into her head as she gave up and passed out.

The sound of Alrindel's voice echoed through her head as she lay half conscious.

"Stay with us Zelia. Stay with me." His voice went wobbly as he continued, "I can't lose you, not again."

⟶

This time, she felt the pain before she even opened her eyes. She lay there unable to move with a throbbing side.

Nikolas's deep, gruff voice carried across the room. "You expect me to believe she's the prophecy child?"

Eleanor's fruity voice came from the doorway. "It doesn't matter what you believe. Only the truth matters." The bed shifted beside her. "I know you are waking. Try not to move. The arrowhead was hard to find, but

Eadon managed. You will be fine, but you need to heal."

She pried her eyes open. Her vision was fuzzy as she blinked the sleep from them.

"And I mean it this time. No running off to train, fight, or anything else."

"Ah, really?" her voice was hoarse.

Skylar moved to her bedside, across from Eleanor. "Or I will kick your butt."

She laid her hand across her side and winced. "I'd like to see you try."

"Oh, you're on. Once you're healed and not a moment sooner."

"You're awake. That's a good sign." Eadon entered the room with Alrindel close behind.

"Real reassuring Eadon. May I sit up? Lying on my back makes it hard to breathe with the metal plate."

Eadon checked her side, lifting the bandage carefully.

"Yes, but not on your own. You might rip the muscle if you do." He sat her up with pillows behind her, then sat on the bed next to Eleanor. "I take it your armor is magic. It's the only conclusion I can come to for you still being alive."

"It was a gift from a…" she paused. "Well, I guess he's family."

Her perplexed expression made everyone smile.

Even Nikolas cracked a grin. "Nice to know someone else's family is more messed up than mine."

"Happy to help, though we still need to discuss who your father is."

"But not today," Eleanor gave her a soft smile, then stood from the bed. "Come, let's leave Zelia to rest."

Eadon stood to follow Eleanor. "You are to stay in bed, alright?"

"I'm not promising anything, but I'll sure as heck try." She gave him a mischievous grin, and he shook his head as he slipped out of sight.

"So, what do you have up your sleeve now?" Alrindel asked once they were alone.

"Figuring out why Nikolas is here and how much he knows."

"About what?"

"His father, but that can wait for a while longer." She snuggled against him and found sleep and a little slice of peace, eager to take her for the first time in a long while.

www.ingramcontent.com/pod-product-compliance
Lightning Source LLC
Chambersburg PA
CBHW010510100726
47902CB00011B/2152